LOVE NOTES

AIMEE BROWN

Boldwood

First published in Great Britain in 2023 by Boldwood Books Ltd.

Copyright © Aimee Brown, 2023

Cover Design by Alice Moore Design

Cover Photography: Shutterstock

Every effort has been made to obtain the necessary permissions with reference to copyright material, both illustrative and quoted. We apologise for any omissions in this respect and will be pleased to make the appropriate acknowledgements in any future edition.

A CIP catalogue record for this book is available from the British Library.

Paperback ISBN 978-1-80426-812-4

Large Print ISBN 978-1-80426-811-7

Hardback ISBN 978-1-80426-813-1

Ebook ISBN 978-1-80426-809-4

Kindle ISBN 978-1-80426-810-0

Audio CD ISBN 978-1-80426-818-6

MP3 CD ISBN 978-1-80426-817-9

Digital audio download ISBN 978-1-80426-815-5

Boldwood Books Ltd
23 Bowerdean Street
London SW6 3TN
www.boldwoodbooks.com

Thank you Andie Newton for being awesome.
(Didn't think I'd do it, did ya? *I feel it in my bones* LOL)

PROLOGUE
BROOKS HUDSON

Six months ago...

'Ugh,' I groan, rolling over and grabbing my ringing phone from my nightstand. I finally get to sleep and someone interrupts me. 'Yeah?'

'I had a dream,' she says, exaggerating each word.

She had a dream? Fucking hell. I thought divorce meant you didn't call your ex-husband anymore after dark. Business and emergency calls only.

'I also had a dream,' I say, rolling onto my stomach and resting my head on my left arm. 'It was great too. I had an ex-wife that didn't wake me up to tell me about some stupid vision she's had.'

She laughs into the phone. 'You'll never escape me; we have a child together, so like it or not, you get me for life.'

'This is what our parents meant when they said we were too young to get married. I get it now.'

'Will you listen? This seems important.'

'You talk, I'll sleep.'

'Fine. I was in this room. It was all white. White walls. White floors. White rugs. White curtains. White—'

'It was white,' I interrupt her. 'Yeah, I'm following, continue.'

'An-y-way, grumpy, you were there, and besides Alijah and me, you were alone. Nobody else was there, not your parents, not Ty, or Oz, none of your friends. You were *alone* alone, Brooks. And it was one of those life-changing moments. Like, your death.' She says it dramatically as if this is absolutely factual. A real Nostradamus moment.

'Dun dun duuun...'

She laughs, but I'm sure it's less because I'm funny and more that she doesn't enjoy me making fun of her 'supernatural' gifts from the universe. Her reading people's aura and drawing tarot cards in high school was a fun party trick that we all enjoyed. I'm no longer at that point in our relationship and haven't been since she decided I wasn't her pre-destined star-crossed lover. Aka: 'the one', soulmate, twin flame, the Ryan Reynolds to her Blake Lively, the Ben Affleck to her J-Lo.

'After death, you can't call me. Sounds nice. Quiet. Peaceful. Relaxing, even. Where the hell do I sign up?'

'Funny,' she says, not laughing. 'This is serious, Brooks. I think you might die alone.'

'OK, well, I appreciate the warning...'

'Wait!' she says, somehow sensing the incoming blast of silence that is me disconnecting our call. 'There was a woman that walked in as I was leaving. She was beyond devastated. I think she might have been your soulmate.'

This makes me open my eyes, now staring at the ceiling, and not because I'm constantly searching for 'the one'. After marrying and divorcing Norah, I know there is no such thing as soulmates. I don't think anyone on this planet is meant for anyone else. Everything we do is the result of whatever choices we've made. There is no destiny. No fate. No karmic influence taking names and kicking ass. Bad things happen to good people, and evil, more often than not, gets away with it.

I have just one question.

'Please tell me it wasn't you?'

She heaves a sigh into the phone, clearly irritated with my apparent disinterest. 'It wasn't me. She had dark hair, emerald-green eyes, and heels higher than I have ever attempted.'

'I like her already. Now I just need to hop on my trusty steed and search the world for this dark-haired, emerald-eyed, stiletto-wearing damsel and convince her to fall in love with me. I'll do this, of course, in all the spare time I have between work, Alijah and you.'

'You're missing the point. She's your literal soulmate. You won't have to look for her. You'll just find one another. That's how fate works, Brooks. I can't believe we were married so long, and you learned nothing.'

'I learned how not to be married. It's not so bad. A little lonely. But I'm surviving it.'

'I forgot how irritating you are when awoken from a dead sleep.'

'Glad I could remind you. Bye.' I tap the end call button before she can say anything else and flip my phone onto silent.

My soulmate. Like I'm going to run after a woman my ex-wife sees in her dreams. No thanks.

1

MERCY ALEXANDER

Present day

'Most boring couple ever,' I whisper, glancing around at the guests.

This wedding looks like a last-minute backyard barbecue, but I know it's not because this couple booked us a year ago. The whole place is casual. Besides the wedding party, the only man here wearing a tie is Dylan. Some of these people are in jean shorts.

Not that there's anything wrong with a last-minute casual wedding. If it were me, though, and I'd spent this much money on a party to declare my love for some guy, people better wear ties and tiaras. Plus, I prefer dressier events because I like clothes and shoes. It's like window shopping – a happy distraction from my mind spiraling that I'm playing my five hundredth wedding, and with each one, I'm reminded I'll likely never find this happily-ever-after crap. Nor do I want it – or at least I didn't think I did. But now that I'm thirty and helping my best friends plan their wedding, something inside isn't settling into my usual bury-your-feelings ways. My head is trying to revive my heart that's been in a decades-long coma, and believe it or not, it's responding – and it's painful. I'm certain I'd rather focus on who's wearing what so I can de-scribe it well enough to google and find it online later than continue listening to my insides whispering about something I'm terrified of.

'Pachelbel's Canon is a classic wedding song, Merc. Some people enjoy traditional,' Dylan, my level-headed business partner, says.

'Traditional would be black tie. This feels more like Elvis in velvet at a twenty-four-hour wedding chapel in Vegas.'

'Elvis in velvet...' He repeats my words, shaking his head with each one.

Weddings, we play at least one practically every

weekend. Dylan and I run a company called Love Notes. Our shop is in downtown Portland, where we sell and rent stringed instruments and pianos, book gigs, give lessons and do private work for musician hires in our recording studio. Both of us play multiple instruments fluently, and we have a side gig once or twice a month as our stringed duo cover band, Violated. Bach and Beethoven aren't songs you'll find Violated playing. We shock the fancy right out of folks with pop, rock, rap and alternative hits. That's right; I can play Nirvana on five instruments.

'I don't understand the world's need to pair everyone off. Love doesn't last. At least not for most people. It's why our country's divorce rate is through the roof. I think marriage licenses should have ten-year expiration dates, and if you choose not to renew, you're over automatically. It'd be mostly painless because you knew it was coming, so you've probably discussed it. No one is to blame; your license expired, so you went your separate ways. It seems a little drastic, but I'd bet many people would take the easy out.'

Dylan stares at me, blank-faced, except for the *you're weird, and I don't understand why I like it* crooked grin he's got plastered on his face.

'You've got this romance vibe down,' he says as he positions his cello.

'Do I seem bitter?'

'A tad.'

We get the cue from the wedding planner that our time to shine is now. The bridal party is on their way down the aisle to Canon in D, played via cello (Dylan) and violin (me).

Once the entire entourage of eight bridesmaids, eight groomsmen, a ring bearer named Buster (their Doberman) and a crying flower girl carried by her jean-cargo-short-and-flip-flop-clad father have made it down the aisle our performance ends.

Dylan leans into me. 'Three years,' he whispers.

I scrunch my face, inspecting the couple. I'd already guessed low because the groom had no reaction when the bride appeared at the end of the aisle. That's my favorite part – seeing how the groom reacts to his bride. That one moment can tell me if it's forever or not. But this guy didn't shed even one tear. No heavy *I'm so lucky* sigh. Not even a crack of a smile. He just stood there stone-faced like her father threatened his life just before this moment. He showed more enthusiasm when his best man marched down the aisle, and they fist-bumped as they met. I can't be the only person who noticed this. The couple isn't even holding hands, just standing beside one another awkwardly. Not a great sign, so I see why Dylan guessed low.

We have this game we play at weddings. Not out loud or anything, primarily through whisper conversations as we sit at the back of the room watching a couple we don't know marry and guessing how long they'll last based on the ceremony alone. Some have the vibe of forever, but most don't. Dylan is calling it early this time. Usually, he waits until the end so he has the whole picture because that's the kind of guy he is. He's careful with his decisions, no matter how big or small. He researches anything he wants to buy for months before finally dropping the cash. The man's middle name is responsibility. Whereas mine is, maybe, cynical?

'I'm going eight,' I whisper back, intentionally guessing higher than him for the first time just for fun.

'Eight?'

'They each have at least eight friends, which means they'll go to every one of them for advice when things start to fall apart, and it'll take that long for them to agree. I could point out a dozen other faux pas, but considering he's wearing a white tux with tails and it's not 1988, must I say more?'

Dyl shakes his head.

'We should be playing one of Penny's ballads. Or Phil Collins.'

Penny is my best friend, Hollyn's, mother. She's former popstar Penny Candy, who's actually met Phil Collins. She's trying to make a comeback, but things are moving rather slowly on that front. Maybe I'll suggest she switch over to wedding singer. This wedding could've used her today.

'This is why you don't get to pick the music,' Dylan says.

'Admit it, guessing the demise of couples is my one talent. I always win.'

'You have more than one talent,' he says, eyeing the violin in my lap.

'I can sense a pending breakup from miles away. Remember the couple that didn't even make it to their I-do's? I called that one the moment we walked in.'

'How could I forget the wedding where the police were called before the reception?'

Inviting your exes (yes, multiple) who are still in love with you isn't a great idea, is what I learned that day. Nobody was prepared for what happened when that priest asked the age-old question, 'Does anyone object? Speak now, or forever hold your peace.' A myriad of men and women stood, and it was an absolute dumpster fire from that moment on. A train wreck Dyl and I couldn't look away from, so we played like we were going down with the *Titanic*.

'You got plans tonight?' Dyl asks. 'I was thinking about making fish tacos like those we had in LA that time. I have enough for you and even River if you want to come over later.'

We can't usually talk through weddings, but for this one, we're way in the back of the room, far from any guests, so as long as we keep it a hair above a whisper, I don't have to melt my mind with pre-written vows I could recite in my sleep.

'I also have wine.' He attempts to entice me with alcohol, but I think he's forgotten who he's talking to because I rarely say no to free dinner, let alone drinks. I don't need bribery; free leaves more money for me to add to my shoe collection.

Sadly, this time, I have to decline. 'Can't. Ed found a library doing outdoor movies this summer, and tonight one is showing *La La Land*. I promised him I'd go.'

When Dyl's eyebrows lift, I know he's into it. We met while playing the *La La Land* tour with the Portland Symphony. Dylan's been one of my best friends for five years, and this movie is how it all happened. It's our all-time favorite for totally different reasons. Dyl's in love with the music and the sweeping romantic essence the whole thing has. I love it because it doesn't end in a happily-ever-after. None of my favorite movies do. *La-La Land, Up in the Air, Shopgirl*. Watch them. They're true to life. Yes, it's sad, but life can be a real crapshoot for some people, and through living that myself, I've discovered things don't often go as you've planned, and the romantics hate it. I've tried to picture my own happily-ever-after, but real life reminds me it's not realistic minute by minute. I'm surviving, and only just at that.

'Want to come with?' I ask, knowing from the smile on his face that he's ready to toss the fish tacos to Mozart – his asshole cat – and spend an evening with my brother and me.

'Yeah,' he says with a wide smile. 'Is there anything more fun than mixing a musical with Edie?'

I snicker. 'He's going to sing all the songs not quite under his breath, so yeah, I can think of many more fun things. *Please*, bring the wine.'

After the insanely long ceremony, and as the two of us exit through the cocktail hour, a glass of champagne somehow ends up in my hand. It always does. I'm just lucky like that. Dylan loads our instruments into his car, taking my violin from me and spotting the glass immediately.

'Mercy...' he moans.

'A man just handed it to me as we walked through. It would've been rude to reject it.'

Once we're in the car, I hand him the now-empty glass. 'It's plastic. Filled with mid-grade champagne. Either they didn't want to splurge, or they're broke, and since money is one of the main fights that break couples up, I confidently stand by my less than eight years, and I may even be leaning more towards your three.'

He nods proudly. 'When I win this one, you're paying for lunch at some point.'

'*If* I lose, I'll consider it.'

* * *

Just after nine thirty, Dylan and I are walking down the path from the parking lot to an ornately land-scaped lawn with fountains bubbling at the back of the brick library building. The property is filled with people lounging under the darkening skies. Some in lawn chairs, others lying on blankets, but all of them chattering to their groups happily. Summer has offi-cially started, and the world seems happy. I know I am, mainly because Dyl drove, so I didn't have to waste the gas. And when I asked him to stop by the

Starbucks so I could grab an iced coffee, he volunteered to pay for his *and* mine. Win.

Yes, we hang out even when we're not at work. It would be easier to count the hours I don't see him. Long story short, Dylan secured the apartment across the hall from his when he learned Edie and Carlos had announced they'd bought the 'cutest little craftsman home there ever was' (Ed's words), and they'd be moving into it together – alone.

Now my best friend's little brother, River, and I live together in downtown Portland, splitting everything halvsies in a shithole three-story walk-up with hot water for about 65 percent of your shower, so you gotta move quickly. It's not luxurious, but it's mine, and I feel safe living with and near two guys I mostly enjoy and trust with my life.

It's dusk, but quickly moving into nighttime. Lights are wound up tree trunks, providing a bit of a glow so people can see. The starlit sky is the perfect background, and the light of the moon is mesmerizing. It almost makes the entire atmosphere romantic, which is probably what they're hoping for, considering the movie they chose to play.

'Mercy, girl!' Ed waves frantically like I might miss him. 'Over here!'

His face lights up at the sight of Dylan. I forgot

these two are secretly in love. Not really, but they might as well be because Edie adores Dylan. It's possible he likes him more than me.

'Edie!' Dylan says like they're old friends reunited.

'Dylan Santiago! Oh, how I've missed you at family dinners lately.' Ed's gaze darts to me.

I glare. He would say that out loud. Just last week, he suggested I bring Dylan again because I'm 'more fun when he's around'. He's convinced Dylan is the perfect man, and I am somehow too stupid to see it.

'I'd come just for Carlos's cooking but showing up without an invite seems stalker-ish,' Dyl says as he glances around Ed. 'He's not here tonight?'

Edie shakes his head with a frown. 'He's with his other love, the restaurant.'

'Ah,' Dyl says. 'Well, speaking of food, I brought some.' He pats the backpack slung over his shoulder.

'You made the tacos?' I ask. He could have told me. I'd have helped.

'I had enough and didn't eat yet, did you?'

I lift my shoulders. 'Does a cup of coffee and a hard-boiled egg count?'

'No.'

'Did I hear tacos?' Ed asks, his hands in a prayer position in front of his chest.

'Fish tacos, my specialty,' Dyl says, handing Ed his bag.

'Yum! I'm so glad she brought you!' he says eagerly, setting the bag on the blanket in front of him and patting either side. 'Sit, sit. We'll have so much fun. How've you been, doll? It's been a hot minute since I saw you.'

'I saw you yester—'

'Talking to Dyl, love.' Ed holds a hand in my direction to shut me up.

'So sorry,' I say, a little vexed he's more excited to see Dylan than the little sister he raised.

I silence myself, sitting to Ed's left while Dylan situates himself to Edie's right. The two spread Dylan's perfectly made fish tacos in front of us while chit-chatting about life, and, like the intelligent man I know Dylan is, he pulls the wine he mentioned earlier from his bag.

'Right when I thought he couldn't be more perfect,' Ed says, glancing my way and batting his eyes. I roll mine in return.

Once the movie starts, we quiet, eating in silence with our eyes glued to the wall-sized screen. It's funny how Ed and I react to the love-at-first-sight moment between Mia and Seb. Both of us pulling our hands to our chest with a nearly silent gasp. Even though I don't believe.

We're related even though no one would ever guess we are. Our dad is a pathetic white guy who knocked up my sixteen-year-old mother, who then decided the situation was too bad for her, but she left me there. Ten years prior, Edie's mom left when she found out she was pregnant with him and never looked back. Ed wasn't even allowed to see Nick because his mother was the smartest, most thoughtful woman I'd ever met. I used to wish she was my mother, but I got the next best thing because Ed is just like her, from his personality to his looks. He's tall, with light brown skin, a total dancer's body, a complexion to die for, hazel eyes and short black shaved hair. And I look just like Nick (our sperm donor) with dark hair, green eyes, an olive-toned complexion with a splatter of freckles across my face that one foster mom once swore would fade with age.

I don't know what it is about this scene that gets me. I absolutely do *not* believe in love at first sight. Or love at all. But this movie makes me *want* to believe – right until Seb's response. Then I'm reminded both life and love suck. I'll leave this movie tonight in my safe little love-hating bubble and be perfectly happy without ever having to experience it because I already know it's the most painful emotion of them all.

Suddenly, it happens. Ed stands, encouraging other couples to do the same. After he's match-made half a dozen folks with strangers for an impromptu dance party and as Ryan Gosling and Emma Stone sing their first duet together, he extends his hand my way.

'What are you doing? No.' I refuse him immediately.

'Having fun. What are you doing?'

'Pretending you don't exist.'

'Go,' Dyl encourages, pushing me Ed's way.

I glare as Ed chuckles at getting his way. He pulls me from the ground by my hand and dances me across the grass while singing the song like he's in the movie.

'Your part's coming up,' he says between his lines.

I could do it. I know every word. But no way am I. We may share a 'performance' gene, but his is much more extroverted than mine.

'You're lucky I'm entertaining you with the dance at all. I'm in heels in the grass, and I've been drinking wine from the bottle.'

'And you make it all look easy, darling.' He glances

over my shoulder, his smile suddenly fading. 'Dylan looks sad.'

He does have a slight frown on his face. I don't know why. He's seemed happy until now, and I know he loves this movie as much as I do. Not to mention he's easily the best-looking man in this crowd. He's tall, with a head full of dark curls that are currently a touch too long, and he's utterly handsome with his caramel-colored eyes and five o'clock shadow now surfacing a few hours too late. He could probably ask any woman here to dance, and not one would say no.

'He's sad because he's being a party pooper,' I say.

'You inspired him off his patootie and out of his comfort zone. Now he just sits there like a sad little puppy in his Dockers and Ralph Lauren polos, admiring you from afar. He's the perfect man, Merc. When will you wake up and see it?'

'Ed,' I groan. 'We've had this conversation a million times. I've told you; we're just friends now. Nothing more.'

'You two never had fireworks?'

I shake my head. 'No lightning, no heart flips, no fireworks. He's a safe choice and perfect as my backup.'

'You have a backup?'

'If you must know, I've got two. A backup, Dylan,

with the rule that if we're the last singles standing in our group of friends when I'm forty, he's the guy I'll run to. Then I've got a backup to my backup – just in case.'

'In case of what?'

'Have you looked at Dylan? He doesn't exactly make anyone want to pour acid into their eyes.'

He smirks. 'That was like poetry, darling.'

'I'm just saying; he's someone's knight in shining armor. I just don't think he's mine.'

Ed is getting tired of this conversation, and it shows. 'Who is your backup if Dylan falls for some gorgeous maiden who is not you?'

'I don't want to say.'

Ed rolls his eyes hard. 'You're a little bit maddening. I think you've got that heart of yours gagged so tight there's no way it could possibly tell you to fall for Dylan *or* anyone else.'

I sigh heavily. This is Ed's thing. *Fall for Dylan. He's perfect. Handsome. Responsible. The whole package.*

Before I know it, I've overthought his words long enough that he's danced me right to him, and I didn't even notice. His now outstretched hand extended Dylan's way, says he's ready to pass me off. *That's* why he didn't partner Dylan with some unsuspecting woman earlier. He had a plan.

I shoot Dyl a 'don't do it' look, but by the coy grin on his face, not to mention that he's now on his feet, something tells me we're doing this.

'Merc,' he greets me with a guilty smile.

'Here we are...' I take his hand, allowing him to slide his other around my waist.

'You know what I love?' he asks as he dances me towards the back of the crowd.

'Fish tacos?'

He shakes his head.

'Never being late for anything?'

Another head shake and smirk.

'Dockers as weekend wear?'

He laughs, shaking his head again. 'I love how you pretend to hate romance and wear this anti-love armored suit, but your favorite parts of this movie are the romantic parts. Deep down, I know you wished Seb and Mia would've ended up together.'

'Are you kidding me? *Everyone* did. But life is complicated, and when you think the timing is right, it swoops in to prove you wrong. Is it sad? A little. But at the same time, maybe the timing was off so something else wouldn't be late.'

'You think their timing was off?'

'Possibly. I dunno. It's a movie. I'm not investigating it for between-the-line clues like I'm in a college reading class. I'd love for all this romance crap to be true, but my life hasn't been that way.'

'Well, that's because you insist on living in the past.'

'The past is a part of who I am; that's not living in it. You either accept me at my worst, past included, or not at all. If I could escape it, you know I would. But I can't. Unfortunately, I know what it's like to have the people meant to love you unconditionally, not. That armored suit is a shield against Cupid because I can't take one more heartbreak. Pieces of my heart are spread all over this city, Dyl. Because of that, my life's motto has become "keep your heart out of it".'

'I'm aware of your motto.' He rolls his eyes. After a beat of silence and him visibly considering his following words, he speaks softly. 'We spend every weekend at weddings. Have you seriously never considered it being you at the end of that aisle?'

'I play "how long will this couple make it" at weddings and write my obituary in my head during funerals. I don't think we have the same daydreams.'

He doesn't look overly pleased with my response. He kind of looks worried, to be honest.

'Do you picture yourself as the groom while we play weddings?'

'Yeah,' he says.

'Who's your bride?' I ask curiously.

'I dunno,' he says. 'She's still fuzzy.'

'Well, if you're wrong, I'll see ya there in ten years, and I expect tears.'

He chuckles to himself. 'You really think that'll happen? There's no way. You're more than capable of love, Merc. Both giving and receiving.'

'I don't think I am,' I insist, utterly unsure of myself and almost ashamed of the words because I *do* love myself. I just can't picture anyone doing the same with all my issues sporadically surfacing at usually the worst times ever. Even I can barely stand it.

And despite my backup plan, not to mention the second one, I've mostly made my peace that I'll end up the single friend who never let anyone close enough and will die alone, found weeks later with the remote in my hand and the Netflix screen displaying the 'Are you still watching?' screen.

'Maybe you don't think you deserve it, but you couldn't be more wrong,' Dyl says quietly, his breath on my neck as the song ends. 'I've spent five years with you daily. I know you well enough to know at least that.'

As the song ends, we slowly step away from one another, our hands dropping apart last. The walk back to our seats is awkward. But not? This is just us.

We talk about anything comfortably. He knows all my secrets practically. Though typically, he's not so over the top, *you deserve to be loved*.

For the rest of the movie, I'm silent. My eyes are on the screen as my insides fight off a panic attack, jousting style. Why's he talking about love all of a sudden? It's painful and cringy, but something about it intrigues me to the point where I'm considering his words, and it confuses the hell out of me.

2

BROOKS

'We need to talk,' Kristyn says out of the blue.

Shit. The four words I regularly hear have left her lips, and I didn't see them coming. Again.

Hazy shades of pinks and purples fill the sky as the sun sets. A breeze rustles through the leaves of the trees lining the sidewalk. It seems like the perfect night to be suddenly single again. I'm not upset, mainly because this happens every time I date. I should have guessed it when she asked me to meet her here instead of me picking her up. I've never dumped a woman. Ever. Things seem great, then bam! 'We need to talk' enters the ring.

I reach for her hand, testing my theory. Before I

can touch her, she shoves them into her pockets. Yep. She's dumping me.

When I was first divorced, I was excited to return to the dating world. I met my ex-wife in high school, so I'd never really dated. I was intrigued to find out what all the fuss was about. It's been over seven years now, and I'm not anymore. Dating sucks. The pool is shallow, peed in, and I just want out. But not alone? So, there is no out. Let that run through your head every sleepless night for all of eternity.

Why am I suddenly so hot? I pull the neck of my shirt away from my chest, the breeze it creates helping.

'What's up?'

'I don't know how to say this—'

Here we go. I'm finally starting that book I've meant to write when I get home. *How to Get Dumped Regularly Without Even Trying*. A memoir. If I were a superhero, I'd be Dumped Dude. No cape needed, just loneliness, one really soft hand, and the ability to repel women with every life decision I've ever made.

'I'm not ready for the kid thing.' She lifts a shoulder, glancing over at me with a silent *sorry*. 'And... there's no way I could bring you home to my mother.'

Ouch. God. I'm not suitable mother material anymore? The kid thing, I get. It's not for everyone. It takes a huge heart to take on someone else's child. But now I'm offensive to mothers? Damn.

'Why?'

I have to know.

'Don't get me wrong,' she says, suddenly turning to me, her hand on my bicep, her fingers tracing the outline of a tattoo. 'I think you're boiling hot. But my mom won't appreciate all the tattoos. She's going to think you just got out of prison.'

Prison? I feel like I should be offended, but then I remember I was at the jail today. For *work*, but still. Obviously, her mom doesn't know the difference between tattoos you pay a pretty penny for and those done behind bars by a not-so-small guy called Slim, working a tattoo gun made from an ink pen. This isn't great for the self-esteem, I won't lie.

'I was considering asking you to my brother's wedding next weekend, but I can't. My dad would die when he saw you.'

'He'd *die*?'

Over a nice, divorced, single dad with a complicated job and thousands of dollars worth of tattoo ink under my skin? Seems a little over the top.

'Not because of the tattoos, more because you're older and a father, the fact that you've been married before, your job situation...' She says these words slowly, hesitantly, like she's breaking bad news I wasn't already tuned in on.

'But this—' She motions between us, a sweet thankful smile now on her face. 'Has been fun – way, *way* fun. You really know what you're doing in the, uh —' She rocks her head in the vague direction of my apartment. 'You know.'

I've got one talent mention-worthy, and that's it? Jesus. I want to be offended, but how can I? It seems like that should make me feel better about all this. A braggable trait to pad this breakup story when I tell it to my buddies. *She didn't like me personally, but I'm excellent in bed.* Maybe that was the point of her throwing it in the way she did – an attempt at distracting my heart with my ego.

But I'm stuck on one word she used. Older. *Older?* Since when is thirty-six 'older'? Of course, she's twenty-five, so technically, I am older than her, but in my defense, she hit on me the night we met. I'm not out hunting for women a decade younger than me or anything. Am I officially now in the older man category? Fuck.

'I, uh...' I clear my throat. 'I'm hearing that we're ending this after I buy you dinner?'

She grimaces, nodding her head slowly.

'Well then,' I say with a sigh. 'I'm gonna be rude

and skip the first bit.' I pull my wallet from my pocket and hand her a twenty. 'For dinner. Text me, and let me know you got home safe. And, uh, good luck?'

Is that what you say after being dumped? *Good luck*. You'd think I'd be better at this as often as I've been left over the years. Usually, they don't do it in person. Text message has saved me many a time from deciding what to do or say immediately after a breakup. I prefer it to this.

She stares at me, a confused look on her face as I back away from her towards the parking garage my truck is in, jogging across the road and disappearing into the city, never looking back. Why stay?

As I walk, I pull my phone from my pocket, tapping the contact who calls me the most, even though he's rarely got anything new to say.

'You banned me from calling you on date nights, lover-boy. Re-mem-ber? Didn't want me in your head during sexy times,' Oz barks, clearly joking but playing it off like he's not. 'What the hell do you want?'

He always busts my balls before he even says hello. 'I'm headed your way.'

'Oh, now you wanna come play? I thought you couldn't make it tonight 'cause you've got a hot date?'

He mimics my voice with that last part but makes it high and whiny.

This prick. If I hadn't known him since I was nine, I'd tell him to fuck off.

'I said I couldn't play 'cause I wanted to get laid.' I'm kidding – kind of. 'Instead, she ended things, so—'

'*Again?* Damn, bro. I feel like you're breaking records with how good you are at that part. I always knew something was wrong with you, but Portland women are really proving it.'

'I'm going to punch you when I get there.'

'Aww, did Ozie hurt your delicate little feelings?'

'Her calling me an older dude hurt my feelings. OLDER, Oz.'

'Well, grandpa,' he says with a chuckle, even though none of this is funny. 'In the world of dating twenty-somethings, you are older. Older, fatherly, with a nutty ex-wife who's not afraid to show up and hang out like you're friends, and you got a kid you worship. No woman wants that much baggage in a dude.'

'You sure know how to give a pep talk.'

'I've been considering adding "motivational speaker" to my list of talents. Whatcha think?'

'I think I almost don't want to drive off this bridge.'

'My first glowing review. Now get your ass over

here and show that wife of mine how to play guitar like a pro.'

The drive across town takes longer than usual, as it's Friday night. The streets are busy as people hunt for where to spend their evening. I got lucky when Oz bought the bar ten years ago. We've always got someplace to hang out. Someplace cooler than on our couches in front of our TVs. It makes me feel like I've got some kind of life when I spend most of my time working, with my daughter, or trying to catch up on my sleep.

A couple Saturdays a month, though, I try to make time to play guitar with the garage cover band my friend, brother and I started when we were teenagers to compete in a high school talent show (that we won every year after). Don't Panic. That's what we named it.

'There he is!' Ty, my little brother, stands from the barstool he's on. 'The kicked-to-the-curb king himself!' He lifts his beer, toasting my terrible relationship skills.

'He needs to be uglier,' Oz says, a bar towel over one shoulder as he leans against the counter behind him. 'Women expect too much from him. His face don't match his personality.'

'How's that?' I ask, a little offended.

'Women look at you and expect a badass alpha male, yet you're nothing but a teddy bear in a tattoo suit.'

I shake my head, an irritated chuckle leaving my lips. 'Why do I like you again?'

'Opposites attract. You're Captain Boring, and I'm Captain Ozsome. Get it? Oz-some? Like "awesome"?'

Ty and I intentionally stare at him like we don't get it. His reaction to this is funnier than laughing at a joke he's been telling since we were twelve.

'Fine.' He huffs. 'Don't laugh, ya assholes. Before you get your pretty panties in a bunch, you can play tonight, alright?' He steps up to the bar before me, patting my cheek.

My phone buzzes in my pocket, interrupting Oz as he tries to flick me shit over nothing and everything all at once – our usual routine. I know exactly who's calling, too – my favorite person on the planet.

'Hey, Ali.'

Her sweet face fills my screen. Her chestnut-colored curly hair frizzy after a day's worth of activities. She looks so much like Norah – who annoys me at times now, but she's not unpleasant to look at, so I'm not sad our daughter is her spitting image. The most significant difference is that Alijah's crystal-blue eyes sparkle with the joy only a six-year-old still has.

'Hi, Daddy!' she says excitedly. She calls me to say goodnight every night if she's with her mom. When she's with me, she calls Mommy to do the same. 'Where are you?'

'I'm at Oz's.' I pan the camera around me to Ty and Oz, who wave obnoxiously.

She gasps through a grin. 'Is Sophie there?'

Sophie's my six-year-old niece. She and Ali are best friends, so we spend a lot of time at my brother's when I've got her.

'Sophie's home, probably in bed. Like you should be. You ready?'

'Yeah,' she groans.

'You don't want to go to bed?' I walk from the bar towards the back office to hear her.

'My new room is scary,' she says timidly.

Norah and her husband, Levi, bought a house recently. They moved in a month ago. At first, my ex getting married was weird for me. Trusting someone else with my kid isn't something that came easily.

'What's scary about it?'

'I dunno,' Ali says. 'Do you think you could check my closet sometime? Levi says monsters aren't real, but I told him you hunt monsters every day.'

I mean, I'm no Dean Winchester, but I get what she means.

'Different kinds of monsters, Al, but yeah, we'll do a little closet investigation next time I'm there, alright? Carry the phone over, and I'll have a look right now.'

'OK!' She giggles, hopping off her bed and carrying the phone to her closet. 'Let me just get the light.' The camera flips away from her as she scans the closet for me. 'See anything?' she yells.

'Everything looks good. No monsters – wait a second!' I say dramatically, staring at the screen now aimed at toy bins in her closet.

She does this at Norah's place, too? Strips all the Barbies and leaves them naked because she can't get the clothes back on them. After dressing a few myself, we've realized I've not got small enough fingers, so they stay naked at my place. Now it's just one giant tub I affectionately call Barbie's dream nudist colony.

'Is that a naked boy Barbie?'

She grabs the doll, flashing his smooth bits to the camera. 'His name's Ken, Daddy. I can't get his clothes on again. But he needs to wear somethin' 'cause he's going on a date with Barbie tomorrow, and it's got to be romantical.'

The way she says it makes me laugh. We talked about this recently. Dating. Not naked dating, but Mommy and Daddy dating – or in Norah's case, marrying – other people and how it didn't mean we loved her any less. Then she asked if it made me love Mommy less. Yes, it does. But that isn't what I told her because I'm an adult.

Poor Ken, going on a date. I'll cross my fingers for the plastic sucker.

Ali's adorable face fills the screen again, dimples punctuating her smile. 'Want to check under my bed next?'

'Let's do it.'

The camera practically drops to the floor as she flashes me a look under her bed – a couple of stuffed animals, a rogue sock covered in rainbow hearts. No monsters.

'All clear!'

She lifts the phone to her face again. 'Thanks, Dad.'

Ugh, I grab my chest. *Dad?* She seems to be phasing out the word 'daddy'. I'm slowly being kicked to the curb by my daughter, too.

'One more sleep, baby, then you get to be at my place for the week. We'll do something way fun. Sound good?'

'I can't wait!'

'Love you, Ali girl.'

'I love you more! Night, Daddy.' She bounces

around, pressing a kiss to the camera lens before the screen eventually goes dark as she ends the call.

'It's cute you still do that every night she's not with you,' Angel, Oz's wife, says, approaching the bar from the back office where I'm now standing. 'How's she doing?'

'She's the one girl on the planet who thinks I'm cool and hopes the world is full of rainbows, butterflies and only a few monsters that she's sure Daddy can take care of.'

Angel laughs, shaking her head. 'You're perfect as a girl dad. I honestly thought you'd freak over a daughter, but you seem to love it, naked Barbie dolls and all.'

Nobody gives you a book on parenting. It's not easy. It's messy, expensive and you're permanently tired. Things you never expected break your heart. And there's no way I can protect her from all the evil that wanders this planet. It haunts me in a way that gets worse with every passing birthday. When she's sixteen, I don't doubt I'll be that dad tracking her car and trailing her across the city to ensure she's not gotten herself into trouble.

'I do love it, naked Barbie dolls and all. Never tell Oz, but Lijah's my best friend.'

My daughter's name is Alijah. Pronounced uh-lie-jah. We call her a menagerie of things. Ali, Al, Lijah, Brooks's kid, the girl (Oz) – she answers to all of it.

'See, totally cute.' Angel stops walking, momentarily turning back to me. 'Wait, why are you here?' she asks, nodding for me to walk with her. 'I thought you were on a date?' She slides behind the bar with Ozie, who's now busy chatting up some regular customers across the way.

'Yeah.' I sit down next to Tyler. 'Didn't work out. She called me old and dumped me instead.'

She looks from the register with a gasp. 'Old? Offensive.' Angel is two years older than me, so I knew she'd understand. 'Maybe you should raise your lady age preference?'

'I've got no age preference. I just attract the under-twenty-six crowd. I don't know why – they don't seem to enjoy me long.'

'If only the rest of us got that option,' Ty says as he nudges me with his shoulder.

'Funny.' I nudge him back, practically knocking him off his stool, but he saves it and never spills even a drop of the beer in his hand.

Tyler's two years younger than me. Shorter, dumber, uglier. I'm mostly kidding. As teens – hell, even now – that's how I introduce him just for laughs. He took the 'annoying younger brother' to a whole new level. After realizing I was the bigger brother for good, he joined track and field so he could train to sprint away from me after intentionally pissing me off. A move that's saved his life many times over. Yet, as adults, I'd consider him best friend number two.

'Where's your nicer half?' I ask.

Emily is Ty's wife. They married right out of high school, much like Norah and me. Usually, they'd have dropped the kid with my parents, and she'd be here with him. Saturday nights are our thing. Me when I can, the rest of them rarely miss a week. Our circle isn't complete without her.

Angel glances at me with only her eyes, her brows raised halfway up her forehead. I know that face. Someone has a secret.

'Em isn't feeling great tonight,' Ty says uncomfortably.

'If only she'da swallowed... eh?' Oz says with a laugh, now stopping in front of me. 'Y'all heartbroken still? Or did Ali cheer ya up? Do you need a hug, sugarplum?' He extends his arms like he'll climb onto the bar and hug me.

'No thanks.' I shove him away. 'What do you mean if only she'd swa—'

Wait.

I turn to Ty, studying his drink, as he avoids

looking us in the eye. His go-to move when he's done something he doesn't want to discuss. Ozie's words suddenly fall into place in my head.

'She's *pregnant*?'

Ty nods, a slight smile turning the edges of his lips. 'I dunno how it happened.'

Ozie rolls his eyes dramatically. 'First, ya find a lady ya like.' He grabs Angel as she tries to walk past him, pulling her to him, his hands on her waist. 'Then heat things up with a little foreplay.' He makes a crude gesture with his tongue that I don't want to spend too much time thinking about. Angel veers away from him, attempting to escape. 'Then, slide tab A into slot B without a raincoat, and BAM! Baby.' He pumps his hips into Angel's before releasing her, slapping her ass as she walks away with a shake of her head. 'You've done this before, man. How's it still mystify you?'

In case it's not painfully obvious, Ozie's my obnoxious friend. The one who embarrasses all of us regularly. He has absolutely zero manners, looks like the love child of Tommy Lee and Jack Black, but the guy has a heart of gold. It's very deep down and rarely surfaces, but I swear it exists.

'Damn, little bro. You're about to be busy, busy.'

'I'm telling you, boys.' Oz doesn't give Ty a chance to defend his actions. 'If you two would sack up and get a little snippety-snip, you wouldn't have to worry about this anymore.'

'There's nothing wrong with your best friends having kids,' Angel tells him. 'They don't give us shit for not wanting them.'

Oz mimics her voice, repeating her words back to her. She jabs him in the ribs before pecking a kiss on his lips. Those two decided long ago that kids weren't their thing, and I respect that. Parenting isn't for everyone. I can't imagine Ozie with a child. I've got to censor him around mine, so I'm thankful they made the choice they did. As for me, maybe Norah and I didn't plan Alijah, but I don't regret one thing about her. She keeps me grounded, makes me laugh and teaches me all kinds of things I never knew I needed or wanted to know.

'Another kid is a good thing,' Ty says like he's trying to convince himself. 'Probably. It'll give Sophie something to mother. Girl's got an arsenal of fake babies stashed all over the house, so she'll be thrilled to play with a real one she can one day boss around.'

'Well, congratulations, man.' I lift the water bottle Angel set in front of me and tap it to Tyler's beer. 'Now you've got two kids to ruin.'

'Careful – one day karma will have some dude making up for your mistakes with Lijah.'

I pull my head back, not wanting to picture that even a little bit. Words only a brother could say.

Ozie laughs like it's funny. 'Brooksy's sensitive tonight, Ty. We'll hurt his feelings if we don't lay off, then he'll go home and cry into his pillow after having his heart broken for the millionth time this year,' he suggests.

'My heart ain't broken.'

It's not like I loved Kristyn. I'll be just fine in a few days.

'Maybe you should challenge yourself,' Angel suggests. 'Next time you see a woman you're interested in, get to know her. Be friends first and see where it goes. The problem is that you immediately jump into relationship status before you really know these women, hoping they're "the one" so you can quit dating. Take your time with the next one.'

'That's a lot of words to say "stop being desperate",' Oz says.

'I'm not desperate and don't believe in "the one". I'm just looking to hang out with someone prettier and nicer than you two.'

Tyler and Oz both laugh. 'Prettier than Oz?' Ty says, blowing him a kiss. 'Never gonna happen.'

3

MERCY

'Pants, pants, I know I wore pants over here,' I whisper to myself, summoning them to find me as I scan the dark room with the flashlight on my phone. I grab my heels as I come across them. Shamefully I never even took my top off. My bra's still on – in case you were wondering how magical the events leading up to this moment were.

There they are! I yank my jeans from a doorknob, pulling them on.

My gaze moves to a pile of mail on his coffee table near me – a guy whose name I don't even remember because I only met him a couple of hours before I ended up here. I glance at an unopened electric bill, a bright red urgent stamp on the front. I guess we have that in common.

'Jared Whitley.' I whisper his name, seeing if my tongue recognizes it. Nope. Interesting. I could have sworn he said his name was Jason. God, did I call him Jason? No. I don't think so. Wait, did I call him any-thing? My head swims a little. I had way too much wine earlier. I stop, steadying myself after nearly falling over as I slip my last shoe on.

I tiptoe to the door, turning the knob, then realize I should probably tell him I'm leaving. In a way that does not involve waking him up. Hmm. After what we just did, a wave he'll never see seems a tad imper-sonal. I glance around the room.

The mail!

I walk to his coffee table again, grab the delin-quent envelope, a pen, and scribble out some words – minus any way for him to contact me because I fully plan to ghost him – before slipping out his front door.

Thanks for the B-level performance.

I'm kidding.

I didn't write that – mainly because it was a C at best.

Thanks! Later. Lemon

Yeah, Lemon is my hook-up name. Lemon Rockefeller, to be exact. It sounds important, doesn't it? Like I'm some kind of princess patiently waiting to become the queen.

I glimpse my phone as I exit his place, glancing up and down the street, unsure of where I am. Two after midnight? Hell's bells, I am way too easy. I met up with this guy at eight, and I'm fleeing his apartment Cinderella-style at midnight like I'll turn into a pumpkin at any moment. I should be playing hard to get because I am a treasure, maybe even a diamond for the right guy – *if* he exists, which I seriously doubt.

Why'd I let him drive? No way can I hike across town in these heels. I like my toes and won't have any if I do. I need an Uber driven by someone who won't take advantage of a single lonely girl walking the streets in the middle of the night in a city riddled with crime as of late.

Wait. Do I even have any money? I tap into my bank account app. Enter my passcode and immediately groan when it lets me down again. The balance is a few zeros short of what I'd prefer. I have thirty-seven dollars to my name until next Friday. Practically a week from now. I should have never bought these shoes. I can't risk an Uber. What if I run out of coffee?

I scroll through my contacts, sing-songing through

them in my head. Edie and Carlos are both at work. Dax and Hollyn are probably in bed. There's zero way I'd ever hear the end of this from River. My thumb hovers over Dylan's name. He'll make fun of me, but he's the only one who'll expect nothing less. Reluctantly, I tap his number and pull the phone to my ear.

'I thought we weren't allowed to do booty calls?'

Instant regret.

'Ha-ha. *Not* a booty call. I need a ride.'

He snickers into the phone like he already knows where I'm going with this. So, it's not the first time I've called in the middle of the night with an SOS.

'What happened to your car?'

'I made a rookie mistake and let a guy bring me back to his place.'

'If only you were a rookie at this game, eh?'

'Shut. Up. At least I get laid, unlike some people I know.'

'I get laid,' he says defensively. 'When I want to. That's beyond the point, though. Do you really think that attitude will get me to put on pants and come pick you up?'

'Come on, Dyl,' I groan, walking down the sidewalk. 'You live across the hall. I'm a little bit drunk. I'm broke. I'm wearing brand-new heels that I'm pretty sure I'm bleeding into because I didn't take the time to break them in. What if I'm kidnapped? You'll feel terrible.'

Please work.

'Where are ya?' he moans.

Woo! Success! I knew that would get him. I glance around, spotting a street sign. No way.

'Shit.'

'What?'

'North Portland. I'm in Kenton.'

'Good God, Merc. You pick the worst neighborhoods to walk-of-shame home from every time. Listen, stay in the streetlights because once someone kidnaps you, it's just a hop, skip and a jump to toss you into the river, and then we'll never find you.'

'Once someone kidnaps me?' I raise my voice. 'How about we don't speak my disappearance into existence? Now, please, Dyl. You're the only person I can count on at this moment, so get your pants on and get here.'

He bellows a laugh into the phone. I'm glad someone finds this funny.

'Pretty please?' I say sweetly, hoping it helps.

'Can you not get to a train station?'

'I'm sure I could, but don't you think that's the first place a criminal will look? The lonely girl getting on the train in the middle of the night seems like the perfect victim.'

'Hide any gang colors you're wearing, stay out of the parks, taser to the balls or neck, and you'll probably be alright.'

'I'm going to use that taser on you,' I grumble. 'Wait!' I stop walking, looking for the music drifting my way. 'I hear music...' I glance around, spotting the lit-up bar a block over. 'There's a bar nearby. It's called Oz? Looking it up now.' I flip the call to speaker, pulling up the bar's website on my phone. 'Their motto is "music, booze, regrets".' I glance over at it. 'I like it already.'

'You sure that's not your motto?'

'It's calling to me, Dyl.' I walk towards it. 'I'll wait there.'

'Do *not* throw your panties at the stage!'

'Won't be a problem; I'm not wearing any. I couldn't find them when I left.'

Dylan groans like a disappointed father. 'Just going to blow by that, but trust me, I've got thoughts. Until you see my face, *stay there.*'

'Thank you! Thank you! Thank you! See ya soon.' I click out of the call, shoving my phone into my pocket and making my way to the bar.

The place is packed. Cars lined up on the curb out

front. It doesn't look like any place special. A hole-in-the-wall dive bar, really. I push through the door and stop in my tracks. Whoa. *Not* a dive bar. How have I never been here before?

A rectangular-shaped bar is in the center of the room, with stools on all sides. It's made of white stone and is lit from within, making it glow around the veins in the rock that are a dark purple-gray. The stage is lifted a foot off the ground at the end of a long windowless room to the main bar's left. Eggplant-colored leather booths line the walls. Table and chairs fill in the rest of the space. Square neon fixtures hang randomly from the ceiling like giant chandeliers giving the room a warm glow. The soft light of white glass lamps illuminates each table. The entire place is very swanky cool.

Since Dylan will be a while, I should probably grab a drink so I don't look like I'm loitering. Cash, cash. I dig through my pockets as I approach the bar.

'Whatcha want, sugar?' A tall, dark-haired woman, bouncing with the music, stops in front of me.

'A glass of whatever is cheapest.' I slide a crumpled five-dollar bill across the bar. She grabs it, tucks it into the front of her shirt, and fills a glass with something from the tap.

I sit on the stool next to me, turning to watch the

band. A heavily tattooed man is playing lead guitar. A tattoo-less bassist is on one side of him, singing backup for the woman center stage, and a guy who never left his emo years is on drums. Musician to musician, they're all excellent.

I'm mesmerized by how well this guy plays guitar, though. Like he's done it for decades, but he doesn't look that old. When my gaze finally reaches his face, our eyes meet.

Oh, shit – I *know* this guy.

He flashes me a smile, losing his place for a moment before recovering with a laugh that displays a single dimple on one cheek. Yep, that's him. How on earth did I not know *this* about him? Probably because he doesn't even know my real name because we had a no-strings-attached 'relationship' five or six years ago. I don't even remember why it ended. Here we are, years later, and he's found my one weakness without even trying. He could be the worst guitar player in the world, and I'd still be grinning back at him like I've got a hanger in my mouth because he's cute, if I remember right, wasn't terrible in bed and has a guitar in his hands. Musicians are my weakness.

I know this guy as Drake Ramoray. That's right; he stole an alter ego from one of the greatest shows on earth. It immediately made me laugh, and I called him Doctor for our entire 'relationship'.

He meets my gaze again, a slight shake of his head and a grin he can't contain before he looks away. Is he flirting without words?

No. We haven't talked in years. And even then, our conversations were primarily breathless.

Our eyes meet again. This time, I smile involuntarily. This feels flirty. Fluttery even. Interesting.

As the song ends, the woman who seems to be the lead takes to an electronic keyboard. How am I only just noticing the piano set up near her? Instruments are my thing. I see them everywhere I go. But tonight, a gorgeous tattooed man I've seen naked performs before me, and – *poof* – I only see him.

What in the hell is wrong with me?

I lift the glass of beer in my hand, holding it at eye level and inspecting it like I could see a roofie. I've been holding it the whole time; there's no way someone drugged me. It's just beer mixing with the wine from earlier. Ugh, I hope that doesn't all come back up later.

My attention is back on the stage as the band flawlessly moves into a Goldfrapp song. The lead is pretty. Soft brown skin, black-as-night hair cut chin length and worn straight but messy. Rings are on all her fin-

gers, and a hoop is in one nostril. Her voice is en-
chanting. These four aren't new to this.

'Hey.' I call the bartender over with a wave. 'Who
is this?'

'They're called Don't Panic. My brother-in-law's
band. He owns the bar, my sister, Angel, is his wife
and she's lead singer. They've played in-house every
Saturday night for the last decade. Good, huh?'

'This is the only place they perform?'

'Yeah,' she says with a nod. 'Super popular. We've
got regulars that never miss a show.'

'I can see why,' I say, primarily to myself, turning
back to them.

The good doctor looks my way again, flashing that
adorably dimpled smile. Damn it – he's still cute. A
dark-gray baseball cap covers his short sandy blond
hair, and a bright blue T-shirt with the word 'YES' in
all caps fits him in a way that's holding my attention
too well. Gray jeans. A pair of black Doc Martens on
his feet. A black bracelet on one of his wrists and a
slight five o'clock shadow on his handsome face. He's
probably six-two, medium build, average but firm.
Can you see firm from afar? I feel like the vague memories I have of him, and his shirt is helping me say –
YES – I can. Tattoos start at the left side of his neck,
disappearing under his T-shirt and covering his arms

(and his chest/back/stomach) to his knuckles. The tattoos are primarily flowers, old-school flash art, and even a giant tiger on his back, and I've spent hours memorizing them. Visions of him, tattoos in full view, dance in my head.

Oh my God, Mercy. Stop.

I swear I'm not usually this horny. I realize I've just snuck out of a guy's apartment – like a vampire trying to escape the sun – but I'm not usually daydreaming about a new guy moments later.

His adorable grin forces one from me as our eyes meet again. I can't seem to look away.

'Want another?' the bartender asks, pulling me from the guitarist's spell.

Jesus, did I drink this already? I glance at my near-empty glass.

'Another, sure.' Definitely, yes. I should drink whatever this is away. 'Which one's your brother-in-law?'

'Drummer,' she says, filling a new glass. 'Ozie. But I grew up with all of them.'

Interesting. So, if I got ballsy and decided I needed to know who the guitarist actually was without making a fool of myself, she's who I'd talk to.

Out of the corner of my eye, I see my driver walk through the front door. He got here fast. Either he wasn't at home, or he ran every light to get here in record time. He glances around the place, his gaze lingering on the band for a moment before finally landing on me. He flashes a smile along with a playful roll of his eyes as he makes his way to me.

'I don't know what I was expecting, but this wasn't it,' Dylan says.

He requests a drink from the bartender, instructing her to add me to his tab before turning to watch the band.

'They're good,' Dyl says after watching them for a few.

'Right? And me being me – I'm pretty sure I've hooked up with that guy?' I point the guitarist's way, leaning into Dylan so he can hear me.

'You're *pretty* sure?' He scrunches his face like he can't believe me.

'It was a long time ago. I was young.'

'How do you explain why I'm here tonight, then?'

I stare at him, hoping an answer comes to me. 'I'm, uh – complicated; you know this.'

He nods, glancing back at the stage. 'Let me guess... drummer?' He laughs, knowing damn well I'm not into the probably late-thirty-something guy wearing too much eyeliner.

'No.'

'Scrawny or tattoos?'

'Tattoos.'

Dylan cocks his head. 'I'm a straight dude – I don't see what you see.' He lifts a single hand. 'Tell me you're not concocting a bathroom seduction plan while I'm here? 'Cause that'll be a tad awkward. 'Thanks for boning my friend while I waited to drive her home...'

I laugh out loud. He knows me too well. 'I can't sleep with him. At least not tonight because I promised myself I'd never do two in a day. A girl has to have some standards.'

The bartender hands him his drink.

'You have no idea how glad I am to hear you finally say those words,' he says, sitting on the stool next to me with a smirk.

'I'm just admiring the memory of him from afar. Perhaps we should try to get you laid while we're here?'

'Can't,' he says, a now cocky grin plastered on his face. 'I swore to myself that I'd never let you set me up again. One urgent care visit for a mystery rash was enough.'

In my defense, that girl seemed like his type. Sweet, soft-spoken yet perky, and pretty in an innocent way. How was I to know she'd rolled in a field of poison oak before their date? Besides that one snafu, they were a good match. But when Dylan broke into a red bubbly rash all over his body the next day, he freaked, thinking he had some kind of STD. All went well in the end. He got laid, and it only took two tubes of cortisone cream before he was good as new. After about a week, that is.

He's completely ignoring me as his head rocks with the beat – Dylan's one of those musicians who hears every single note. Right now, he's downloading this into his internal files, and he'll be playing these songs at the shop tomorrow by ear. I won't be surprised when he tells me he emailed the band to let them know we have a hirable recording studio. He's all about business opportunities. He even carries a stack of business cards in his wallet.

'It's not that I *can't* get laid,' he finally says defensively. 'I'm just too much of a gentleman to ask some random woman to join me in the bathroom,' he adds, an unmistakable judgmental tone in his voice.

I roll my eyes, but I can't argue because he's not wrong. He is a gentleman. He also thinks 'damaged' women can be fixed with proper attention and behavioral awards. He's not feeding me M&M's every time I do something he approves of, but yes, he's tried that fixing shit on me. But sparkling with perfection isn't my thing. I'm more of a fool's gold kind of girl. There's some sparkle outside, but dig a little deeper, and the darkness comes to light.

'Tattoos is a guy named Brooks Hudson,' Dyl says, leaning into me.

I glance over at him, horror probably all over my face. 'What are you doing? I can't know his name! We were no strings attached. His real name is a giant string.'

He pinches his eyebrows together. 'Pretty sure you could close your eyes and picture him naked – but knowing his name crosses the line?'

I hold up an offended hand like I haven't already dreamed of precisely that.

'I don't give random sleepover guests my real name. You know this.'

'That's right, Lemon Rockefeller. I forgot you were a citrus heiress.'

I chuckle; the name I chose still makes me laugh, and the guy I first tested it on didn't even notice we were standing next to the lemons when I made it up.

'I don't want some rando hunting me down unless he needs to warn me of the three scariest letters on the planet.'

'S-T-D?'

I roll my eyes, sipping my drink and ignoring him, but he's not wrong.

'As disturbing as that is, usually when we go to bars together, I act as your wingman, so I wanted to help you out. While you were probably creeping him out with that stare, I talked to the bartender. She grew up with him. He's thirty-six, divorced, recently dumped and chronically single. He started playing the guitar at ten. Never wanted to be a rock star, just does this to blow off some steam.'

He's a literal guitar hero to blow off some steam? I could think of many other ways he could blow off some steam, including me, less clothing *and* his guitar.

'Peas in a pod, you two, and he doesn't even know who you are yet,' Dyl says with a nod.

I glance up at the stage again, trying not to let my stare move back into what he just called creepy. Drake, or rather, Brooks Hudson, glances at me again. His eyes dart to Dylan, who's sitting way too close. I catch Dylan lifting his chin, the universal silent guy greeting.

'Don't do that.'

'Why?'

'He's gonna think we're here together.'

'We *are* here together.'

'I mean romantically.'

Dyl rolls his eyes as he stands and walks away from me like I'm annoying him.

Great. Now it looks like he's just dumped me.

Right then, a couple of men bolt from the bar, sprinting through the place, heads following. Is this a fight heading outside? Who really cares; they're taking it outside, and my eyes are on Brooks Hudson.

Moments later, lights and sirens are wailing by. Good thing I'm not walking home.

There's a slight shuffle on stage as Brooks hands off his guitar to the singing woman. Flawlessly, without missing a word, she takes over, and he disappears out a side door near the back of the room.

The fluttering within that I was starting to enjoy suddenly settles in my chest, like fall leaves dropping to the ground in the wind, leaving me with my usual black hole heart sensation. Why did he just bolt? And why am I upset about it?

4

BROOKS

'What is this place?' Ali asks, sitting next to me, swinging her feet in her chair. We've been here thirty minutes, and this is the first time she's questioned it.

'It's a Mexican restaurant. Tequila Mockingbird.' I laugh to myself at the name. Someone was creative.

'They got good tacos,' she says, taking a bite of a crunchy shell taco and dropping half the contents onto her plate. She doesn't even notice as her eyes are on my phone playing one of her favorite shows.

Norah and I exchange our daughter with a family dinner every Sunday night. Nor suggested it after she and Levi got engaged. We figured it would be best for Ali to see that we all get along. I even went to their wedding. I hope this shows Alijah that she can trust us and not try to play us against one another. Not that six is the age plotting against your parents begins, but why not attempt to get ahead of it?

'Heard ya got dumped again?' Levi says with a smirk.

We're friends, Levi and me. Not because I chose him but because Norah did, and he's voluntarily helping raise our daughter. We have mutual respect for one another. He calls me for fatherly advice. We spend holidays together. He and I have even watched a couple of games together. Norah could have picked way worse than Levi.

'I should have never told her that.'

'Yeah, she's not great at keeping secrets,' he says under his breath as Norah walks our way from the bathrooms.

'What's "dumped"?' Ali asks.

'It's your daddy's middle name,' Norah says with a smirk, sitting across from me.

Lijah raises a single eyebrow, exactly like I some-times do.

'Ha ha.' I don't laugh, turning to Alijah to explain. '"Dumped" is – well, it's when you like someone, and they like you back – until they don't?' I cock my head, unsure of my answer. 'Then they ask you to go away.'

She scrunches her face, clearly displeased with this. 'Someone doesn't like you back?'

I nod, appreciating her disbelieving tone more than she knows. 'Shocking, isn't it? I'm a delight.' Norah guffaws. I shoot her a glare before glancing back at Alijah. 'That said, yeah, some people don't like Daddy.' I lift both shoulders like it's a complete mystery to me too.

Maybe that's my book? *How to Explain Your Dating Life to Your Children* – Some People Don't Like Daddy. Boom. Written in one sentence.

Ali picks at her plate, eating grated cheese by the piece, visibly stewing on my words until she finally looks over at me with a smile.

'I like you, Daddy.' She sets her hand on mine. 'I won't dumped you.'

My God, that is the sweetest thing she's ever said in all her six years.

'Well, you're my favorite girl on the planet, so I'm glad to hear that.' I lift her tiny hand to my lips, earning a giggle.

Had Norah and I not accidentally gotten pregnant on what was probably the last time we slept together before she suddenly decided she'd had enough of me, my world would be a whole lot darker than it is right now.

You can't imagine how shocked I was when I found out I was having a baby five months after Norah kicked me out while sitting in her divorce attorney's office. She already knew the sex and was afraid to tell me because I might think the baby wasn't mine, so she had her lawyer do it. Did that fear prevent me from offending the hell out of her and having a paternity test done anyway? No. But Ali will never know because Norah swore to take it to the grave. Looking back, I'd be lost without Alijah. She's the reason I am who I am.

'How's it going tonight?'

I glance at the waitress speaking a couple of tables away from us.

'Oh. My. God,' Norah says under her breath, her eyes wide and on me.

'No. Freaking. Way,' I say simultaneously, slowly lifting an eyebrow at her words and her at mine. 'What?'

'*That's* her.'

I try to look at her without making it obvious because it *is* her. Lemon. The woman I had a quick fling with right after Ali was born. A fling that had strict rules because neither of us wanted a relationship. That *was* her at the bar the other night.

When she turns from the table, her gaze lands on

me. She stops, her jaw dropping open through a smile. The surprise on her face slowly morphs into her seeming happy to see me.

Good God, she's even prettier than I remember. Her straight dark brown hair falls below her shoulders. One side is tucked behind her ear, revealing multiple silver hoops. Her eyes are emerald green; the smokey gray and sparkly green eye make-up hypnotically accentuates them. Pink fills her cheeks, almost masking the splash of freckles across them. She's wearing an oatmeal-colored blouse tucked into a pair of black skinny jeans, and without the electric blue stilettos she's wearing, I think she's around five-six, five-seven? Super feminine, average build, perfect curves. Solid twelve out of ten, if my memory serves me correctly.

'Doctor.' She acknowledges my alter ego with a smirk, walking away, glancing back at me with that same curious grin she had the other night.

'Doctor?' Norah asks. 'You know her?'

Know her? No. I don't even know her real name, but I do know other things, and I can't say I hate the memories.

'Hello?'

Norah's voice bounces around my skull while my heart does the same in my chest, making breathing hard. That is the exact feeling I got when I saw her at the bar the other night. I've never had that before.

Once she's entirely out of sight, I breathe, rubbing my hand over my chest. If I have a heart attack right here, at thirty-six, in front of a woman I can't quit thinking about, I hope I die.

Norah's concerned stare catches my attention, and only then do I realize I'm rubbing my chest like I'm actually in pain. I readjust my hat then drop my hand.

'What's wrong with you?'

'Nothing,' I say as casually as possible, but I know I've failed when Levi's gaze meets mine. He lifts a judgmental eyebrow. I shake my head, hoping he'll let it go.

My heart has slowed just enough that I'm stunned silent. I haven't thought about Lemon in years; now, she won't get out of my head, after I've somehow run into her twice in one week.

I glance back. She's standing at the bar, obviously trying not to look my way, and when she does, it's an instant grin. I want to talk to her, but not in front of my daughter and ex.

Suddenly, she's headed my way again.

'You guys good?' she asks, stopping at our table and glancing around before settling on me.

Norah and Levi both look at me.

Say something intelligent, Brooks. Be witty. Charming. Make her laugh.

'Yeah – yeah,' I stutter out.

Smooth. I'm sure she's impressed that you've ogled her twice now and have only managed to say one stupid word to her. Speak, for Christ's sake. Now's your chance. Say something. Ask her name. AN-Y-THING.

I open my mouth, but no words leave my lips. They're all jumbled up in my head. This isn't like me. I don't freeze up in nerve-wracking moments. It's kind of why I'm good at my job. I'm the guy who can keep his cool in any situation. The problem is none of what's going on in my head or chest right now seems normal.

'Just let me know if you need something,' she says, never taking her eyes off me.

I nod as she flashes me a grin before walking back to the bar. She's giving me every opportunity, and I'm sitting here like a brainless idiot, letting them pass me by until things are super fucking awkward. Way to go me.

'What was that?' Norah asks, witnessing the whole thing.

'What?' You're damn right I'm playing the innocence card here. Maybe she'll buy it?

'That,' Norah says, nodding in the woman's direction. 'What was *that*? Do you know her? Because I think I might.'

'You might?' I glance at the bar, but she's gone. 'How? I don't even know her. I mean, I... for a while, we, uh...' Suddenly, I remember I'm talking to my ex-wife and about to tell her about a two-month fling with a woman whose name I never knew. Nope. I can't do that. 'It's nothing.'

Norah laughs. 'Brooks, you're stumbling over your words because of a woman. It's not nothing.'

'No, that's not – hold up – how do you think you know her?'

'She's the woman from my dream.'

The woman from her dream?

'What drea—' Mid-word, the whole conversation comes rushing back to me. 'No way.' I glance at Ali, who's luckily missing the entire embarrassing episode as she's got my phone in her hands, her attention on the video still playing – saved by *WordGirl*.

'It's her,' Norah says. 'I'm one thousand percent sure, and you know I'm never wrong. Now spill it. How do you know her?'

I lean Norah's way to fill her in – talking under my breath, hopeful Ali doesn't overhear. Because if I don't appease this woman now, she'll be texting me all night, attempting to pry it out of me.

'I played at Oz's on Friday, and she walked into the bar. She smiled, and I smiled back. We kept catching each other's gaze. It felt like we were silently flirting, and I've been thinking about her ever since.'

'That's why she thinks you're a doctor?'

'It's possible we had a thing a while back. A no-strings-attached thing, so she never knew my name, *Sunny Knight...*'

Levi bursts out a laugh. 'Norah was Sunny Knight when I met her,' he says. 'You used the same name on everyone?'

'Yeah, why not Rainy Drought, Nor?' I ask, both me and Levi laughing.

The way she glares through her pinched smile says she's amused but refuses to give me the satisfaction.

'Lying is easier when you make it simple,' Norah says with a guilty grin before her gaze moves back to me. 'So you spent some evenings romancing a woman who never knew your name. Then recently had a moment of eye contact, and now she's got you all tongue-tied?'

'I'm not tongue-tied,' I argue, slightly irritated she's witnessed this. 'In my defense, you just told our daughter that "dumped" is my middle name.'

'It's not a lie. Every woman dumps you. Even I

don't understand why and I was one of them. Why'd you stop seeing her?'

'I don't remember. I got busy, and it just ended...'

'Brooks. My God, you were staring at her with cartoon heart eyes. Strange things happen with "the one".'

'*The one?* Stop right there...'

She rolls her eyes, not even pretending she'll stop talking. 'We always know subconsciously when we've met them. That's why people tell their friends and family they've met the person they'll marry after only the first date. We just know.'

'That little feeling's not always right. Evidence I'd like to bring to the table: I once thought *you* were the one,' I say sarcastically. 'You're reading way too much into it. I want to talk to her, but I've already shown her my worst side.'

'What did you do to her?' Nor asks like it must be something real bad.

'You do not get details. I meant – I've shown her I'm some douchey dude who "romances" women and then disappears. We never even went on a date...' I'm having to remember our daughter is sitting right next to us and we need to watch what we say.

'Romantic,' Nor says sarcastically.

'I was in a weird place then. We'd just had Alijah,

and I had no normal. I don't want to come off as a stalker.'

'You do that by speaking, not just staring at her blankly. Wait.' She stops talking, a single finger in the air like she's just had an epiphany or, worse, a vision I'm certain I don't want to know. 'This is a giant flashing neon sign and you're afraid because you don't want to get hurt again.'

'Daddy's not afraid of anything,' Ali interjects, never looking up from the phone. A reminder that she listens to everything even when it doesn't seem she is. Shit. I just called myself a douchey stalker. That'll be fun to explain.

I motion Ali's way proudly. 'The one woman on the planet that gets me – not to mention the smartest girl at the table – has spoken. I second her words. I'm not afraid.'

Ali beams proudly, her eyes never leaving her show.

'Then go talk to her,' Norah challenges me.

'I think she has a boyfriend.'

'Why do you think that?'

'There was a guy with her at Oz's.'

Norah glances at the bar and my head follows. There she is again. Making drinks and not even realizing we're over here discussing her.

'She seems interested,' Norah informs me as if she doesn't believe it. 'With all these stolen glances I'd bet she's still swimming in the singles pool.'

'She's working, Nor.'

'So?'

'What if she thinks I hunted her down instead of this being a random coincidence? I don't want to make her uncomfortable.'

She sighs dramatically. 'You've seen this woman in what I can assume were some pretty revealing positions, and you think talking to her might make her uncomfortable? Just don't be creepy, you weirdo.'

I'm slightly irritated she's calling me out like this. Yeah, Norah and I are friends raising a kid together. We have a history that goes back to our teen years, but usually, our conversations revolve around Alijah, our upcoming schedules, or sometimes her stupid visions. *Not* my love life.

I look everywhere – the silence hanging awkwardly over our table like a raincloud about to burst – avoiding Norah's stare. I am not afraid of this, damn it.

'Fine,' I say, glancing back just as she's rounding the end of the bar carrying drinks to the table she was at earlier. 'Once she's delivered these drinks, I'll talk to her.'

Levi lifts a fist in the air. A silent *you got this.*

'How'd my life become me hanging out with my ex-wife and her new husband?' I blow out a nervous breath, adjusting my hat again and avoiding eye contact with anyone around me.

While Lemon speaks to the table she's delivering to, I make myself look busy, my eyes on Ali's show. My ears are on her, though. Her voice is intoxicating. She's confident, light-hearted and funny. I remember that laugh. She was so fun in the bedroom. It was never uncomfortable.

She glances at me shyly as she walks past, a slight smile on her face when our eyes meet.

Do it, Brooks. Talk to her. Speak! See if Norah's right. God, I can't believe I'm considering advice from my ex-wife.

I stand from the table once she's returned to the bar. 'Can I borrow this?' I ask Ali, taking my phone from her.

'Yeah,' she groans.

Considering I can barely think straight, my chances of playing this smooth are slim. Asking for her number and having her program it into my phone seems foolproof. Will she think I'm a total asshole when she realizes I never even initially asked for her number? Maybe. It's not like I was sending over *wanna do it?* texts at midnight; we did chat, mostly through a hook-up site. The possibility of her thinking I'm some booty call asshole is a chance I've got to take, or I'll never forgive myself. I'll ask for the opportunity to prove that I'm not that guy. Easy-peasy.

'I'll be right back,' I say to Norah, who excitedly claps her hands in front of her chest. 'Stay here,' I command. 'Don't let her move,' I say to Levi. 'Hold her down, tie her up, sit on her, whatever, just keep her here. The last thing I need is help from my ex.' I pat Norah's head, hoping she listens but knowing her too well to believe it.

In the time it took to keep Norah at the table, Lemon – as I know her – has disappeared and only the Hispanic man working the bar with her remains.

'What can I get ya?' he asks as I stop at the counter.

'I'm looking for a woman that works here. Dark hair, green eyes, beautiful?'

He chuckles, shaking his head. 'She don't work here.'

I glance over at the table she just delivered to, confused. 'She just carried out a tray of drinks... pretty sure she works here.'

The bartender leans forward. 'I mean, that's what she's commanded I say to anyone who asks about her,' he whispers, glancing around guiltily. 'She don't work here, man,' he shouts with a heavy accent; the grin on his face says he's enjoying this.

After a beat of silence, he leans across the bar, covering his mouth with one hand. 'Technically – and you didn't hear this from me – she really don't work here. She's a classical musician. A prodigy or something. Her family owns the place. They let her fill in when she's spent all her money on shoes or some crap. Worst bartender I ever had.'

He suddenly looks me over. 'She spill a drink on you? 'Cause it wouldn't be her first casualty. What was it? I'll get you another on the house; just don't question her, or she'll offend everyone in the room.'

She's a classical musician? A prodigy? The worst bartender ever who might offend the whole room with a complaint? I've never been so intrigued. When he's done speaking, I realize I've got an ear-to-ear grin.

'No. She didn't spill anything on me. I just wanted to ta—'

Right then, my phone buzzes in my hand. I glance at the screen, dropping my head in frustration. Travis Seiver. Damn it. Work. I flash the guy my phone, holding up the universal *give me a sec* finger as I step away from the bar to take the call.

'What's up?'

'There was a scuffle at your trap-house while you

were on your little staycation, and now I'm involved. Dom opened his mouth.'

'Damn it,' I growl in frustration into the phone. What am I madder at? The fact that I might have a criminal making my life hard or that my heart is still all aflutter in the presence of a woman I know very little about but suddenly want to?

'Catch ya at a bad time, muffin?' Seiver asks, clearly not sorry for anything.

'If you must know, yeah, ya kinda did.'

'You know the shit that comes with this job, Hudson. We're married to it. Take care of this before the gossip spreads through all the wrong people, and I fire you.'

'Fire me for what? I can't make Dominic shut up.'

'Try, or I'll find something.' The phone goes silent, me not realizing he's hung up on me until it rings again, this time directly into my ear.

'Now what?'

'I told you Dominic as an informant was a fucking wildcard!' Andrews, my partner, barks the words through the phone, forcing me to pull it away from my head to save my eardrums. I should have known the next call would come from him. He's never hesitated to let me know when I've failed before.

Andrews and I are undercover detectives with the

drug and organized crime unit for the local police. We investigate drug rings, murders, organized crime and all that stuff no one usually wants to be a part of. We work on shift together, but after working what felt like hundreds of hours a week the last few months, on this one case, I finally convinced Seiver I had everything under control. We were sitting in what I thought was the calm before the storm, and he gave me a few days off. I'm not on the clock this weekend, yet I've been urgently called out twice now.

'Anyone else having issues?' I ask.

'Not to my knowledge. Marky Mark and the druggie bunch packed up and moved everything. I figured our safest bet was to let the shitstorm settle. But Seiver's pissed—'

'Yeah, he recently told me as much,' I interrupt him, a little irritated Andrews was filled in before me. We're both off this weekend. He's spent the last five years training me to take his spot when he retires – which is coming soon. Seiver needs to stop convincing himself I can't do this job on my own.

'Ole Domi wants a word. He says you made him a promise you didn't keep. I don't know how far his words have traveled, but you might want to watch your back.'

I drop my head. Sometimes my informants give

me serious grief. This is feeling like one of those moments.

'Go stroke Dom's hair and tell him everything will be alright, and I'll deal with Seiver.'

Andrews has been doing this job for decades; he's tired. He's got one year left. He prefers to be what I affectionately call my getaway driver instead of the guy befriending drug lords and criminals. That leaves the tricky parts for me. Like smoothing shit over with a prisoner I've somehow convinced to rat out his buddies and bosses. This'll be a fun time.

'I'll take care of Dominic and call ya,' I say, hanging up as I walk to Norah's table. I pull my wallet from my pocket and hand her all my cash. Eighty bucks. 'This is for dinner. Can I pick Ali up in the morning?'

'Go,' she says, a knowing look on her face. 'We got her.'

'Thanks.' I point to Ali. 'Love you, girl.' I lean down, pressing a kiss to her forehead. 'Daddy's gotta work, but I'll see you in the morning, alright? Cake pops and hot chocolate for breakfast, deal?'

'Deal!' Alijah squeals, bumping her fist to mine while flashing my favorite grin, a hint of disappointment mixed in.

She has no idea what exactly goes on when I'm at

work. Hopefully, she won't for many years. Keeping it from her was a decision I made a long time ago, and Norah agreed. She knows I work in law enforcement and sometimes arrest 'monsters' (what she calls bad guys) – that's it.

I glance at the bar as I leave, not seeing the woman whose name I still don't know. I want to talk to her; instead, I'm fleeing the scene for the second time. If this is Norah's so-called fate, we'll meet again. Pretty sure that's how all this destiny shit works.

5

MERCY

After taking a break to settle my fluttering heart, I step out of the kitchen and back into the bar with Julio. I wish I didn't know Brooks's name because now it's personal. I want to know why this is happening. I want to talk to this man. I glance out at their table. Empty.

'He *left*? Again?'

Damn it. This makes my chest feel like hardening concrete. I preferred the butterflies.

'If you *know* him, why were you only eavesdropping and not talking to him?' Julio asks.

'Because I don't know him – only his name. And his penis.' I say that last part quietly and into my towel.

Julio lowers his chin.

'We may or may not have had previous relations, but it was years ago. Now, I've randomly run into him twice, and each time there's a weird buzzing-fluttery sensation in my body that I don't think was there before.'

'Just in your loins or everywhere?' he asks with a half-cocked grin.

I glare. 'Everywhere...' I say, as I wipe down the counter.

Julio's eyebrows shoot up his forehead. 'Love at first sight?'

'That's not a thing, and I've laid eyes on him before, so not possible. Guess again.'

'Lust after previous fucks?'

I laugh at the ridiculousness of it but also nod my head. 'That seems more me.'

My brother says I need to rein in my cynicism towards love. I say a healthy dose of cynicism is what saves breaking already damaged hearts. But what the hell do I know? Love isn't an emotion I've experienced often. My parents didn't love me. Pretty sure my foster families only liked me at best. There's my brother and friends, and sure that's a good kind of love to have, but now that I've hit thirty, the thing on my mind is currently dying alone. Unloved, never *having* loved, and a real pitiful story someone will someday tell without enthusiasm.

For reasons I don't understand – considering I hate weddings – I'm helping my best friends plan theirs, and my mind's wandering on sleepless nights. Now, not only am I worried that I'll die alone, but what will I do when everyone I know is partnered off, and my heart still hasn't excavated itself from the concrete slab it sits under?

It's why I'm questioning this feeling I'm having in Brooks Hudson's presence. Did I feel like this when we were sleeping together, and our conversations consisted of small talk and semi-full sentences during mind-melting sex? I don't think I did. How is he doing this without a guitar hanging around his neck? Is it his adorable smile? The tattoos? The way he stares into my eyes like he can see my soul?

Settle down, Mercy. Put your feelings box away and forget him. It's nothing. You're just horny.

'You got visitors,' Julio says, glancing at the front door.

He came back for me! Holy guacamole. Nobody's *ever* come back for me. Before I look his way, I smooth out my apron, ensuring nothing is out of place. This is so exciting.

'Merc!' Hollyn says when my eyes meet hers.

I drop my shoulders, a disappointed groan leaving my lips.

'Uh, thanks?' she says, clearly offended.

'Sorry, it wasn't about you.'

No way am I telling her I was hoping she was the handsome blond man I spent weeks sleeping with, never told her about, and now can't get out of my head. Mainly because she'd never believe I was pining after some guy. I don't pine. I take care of business and then move on. If she knew how much I've been dreaming about Brooks Hudson, she'd insert herself into the situation, attempt to hunt him down, and it'd blow up from there.

'What are you guys doing here?' I ask.

'Dax didn't feel like cooking tonight,' she says.

'Hols has no interest in learning, either,' he adds, winking her way.

She stands on her tiptoes, pecking a kiss onto his lips.

These two are sickeningly in love. They got engaged last month, after reuniting a year ago. Growing up, Dax lived next door to Hollyn. He's best friends with her little brother, River, and I'm best friends with her. He crushed on her his whole life, then never told her, like the stargazing, flower-loving dork he is. Last spring, he picked her up after a bad breakup, and here we are a year later. They're in public-displays-of-affection-that'll-make-you-want-to-gouge-your-eyes-out levels of love. The fact that she's actively planning their wedding isn't making it better, either.

'Also,' Hols says, turning back to me as she pulls her phone from her pocket, 'I want your opinion on some dresses.'

'OK!' I say with enthusiasm.

She's my best friend, a sister really; of course I'm excited she's getting married. Just not brainstorm-a-pro-and-con-list-for-every-dress-she-falls-in-love-with excited like she is. But I won't ruin this for her. Maybe choosing a giant white dress isn't one of my daydreams, but it is hers, and because I love her to death, I'm going to suck it up and help plan this wedding with a smile.

'Well, saddle up, kids.' I motion to the barstools. 'Want an entrée? I'm starving, and I'm sure Carlos has nothing better to do...' I joke loudly, but only because I see him walk past the saloon doors that separate the bar from the kitchen. We're just after the dinner rush, so he's finally got a break.

His steps stop, then he appears, staring at me over the doors. 'Everyone has drinks, right, *amor*?'

Carlos is a couple of years younger than Edie, who is a decade older than me. Ed and I didn't grow up together; I'd only met him a few times before the nightmare that put me into the system. Because Ed's mother took an interest in my case when it hit the news, she convinced him and his boyfriend (now husband) to step in. They spent a few years working their patooties off to gain custody of my untrusting, mouthy thirteen-year-old self. Picture that and two twenty-something gay men attempting to raise me like they knew what they're doing – it could've been a TV show. I loved every second of it. Those two are the only family I have, besides the one in prison, whose prior actions still infiltrate my life in a way I wish they wouldn't and is the human garbage responsible for my missing heart and probable promiscuity.

'Yes, brother-father number two, everyone who wants drinks has drinks.'

He rolls his eyes to the ceiling. That's the one thing I say that he can't stand. *Honey, I think TLC just called*, is how he usually responds.

'She hasn't even spilled one yet,' Julio interjects. 'I've even only seen her knock back a single shot.'

I gasp. How dare he out me for the shot *he* poured an hour ago the second I walked in. I shoot him a glare.

'What's that saying? Snitches get stitches?'

Julio laughs as if he's done nothing wrong. 'I think that's it, yeah.'

'Fine, I suppose I'll feed you,' Carlos says, stepping into the bar with me and greeting Dax and Hollyn. 'Look at this!' He beams, pulling her left hand closer to inspect the rock on her finger. 'Oh, Mercy, girl, find you a boy who loves you like Dax loves Hollyn. Have you seen this ring?'

'I saw that ring before she did. So, yeah. I also know I'll never wear one, so get your fix now.'

Carlos rolls his eyes. 'She's so cynical. You think there's a man on the planet who could put up with her?' he asks, glancing back at me with a sly smile. 'You two should set her up with a nice guy.'

'No set-ups,' I remind him. 'You and Edie signed that contract.'

'Contract?' Carlos laughs. 'She wanted us to sign in blood,' he says to my friends.

'That was a joke.'

It wasn't; they meddle too much, and I was trying to teach them a lesson. It backfired and now the contract he speaks of is displayed on the front of their fridge under a *You're a superstar* magnet. They make fun of it daily and then go through their contacts to find anyone who might know some pathetic man who'll make my heart sing. It's never going to happen.

'I'm not allowed to set Mercy up,' Hollyn tells Carlos. 'She's afraid I'll pick someone who wants to give her one of these rings.'

'She don't need setting up anyway,' Julio says, as he finishes making the drinks his table ordered. 'A guy was in here looking for her earlier.'

Hollyn's jaw drops open, her overly interested smile screaming, *we're talking about this.*

I glare at Julio. 'We're no longer friends.'

'Were we ever?' he asks with a sly grin.

'A guy was in here looking for you?' Carlos and Hollyn ask in unison.

'How did I not notice this?' Carlos asks.

'You didn't notice because he wasn't *looking* for me. He was here with people and happened to run into me—'

'He called her beautiful,' Julio says, finally walking away to deliver his drinks.

I'm going to kill him. Right after I settle my heart from the gallop it's on, that is. Brooks called me beautiful? A smile creeps up on my face unexpectedly at his words. I don't get that one often. Usually, my mouth ruins it for me. I take a breath, realizing my heart is beating so hard I can barely breathe.

'Spill the tea, sister. Who is this guy?' Carlos asks. He stares my way, his eyes wide, and the goofy grin plastered on his face tells me Edie will know every word out of my mouth, so I better be careful what I say.

I heave a sigh and then give them the footnote version of how I don't actually 'know' him, and they all listen like it's interesting.

'It was a total missed connection, and now all I know is that he keeps disappearing before I can talk to him.'

'Ooh,' Hols swoons. 'It's like that John Cusack movie. *Serendipity*. He and Kate Beckinsale, I can't remember their character names, anyway, they know they have this connection, they never exchange names, and for the whole movie, they miss each other. For *years*. It was absolutely maddening and romantic all at once.'

'Might I suggest watching something scary once in a while to balance out your newly found lovesick ways?' I pat her hand, earning a glare.

'Or perhaps you could admit that you're craving love lately.'

'I will admit nothing of the sort,' I tell her. 'The bar thing was a total fangirl moment. I was attracted to his ability to play the guitar. You know me. I'm not looking for anyone; I just happened to run into him, and we have a stringless past that we tied up neatly with a bow. Yet, whenever I see him, I'm somehow stunned silent...'

'Should have knotted it 'cause it seems like that bow may have come loose,' Dax says partly under his breath.

I glare his way, intentionally making his drink badly, then set it in front of him confidently. He smells it before tasting, scrunching his face, then coughing with the first sip.

'Damn... it's a good thing Hollyn's driving.'

'When you're around him, you're stunned silent?' Hollyn asks, completely ignoring my attempted poisoning of her fiancé.

'What would I say? "Remember when we did it in your SUV because we couldn't wait? I know you lied about your name when we met, as did I, but my friend has done some research, and now I know way more about you than you know about me. Can you explain the weird fluttery feeling in my body every time we're in the same room?"'

Hollyn cocks her head, scrunching her face as if she now gets it.

'I don't need to make things any more awkward than they already are.' I force myself to look Hollyn in the face, only to realize she's wearing a lovesick smile more now than ever. What is this face?'

'Did you just say you have *feelings* for this guy?'

'*No* – I said I had a fluttery feelin—' Shit. 'That's not what I – really, I meant...' Finally, I give up. No words will fix this. 'Can we talk about anything else? Wedding dresses? That's what you came for? Let's see 'em.'

Yes, I'm changing the subject because I'm already spinning this story into something that'll keep me up all night. Brooks called me beautiful. He used to say it when we did it but I was naked, he wanted in, of course he's going to say it. This time I'm fully clothed and have hardly spoken a complete sentence to him. That makes my heart twirl. I can't explain it, but I doubt I'll need to because, chances are, I'll never see Brooks Hudson again with my luck.

6

MERCY

I have a new ukulele student starting today. It's the instrument I teach the least – partly because YouTube is pretty good with the how-to-play-ukulele videos. The shop's front door dings open while I'm in the office replying to work emails.

'That'll be your new student,' Dylan says, appearing in our office doorway and glancing at the wall calendar. 'Ali Blackwell, six years old, her uncle Nate signed her up as an early birthday gift.'

'OK, I'll be right out,' I tell him. It takes me a moment to finish what I am doing before I enter the shop's main room. 'Hi!' I chirp as if I'm the happiest woman on the planet. Truth be told, when I'm at work surrounded by instruments, I am.

'Hey,' the man says. 'This is Ali, my niece.' He nods towards a little girl with shoulder-length curly light brown hair, crystal-blue eyes, a dimple in her left cheek and the most adorable little outfit completed with a pair of child-sized Doc Martens boots. A brand new ukulele is in her hands, and she strums it like she's already been practicing.

I kneel, balancing on my heels. 'Hi, Ali. I'm Miss Mercy. Are you ready to learn how to play the ukulele?'

'Yes!' she says excitedly.

'Great.' I stand, turning to her uncle. 'We'll be about thirty minutes if you have something you need to do. Or you can watch.'

'I'm going to go to the bank,' he says, ruffling the little girl's hair.

'Uncle Nate!' She giggles, now smoothing down her hair.

Once he's gone, I walk Ali to the seating area where I teach guitar, ukulele and cello lessons. I even do all of it without swearing. Dylan's rules.

'Have you ever played the ukulele before?' I ask as she sits down.

'No,' she says. 'But my daddy plays guitar and sometimes lets me play.'

'That's cool! So, you know how to strum?'

She nods enthusiastically. 'Can you show me a song?'

'Sure. You know, I learned to play the ukulele even younger than you.'

'You did?' she asks curiously.

'Yep,' I confirm. 'I was five, and it was a song sung by Kermit the Frog. Do you know who that is?'

She nods, a massive grin on her face. 'Can you still play it?'

'I can,' I say, instantly wishing I'd not mentioned it. Leave it to me to pick my most painful memory as an example.

'Can I hear it?' she asks.

'Um...'

Fuck. Fuck. Fuckety. Fuck.

You can do this, Mercy; you don't want to. But you can. She's just a little girl, and it's just a song. It's not that big a deal. Reliving the memories will be worth the pain if it gets her excited about playing the ukulele.

Yeah, not that big deal, I argue with myself. It's just me opening up my past and allowing the memories to bombard me like a serial killer coming at me with a knife.

'Absolutely,' I finally say, grabbing my ukulele off the countertop. I sit on the rolling stool before her, positioning the ukulele in my hands while showing her how to do the same, and take a deep, cleansing breath.

I start the song, 'Rainbow Connection'. Ali's grin grows by the second as I sing the words. I try to focus on the words only, but memories flash through my head like a movie on a drive-in theater screen. I performed the song for Nick, my father, while it played on the tape player in the background. He clapped when I was done, rewound the tape, and in a rare sober moment, danced me around the living room, singing the song with me. The two of us giggled as we danced, me strumming the tune on my tiny blue ukulele, and at that moment, I felt safe. Loved, even.

I've never experienced anything like it again and have forced myself to steer clear of the emotions to forget the pain they bring me now. The good mixed with the terrifying is like fire and ice running through my barely beating heart.

Stop thinking about your past before you trigger your anxiety and freak this sweet little girl right the fuck out.

I finish the song, glancing at Ali, who is beaming. 'I wanna play that,' she says excitedly.

Of course she does.

'OK,' I say, not wanting to tell this girl no.

For the next thirty minutes, we work on the basic chords of the song's beginning, and to my surprise, she's a natural. She picks it up quickly and plays the chords without my help by the time her uncle returns to collect her.

'You're a prodigy, girl,' he says, extending a fist to her that she bumps proudly. 'I knew you would be.'

'It's fun!' she says.

'See you again next week?' I ask.

'Yes,' she answers excitedly, taking her uncle's hand and exiting the shop, telling him all about Kermit the Frog and 'Rainbow Connection'.

* * *

Now that I'm off work, I realize I've not eaten all day. What do I have that could be classified as dinner? I stare at the kitchen clear across the room. If only I didn't have to get up.

The TV blasts some documentary River's watching. Yes, I live with River. I couldn't afford the place on my own, and he was tired of sharing an apartment with Dax and Hollyn, so now we split everything and try not to kill one another with our similar personalities. He lounges on one side of my couch nightly, commandeering the remote, and I sit opposite him, usually surfing the web on my laptop and casually watching whatever he's chosen.

'*What?*' he groans, obviously sensing my attention on him. He's the little brother I never wanted and plays the part well.

'It's your turn to buy dinner, Spicoli.'

If model Christopher Mason and Ashton Kutcher had a baby, that baby would River Matthews. I'm totally making this dinner thing up, by the way. It's a little game we play. Sometimes he bites. Plus, I'm sure he owes me.

'Got a pizza on the way, swamp donk. Maybe I'll share.' He glances at me for my reaction to this new pet name.

'Swamp donk?'

He laughs – 'He he. I like that one.'

I roll my eyes. Note to self, find a more offensive name for River. Back to my laptop, I stare at the flashing cursor. Am I that girl, googling a guy I don't know? It seems that way.

'You ever investigated someone you don't know online, Riv?'

He laughs. 'So often, I've considered starting my own internet stalking company. Cyber PI. Sounds like a cool TV show, doesn't it?'

'It sounds like you'll need a bad eighties mustache and really tight jeans. Word to the wise: it's a fine line between stalker and private investigator; keep that in mind.'

He rolls his head my way, his golden-blond shoulder-length wavy hair slicked into a man-bun, his eyebrows raised halfway up his freckled face. 'If you're looking for my sex tape, it's at www dot—'

'Ew, no.' I hold a single hand his way. 'I'm sorry I asked.'

He tosses the remote onto the couch, then walks to the kitchen, staring into the fridge, despite having a pizza on the way. The man constantly eats yet never gains a pound.

'Who you stalking?' he asks.

'Nobody.'

Brooks Hudson Portland, Oregon. I type his name into the search bar. That's right; I'm lying to my friend.

Also, yes, I'm still thinking about him. Him being Brooks Hudson. I have zero answers to my questions, and I can't get him out of my head. It's not just dirty thoughts, either. I'm imagining getting to know the guy. In one daydream, we went on a picnic. *A picnic!* I don't do romantic picnics. When Dylan brought food to the movie the other night, I drank all the wine, straight from the bottle. That's me at a picnic. I've pretty much wracked my brain for any other man this has happened with, and zilch. That scares me.

All kinds of articles on Brooks Hudson pop up, but

none appear to be about the guy I'm looking for. Maybe try – *Brooks Hudson Don't Panic Portland, Oregon*? I hit enter.

The website for the bar Oz pops up, along with their social media and schedule. I tap their Facebook account, scroll through photos, and stop on a band video. There he is. Brooks Hudson. Exactly as cute as I remember. My computer is on mute, but even so, he's also as talented as I remember. The caption reads: *Don't Panic performs every Saturday night. Come see us next week!*

I watch the video again, smiling to myself like a weirdo. Wait a second – what the hell is that? I touch my chest. Fluttering. Butterflies? Caged in my chest, making everything inside all wobbly while watching a video of him – it's happening again?

What. In. The. Hell?

'Come on,' Riv says, dragging out the last word. 'Who ya looking for, Merc?' He drops onto the couch right next to me, breaking every don't-invade-my-space rule we have.

'You sit down like a twelve-year-old,' I say.

Without asking, he grabs my laptop, pulls it to him, and shoves me into the edge of the couch so I can't reach it, holding me in place while he snoops. 'Ho ho ho, what do we have here?'

'Listen, Santa, I don't need your help.' I grasp for my laptop, but no dice.

He ignores me, pressing play, turning up the volume and watching the thirty-second clip.

'Not bad,' he says with a nod of approval. 'You're looking for this band why?'

'I just stumbled across them.' I reach for my laptop again, but he pulls it away. Then he does what I should have suspected he'd do. He checks my internet history! There should be a law about this! Clearly, he's a pro at deleting his own because he tapped into it faster than I could even say the words 'internet history'. *And* now he's laughing at me.

'You're a self-proclaimed anti-romantic, yet you watch "romantic porn for women"?' He squints at the screen to make sure he's reading it right. 'Who even are you? And who's Brooks Hudson, Merc? What did he do to be stalked by you? Do Daxy and I have an ass to kick?'

'I think we all know I could do more damage to a man than you and Dax could. It's nothing.' I grab my laptop back, close it and hold it tightly against my chest, but he doesn't go away.

'We both know I got nowhere to be,' River says, settling into the couch next to me. He crosses his ankles on the coffee table and rests his hands behind his head, one of his elbows now in my face.

I shove it away, but he doesn't budge.

'Who's the guy?'

'You're a total child.'

'Man child,' he corrects me, using a name he hears from me often.

Seriously, he's twenty-eight going on sixteen. He's been tormenting me since I was eight, and never got the memo that people are supposed to grow up.

Knock. Knock. Knock.

Thank God, saved by an unexpected guest. The front door swings open, and in walks Dylan. Our apartments being across the hall from one another is an open invitation.

'I, uh...' He stops at the kitchen island, waving a single piece of mail in the air. 'The mailman put this in my box, but it's for you.' For a moment, he stares at it, his brows furrowed before he finally walks it to me, a grimace on his face.

I lean forward, setting my laptop on the coffee table. 'It's mail, Dyl. Everyone gets it. It's not that unusual.' I grab the letter from him, glancing at the writing across the front, expecting a bright red late stamp that he's judging me for. But that's not what's shocking about this letter. It's worse. Much, *much* worse.

'Oh no,' I say breathlessly, dropping the letter onto my lap like a ball of fire.

'More unusual than ya thought?' River asks, now grabbing it.

'Why are you two sitting so close together?' Dylan asks.

'To annoy her mostly,' River says, inspecting the letter. 'Is this...' He glances at me, his jaw dropping open, then back to the letter. '*No.*' He tosses it back at me, where I drop it onto the floor, trying to escape it. We're both now off the couch, staring at one another as if we've just seen a ghost.

'Why would he write you?' Riv asks, panic in his voice.

'I don't know?' I glance at the envelope on the floor between us. My name, MERCY MAE ALEXANDER, written in blue ink, stares back at me. I bet this is the first time he's ever written it.

River's head snaps towards the still opened front door. 'You left the door open, Dyl!' He runs to it, locking all three locks. 'He knows where we live!'

'So?' Dylan says as he watches us panic.

Our heads move back to the letter. 'What do I do?' I ask.

'Uh, read it?' Dylan asks, the three of us standing around the letter like it's a bomb we're considering disarming and he's the only one with any brains here.

'Why would he write to me?'

'Maybe he's out?' River suggests.

'It's only been twenty-two years. He got *fifty*,' I remind him.

'Good behavior?'

'He's a *mur-der-er*.' I exaggerate every syllable. Dylan grimaces as I say the word.

'Right. He's probably not that well behaved,' Riv says, nervously running a hand over his head.

'Why are *you* freaked out?' I ask. 'He's not your father.'

'But I live with you, and he clearly knows where, so when he comes to execute the witnesses – I'm a goner.'

'Newsflash, dumbass: you didn't witness anything!'

'I'll witness him murdering you!' he yells back, the stress in our apartment currently at an all-time high.

'Stop!' Dylan hollers, the only reasonable person in the room.

He kneels, inspecting the letter without touching it. 'Nick Alexander, #14273.' He points to the envelope. 'That must be his inmate number. Salem, Oregon. This came from the prison. He's not out.' He stands, his hands on his hips as he looks between me and the letter. 'Want me to open it?'

'And release a demon into my apartment? *No*. Let's just – uh – I dunno. I need to think.' Suddenly, I'm pacing, and I never pace. Not unless it's really bad. Is this really bad? It feels really bad. 'It's just a letter,' I say to myself. 'Words aren't scary. Depending on how they're arranged, I suppose.'

'Unless they're individual letters cut out of magazines and glued on,' River interjects, lifting a shoulder when I glance his way.

'Or written in blood,' I suggest.

'Or—'

'Good God, enough!' Dyl shouts, interrupting River, throwing his hands to his sides. 'Words are scary; I get it; settle down. It can't be that bad. It's *just* a letter. Read it.'

'I'm not reading it.'

'We could put it in the freezer?' River suggests, lifting both hands.

'What? *Why?*' Dylan asks.

'Inside that envelope may be a curse or a hex or anthrax. Leaving it on the floor will burn the whole building to the ground. Put it in the freezer to prevent that.'

The way Dylan rolls his eyes screams he's not sure why he's friends with either of us.

'No, *Joey Tribbiani*,' he says with half a laugh. 'We're not putting it in the freezer to cool it down. It's a letter! Not a fire-starter or a curse or a hex *or* anthrax – by the way, where would a prisoner get that?'

River shrugs. 'Where do prisoners get drugs?'

Dylan waves a hand like he's not impressed with either of us. 'Maybe the guy found his soul and finally decided to apologize to his daughter.' He looks at me, concern all over his face. 'Why not read it?'

There's no way this is an apology. If it is, it took twenty-two years for him to find the words I needed back when I was a child. I've mostly made my peace with things and built big internal walls to hold back the bad this man created. I can't read anything he has to say. The walls will shatter, and I'm not ready to deal with whatever spills out of that. Not yet. I'll bring it to Edie. He'll know what to do because Nick's his father too. Maybe *he* got a letter? I have to find out.

I grab the envelope from the floor. 'I'll take care of it,' I say, slipping my Birkenstocks on, grabbing my purse from the kitchen island and shoving the envelope inside.

'Where are you going?' Dyl asks.

'To talk to Ed. He's better at this stuff than I am.'

'I'll come with you,' he volunteers.

I stop at the door, turning his way. 'I don't need a babysitter. I'm fine. You said it yourself: it's just a letter – nothing to be afraid of. I just—I need to think about this. Take a walk, get some air and talk to Ed. *Alone*, alright?'

That is the biggest lie I have ever told. I am not fine. My heart is jumping in a way that feels very call-an-ambulance serious. My breathing is speeding like I'm about to need a paper bag if I don't flee the prying eyes in front of me.

'Fine,' Dyl says. 'Just text one of us later to let us know you're good?'

'Will do.' I march out the front door, nearly sprinting down the three flights of stairs to the side-walk below. I lean against the building for a second, trying to remember how to breathe. 'This is fine,' I say, forcing myself off the wall. 'Everything is fine.'

Never in a million years did I expect Nick to contact me. As a kid, sometimes I'd pretend all of it was a nightmare and he was just a father with a job on the road. A rock star. One day he would show up and save me from living with strangers. The things kids do to cope, right? A daydream was much easier to believe than my father being in prison for murder. I'm terrified to know what this letter says. And just as terrified not to know.

Breathe, Mercy. Just breathe.

'It's just a letter,' I remind myself again, quickly walking towards Tequila Mockingbird, where I know Ed is tonight. I talked to him earlier, and he was headed to see his favorite chef. 'Everything will be perfectly OK because Nick's still in prison,' I tell myself. 'Only his words escaped.'

As I talk myself out of a panic attack, out loud, in public, like a real weirdo, my bag crashes to the ground, dumping its contents all over the sidewalk as I ram into someone after turning the corner.

'*Fuck-er!*' I yell, the inner turmoil surfacing in one very *what the fuck did you do* tone.

'I'm so sor—'

I glance up at the man I've just crashed into head-on-collision style.

'Holy shit,' he says, shock on his face. 'Lemon.'

Oh.

My.

God.

'Brooks Hudson? Er, I mean, Drake Ramoray?'

7

BROOKS

'*How* do you know my real name?'

My hands are on her shoulders, preventing her from being knocked over after we just ran into one another. Her hands are somehow on my chest, one of them gripping my T-shirt, and neither of us moves. We just stare at each other in shock. She smells good, like green apples, pink sugar and coconut sunscreen.

Stop smelling her, Brooks, and speak.

For a moment, she looks a combination of panicked and confused.

Probably because you're freaking her out – hands off her.

'I'm so sorry.' I make sure she's steady on her feet before releasing her.

'I just swore at you,' she says nervously, releasing my T-shirt and patting my chest before suddenly realizing what she's doing and pulling her hand from me as I step back. 'Sorry.'

'Don't be. I am a fucker.' I try to make light of the situation, laughing at myself. I'm totally at fault for nearly mowing the woman over because I wasn't paying attention at all. 'I should have been watching where I was going, but my head was on...' I readjust my hat. 'You.'

Her smile screams surprise as she lifts a single eyebrow. '*Me?*'

I nod. 'I'm not usually this awkward, I swear, but I've seen you a couple of times now, and I can't quit thinking about you.'

She smiles shyly, kneeling to pick up the things spilled from her bag on the sidewalk.

'It's weird, right?'

I kneel to help, my eyes on her. 'A little, yeah...'

She looks at me suddenly, her gorgeous emerald-green eyes searching mine. 'You noticed me at the bar too?'

'Considering you were easily the most beautiful woman in the room, yeah. I noticed. As did half the men there, I bet. How do you know my name?'

'I told my guy friend we once had a thing, and he took it upon himself to ask the bartender about you.'

Her guy friend? Did I get fortunate, and the man with her at the bar wasn't her boyfriend?

Hold on – she asked about me?

'How much do you know?' I ask nervously.

'I know you're Brooks Hudson. You play with the band Don't Panic at a bar called Oz. You're thirty-six, divorced, recently dumped, chronically single and have played guitar since you were ten.'

My jaw drops into a grin, and I don't mean to bellow a laugh that earns one out of her, but I can't help it. I turn my attention to picking up her things, a pen, a compact mirror and a letter. She grabs the letter quickly, looking suddenly horrified as she shoves it into her bag.

'Well, that's a lot.'

'Did I freak you out? Sometimes I'm too honest,' she says as we stand, her escaped possessions now back in the safety of her bag.

'I always liked your openness. But if we're being too honest, you might freak when I tell you I just spent an hour drinking alone at Tequila Mockingbird, hoping you were working tonight, and I'm not a drinker.'

Alijah woke up with a fever this morning, so I met

Norah at the doctor's this afternoon. It's probably just a bug, but we decided to go ahead and skip the family dinner and exchange houses early. She's now back with Mommy, a pediatric nurse, so she's in good hands. That meant I had some time to myself, and of course, my mind wandered right to the woman standing in front of me – as it has so many times over the last week. So, I went to the restaurant I had run into her previously, hoping she'd be there.

'You're actively stalking me?' she asks flatly.

'*No*,' I say quickly. 'No. Just was hoping to see you and say actual words.'

She laughs, lifting a curious eyebrow while attempting to hold the growing shy smile on her gorgeous face. A smile that makes my heart race.

'I don't believe in fate, but this seems kind of...'

'Like fate?' I finish her sentence.

She nods.

'Do I get to know your name? *My* cover is blown, so it's only fair...'

'Oh.' She laughs nervously. 'Mercy,' she says as her cheeks grow pink. 'I'm Mercy Alexander.'

'Way better than Lemon. It's nice to meet you, Mercy Alexander, finally.' I extend a hand her way. Hesitantly, she takes it, electricity shooting from her to my chest. She flashes me a wobbly grin. Maybe it hit her too?

'Likewise, Brooks Hudson.'

Ask her out before she disappears, and only regret remains. Dinner? Probably too soon. Drinks? I don't want her to think I'm trying to get her drunk. Maybe coffee? Seems harmless.

'Do you drink coffee? At night?' The words don't leave my lips as smoothly as I'd hoped.

'I do,' she says with that perfect hint of a grin. 'I also just ran out on pizza delivery in a huff over something I shouldn't get into right now, or you'll surely run for the hills, so I'm starving. Do you happen to eat at night?'

'I do eat at night. All times, really.'

She glances around the street. 'Pizza and beer?' She points to Pizza Schmizza, a local pizza and beer joint famous within the city.

'Let's do it.'

Ten minutes later, we're sitting at a table, a silence that should be awkward all around us, but for some reason, it's not. Every time I see her, she's prettier than the time before and casually cool, like we've been hanging out this way for years.

'So, we know a lot about one another?' I break the silence.

'In some ways, yes,' she says with a wide smile.

I lift a single shoulder. 'I mean, I may have asked about you too.'

Her eyes widen. 'Who talked at the restaurant?'

I laugh. 'A guy named Julio.'

'I will murder him. What did he say?'

From the way he talked about her, I expected this. 'You scare Julio a little.'

She smirks at this news, looking proud of herself.

'He confirmed you're thirty and a classical musician – the word "prodigy" may have come up. Your family owns the restaurant. You're a terrible bartender. You buy too many shoes, and me calling you beautiful the other day made you blush.'

She leans back with a guilty grin as a server delivers the pizza we've ordered to the table.

'I *may* have blushed,' she admits when the waitress leaves the table. 'Could have been the lighting.'

I chuckle. She doesn't want to admit my words made her blush. That's cute.

'I don't usually get the word "beautiful" from men, so when Julio told me, it caught me off guard,' she says, already helping herself, taking a bite of pizza without waiting on me. She's the opposite of nearly every woman I've dated who ordered a side salad and water at dinner and then barely touched either.

'Whoever those men are, complete idiots. All of them. You're gorgeous.'

She looks me dead in the eyes and cocks her head. 'Thank you,' she says softly. 'Is this where I tell you how handsome you are?'

'Only if you want to.'

'I think you know you are. I mean, I spent months with you as my primary booty call, so obviously I'm attracted to you. I could even close my eyes and picture you naked, right now.' She does exactly that, sending heat up my neck to my ears.

I laugh out loud, more embarrassed by her picturing me naked than I expected. 'Now it's my turn to blush?'

She smirks. 'It's only fair.'

I readjust my hat before grabbing a slice of pizza and setting it on my plate, completely unable to focus on eating right now.

'Why do you keep running away from me?' she asks between bites.

She noticed that, huh? 'My job. It's complicated at times.'

'You have a complicated job? What are you, CIA?'

'No.'

'Secret Service?'

'They protect the President – who doesn't live in Portland.'

'Thank God. Why'd your girlfriend dump ya?'

I laugh. 'Jumping right into it, are we? Seems a little risky laying my flaws out on the table immediately instead of letting you discover them later on.'

'Who says I want to see you again?' she asks with a wink. 'I'm kidding. Truthfully, I may or may not have thought of you a few times over the last week as well.'

I swear my heart is glowing in my chest right now. 'Are you leaning heavily towards "may" or "may not"?'

'Um... the former?' she says like she's either unsure of her answer or, just like me, hoping it doesn't freak me out. It doesn't. 'We keep running into one another. Maybe it's a sign we're supposed to be friends?'

Angel's words at the bar play through my head. *Maybe you should get to know a woman and be friends first.* Now Mercy herself has mentioned it. Perhaps they're right?

'I feel like we've got a good start on the friend thing already.'

She looks at me like she's both intrigued and confused as hell. 'After three accidental meetings you'd consider me a friend?'

'That and the two months we spent sleeping together every Saturday night.'

She bites her lips together, laughing through only her nose. 'That worked as well as blackmail. Welcome to my tiny friend circle, Brooks Hudson. So, spill it. Why did a girl dump you?'

'She said I'd offend her parents with my tattoos, some other stuff about my job, and things I won't get into as it's nothing new, and then...' I pause dramatically, watching her slowly lift her eyebrows. 'She said I was old.'

Her laugh is upbeat and sincere. '*Old?* Damn woman,' she says. 'Cut a guy, would ya? That must have grated your ego like a wood-chipper! How old was this woman?'

A wood-chipper. I laugh. 'She's twenty-five.'

'More than a decade younger? Touché, old man, I don't want to say age matters – because I don't believe it does unless you're *under*age – but it sounds like you're in two different stages of life. You have responsibilities she can't relate to, and when you can't relate to something, you can't articulate how you feel about it properly, so instead of telling you what *her* problem was that caused her to pull the plug, she picked out the easy things. The superficial shit that made it seem like you were at fault. Trust me; I'm a pro at finding the superficial shit.'

I sit up straighter, leaning on the table with my elbows. 'Beautiful, hungry, funny, decent in bed and smart. The more you talk, the more I like you.'

'Decent?' she asks, clearly offended.

'It's been a long time,' I say with a shrug.

Her smile says she's still interested.

'Do you want to hang out sometime and get to know the clothed side of each other?'

'I dunno...' she says hesitantly. 'It sounds so dirty...' She scrunches her face playfully. 'We weren't really "friends" before, so I feel like I should warn you I'm as complicated as women come.'

'I got that feeling about you too.'

She laughs to herself.

I stare across the table at her, sipping my beer and setting it down slowly. 'You don't scare me, Mercy Alexander.'

'Then I guess I'll try harder,' she jokes.

'So, you *do* want to see me again,' I say proudly.

She rolls her eyes slightly, smiling as she picks up her pizza, shaking her head. 'I didn't say *that*,' she says with her mouth full.

I'm feeling pretty confident I'm reading her well right now.

'You said you ran out on your dinner in a huff earlier. Since we've officially been friends for two minutes, I feel like I should ask, are you alright? Maybe it's something I can help with?'

'You are old with more life experience than me,' she jokes. 'Um...' She sets her pizza on her plate and looks over at me. 'I made you be honest, so I guess you expect that from me. It's only fair, right?'

'Seems like something friends might do...'

'You said your job is complicated?'

I nod, confirming it.

'I have a complicated past. Sometimes it drives my present. Tonight, it came back to haunt me, so I ran. That's my thing. Usually, I don't like to get overly involved with people because I've got some demons, so I exit before they emerge. At times my exit is graceful; other times, it's like tonight. I was headed to talk to my brother about one of those said demons earlier, but I bumped into you, and it seemed easier to forget, so here we are.' She grabs the beer in front of her, taking her time with a long pull until, finally, she sets it down with a grin.

'Can I tell you something?'

She pinches her lips, but the smile breaks through as she nods.

'I think you're right. We're supposed to be friends. Let's distract each other from our complicated lives.'

'Do we need to somehow make it official?'

'Like a secret word or handshake?' I ask.

'Or an inside joke. For instance...' She leans closer to me from across the table. 'I've seen your penis.'

I laugh to myself, shaking my head. 'You didn't finish your sentence.'

She grins. 'The verdict is still out...'

'Which part of that was the joke?'

She only lifts her shoulders, a coy smile on her face, before she takes a bite of her pizza, a gleam in her eye that says she's enjoying this. I think I might be too.

8

MERCY

'You agreed to text or sext?' Dylan chuckles at his joke. He's sitting behind the desk we share at our shop, leaning back, his arms crossed over his chest, a single curl hanging over his forehead, and a smirk on his face.

'Who knows? Perhaps both. What's wrong with texting a guy?'

'Nothing besides the fact that it will require you to get to know him, and I'm pretty sure that's one of your forbidden rules in life. No one gets too close.'

'Maybe I've decided to grow up and change my ways?'

He drops his arms, leaning forward in the chair

and resting his elbows on his desk. His stare pierces through me as a suspicious smile grows on his face.

'You've decided to grow up? But you're only thirty.'

'Ha ha.' I hang my bag on the hook in the office.

'I'd be willing to bet you'll be doing him again on your lunch hour within three days.'

'You're not funny.'

'It wasn't a joke,' he says. 'Name a single guy who hasn't rounded second base within three days.'

Shit. He wants to play *this* game? Quickly I go over the men I've 'dated' in my head. Josh, nope. Stuart, never admitting that. What about Ezra? I think we waited a week. Wait, no. We did, but it was to give him time to prove he didn't have bugs down south. There's gotta be someone, *anyone. Think, Merc!*

Weston. *Yes! Wes!*

I suspected Weston was married, so we went on a few sexless 'dates', including long unnecessary walks at sunset and dinner at the mall food court, my treat. Then, he finally invited me over to his place. Which I discovered later wasn't actually *his* place but his parents' because he was *not* twenty-five like he said. He was nineteen. And a virgin. I'm pretty sure I stole his innocence in his parents' bed that night. I'm not proud, but it is what it is.

'Weston Graham. We waited two weeks.'

A cocky smirk grows on Dylan's face. 'Weston?' he asks. 'That your final answer?'

'Final answer? We're playing this game-show style? Alright. Yes. Final answer.' I slap my hand on the desk like an invisible buzzer, locking in my answer.

'Wes?' he asks again. 'Weston. The *virgin* college kid?'

I guffaw. 'I told you about that?'

How do I not remember? I thought I was totally in the clear with this lie. It's one of those secrets you take the grave.

Dylan laughs, shaking his head like he can't believe me. 'Yeah. We're not counting Wes. The kid was trying to work up the nerve to get a piece. That was the hold-up, not your burned-out morals.'

'I'm a little offended. But considering I give you a hard time about your non-existent love life, I suppose you've earned this one.'

He smiles wide. 'Finally. What's the score now, me one, you five thousand thirty-two?' he asks with a wink.

'Sounds right,' I say coyly.

'By the way, Brad Winston called to see how you've been coming along on his pieces.'

My eyes grow. I'm not exactly finished with his gig

– some work for their band Infusion's upcoming album.

He reads my face flawlessly. 'Maybe you should finish that today?'

For a moment, we stare at one another.

'I'm not sleeping with him within three days. We're both busy.'

'Is that what he told you? "I'm super busy; let's text"?'

'No...'

Yes.

Kind of.

He said he was super busy and didn't always have a chance to answer his phone, so he thought texting would be an excellent way to get to know one another. You know, become friends as we agreed. Texting felt like a good idea at the time – less pressure. I didn't have to jump in and could take days to find words if necessary. Seems almost harmless.

The front door dings open, and Dylan stands. 'I'll take care of them. You go finish the Infusion pieces.'

I didn't even admit I hadn't done it yet, and he just knows he's right. I'm one of those musicians who have to *feel* the music to make the recording, and until now, I haven't thought twice about it. But the upcoming deadline has suddenly inspired me.

A couple of hours later, I'm finished in our recording studio and sending the files to Brad Winston himself. A guy I'd never heard of before he called us but have now realized that their band was super popular back in the day, and their fanbase hasn't faded much. I'll be on the credits of three songs, and I have the be honest – this part of being a relatively unknown musician feels good.

I play five instruments well: ukulele, violin, piano, cello and guitar. My brother insists I'm some musical prodigy, but I'm not. I discovered as a child that I needed an escape from my life. Music gave me that.

I lived in a dangerous part of the city with my father in the house he sold dope from. My mom fled shortly after my birth. I don't even know more than her name, as in the rare sober moments my father had, he never wanted to talk about her. But after everything that happened, I almost wonder if he did something to her. I can't think about it too deeply, or my mind goes to some dark places.

Anyway, we had this neighbor. The most wonderful, joyful, round black woman named Lola. She was in her seventies and was a former lounge singer in her younger years. She'd tell me stories that kept me interested for hours on end. They were glamorous and part of a world I couldn't even imagine. She knew my situation and didn't leave home often, so when my house was volatile, I'd wander over to Lola's place, where she sat in her garage and chain-smoked while watching the neighborhood. Sometimes she'd fix my hair in elaborate ways. Other times she'd pull out her now-grown grandkids' toys and let me play with them. Once, she got out her old fancy dresses from her performance days, heels included (it's where my heel obsession started), and let me dress up, pretending to be important.

But the day I remember most was my fifth birthday. She would watch me when my dad wasn't home, which was often. It was never pre-arranged; ensuring I was taken care of wasn't at the top of Nick's to-do list. I'd just wake up to an empty home and stroll to Lola's place. She'd feed and take care of me until Nick showed up again. I don't think he ever even paid her for it.

That particular weekend, I woke up alone. Again. Lola gave Nick until late morning, but when he never showed up, she dropped me off with her daughter to play with her children, then ran to the store. When she returned, she made my birthday a big deal with a store-bought cake, helium balloons and a present. Things most kids learn early on to expect. But I wasn't like most kids; this was my first birthday cake, and I was beyond thrilled. The present she gave me was my very first ukulele. It was bright blue, and I still have it hanging on my bedroom wall. Over that winter, she taught me how to play the song that recently tormented me, 'Rainbow Connection'. It was right then I became addicted to music. My spinning mind stopped, and I focused only on what I was doing.

When I moved into foster care, they placed me with a middle-aged couple without kids. Charlie and Alice Henderson. They were sweet folks that had dinner parties with their childless friends and insisted I 'wash up' before dinner. It was a whole new world for me.

Charlie was a musician with the symphony. A violinist. When he noticed all I did was play the same few songs on the ukulele, he asked if I'd be interested in learning violin. He taught me everything he knew from when I was eight until I moved on to another foster family when I was ten after Alice was killed suddenly in a car accident. Bad luck seems to follow me like a lost puppy.

When I hit send on Brad's email, Dylan walks into the office. He's been out of the shop playing funerals all day, but don't think I haven't noticed the brown paper bag in one of his hands, grease already staining the bottom of the bag, and a drink tray in the other.

'What's that?'

'I figured you'd be hungry, so I grabbed us lunch. Even got your favorite drink.'

'You bought me a strawberry milkshake?'

'*And* your favorite greasy bacon cheeseburger, extra cheese.' He pulls it from the bag, tossing it onto the desk in front of me, then sits in the chair that faces the desk.

I look down at the blue-and-white-check-paper-wrapped burger, cheese sticking to the insides and grease staining the calendar on our desk beneath it. He never brings me lunch anymore. I mean, he brought dinner that night we saw a movie with Edie but usually, we part ways for lunch.

'This seems fancy. The diner is clear in Hillsboro. What made you drive across the city?'

He lifts a hand. 'I figured I'd reward you for completing those pieces in one day.'

There it is. He's rewarding me for doing things his way. I hate it.

'It wasn't *one* day,' I fire back.

The way he lowers his chin like he doesn't believe me reminds me he knows me too well.

'Fine, it was one day.' I take the strawberry shake he's now handing me and immediately get to work, attempting to suck it through the straw. Y-U-M. 'Stop staring at me, perv. I'm not eating a corndog.'

He laughs. 'I'm a dude, Merc. There are certain things men don't look away from.'

'Women do that too, but we're more partial to seeing a man do the dishes or vacuum. Add some dance moves in your underwear to that routine, and you'll for sure get laid.'

'Noted.'

It's possible I forgot to mention that Dylan and I used to have 'relations'. He calls me his ex to annoy me but truthfully, we never really 'dated', just spent a lot of time together because we were on the road with the *La La Land* symphony tour. Like I've told Edie a million times, we may have no spark, but we have a ton in common, so we decided friends was best.

'You never told me what Edie said about the letter from your father.' He changes the subject.

I stop – burger in my hands and midway to my mouth. 'We call him Nick. He was never my "father". He thinks I should read it.'

Lies. All lies. I haven't even told Edie yet. I've just pretended the letter doesn't exist because that's easier.

'If I know you, and we both know I do, telling you to do anything means you'll fight pretty hard not to do exactly that.'

'Not *always*,' I say, defending my stubborn ways. 'I just recorded the pieces you told me to.'

'Only because they were due tomorrow.'

'Still counts.'

We eat silently for a few minutes before Dylan breaks the silence again. 'You text him yet?'

'No.'

'Why not?'

I shrug. 'I'm nervous. What if I start texting him, get close, then say something typically Mercy that makes him realize he doesn't enjoy me after all?'

'There's no way that'll happen.' He seems pretty sure of himself. 'Why wouldn't he enjoy you?'

'Because I'm sharp like a knife as opposed to soft and sweet. Men don't often like strong women. They want sugar and spice and everything nice.'

Dylan stares at me from across the desk. 'You've got the spice, Merc. I'm sure the right man will bring out the sugar. Since when do you worry about someone liking you anyway? You're Mercy Alexander, musician extraordinaire, who says what she wants without regret.'

'I know, but even you hate that part of me, and we're friends.'

'We wouldn't be friends if I hated *any* parts of you. Do you sometimes have a way with words that often leaves me without any? Yes. But it's nothing I'd ever hate you for. I'm sure Brooks will be the same.'

I grin proudly. Dylan is loyal to his friends. He grew up wealthy, and because of that, he never could tell who was hanging out with him for the money and experiences and who really liked him for him. So, like me, he doesn't extend his friend circle often. I'm honestly honored he considers me his best friend. We work so well together, and I trust him. I don't say that about many people.

'Can I tell you something uncomfortable?'

'Is "uncomfortable" code for "personal"?'

'You know it is,' I say.

I sit my burger on the paper, pressing my lips together while I find my words. 'Since I turned thirty, I feel... off track? Does that make sense? People my age are working towards a life they want, getting married, having kids, and besides my career, I have no idea what I want. Though, lately, I dream of something I've previously banned from thought.'

'*Like?*' he asks curiously as he eats.

'Like, I dunno – my own happily-ever-after? Hearing you go on about how I deserve to be loved the other night, seeing the way you look at Cassie—'

'I don't look at Cassie in any "way".' He air quotes that last word with one hand as he defends himself.

Cassie is a musician we work closely with. She plays piano and cello, and she adores Dylan. We're talking heart-eyes and middle-school-crush vibes.

'Oh-kay...' I say like I believe him. 'Anyway, with the many weddings we play, and Hollyn's all-romance-all-the-time attitude, it has me wondering if it's possible for me, and that's dangerous, Dyl. I'm starting to daydream of a romantic fairy-tale life. For the first time ever, I feel like I deserve more, and I blame you and Hols.'

Dylan chuckles to himself, sipping his soda before speaking. 'You blame me for making you finally see your worth?'

'Yes.'

'Happy to help,' he says with a shake of his head. 'You're the most impossible-to-understand woman I've ever met, but despite that, if anyone deserves a fairy-tale life, it's you, Merc.'

'First, you buy me my favorite lunch, then you compliment me. Are you up to something?'

'No,' he says, bewildered. 'Just trying to be nice. I've got some things going through my head, too, ya know.'

'Talk to me. What's on your mind?'

He shrugs, still eating as we talk. 'Work stuff.'

'You know, if you'd think less about work, you might have time to have fun.'

'I have fun,' he insists.

'What time did you leave here last night?'

'I don't know,' he says with his mouth full. 'Eight?'

'We close at six.'

'I had stuff to do.'

'Like?'

Right then, my phone buzzes on the desk, and our eyes move to it. When I see his name, my heart thumps. Brooks is texting me now.

'It's him,' I say to Dyl, feeling a little panicky yet fluttery too.

'What'd he say?'

'Um...' I grab my phone, tapping into the text nervously. 'He says, "Hi, beautiful." That's sweet,' I swoon. 'Then, "Am I allowed to say that when we're just friends? I mean, it's true but is it too romantical? I don't know, you tell me. Anyway, what are you up to tonight?"'

Dylan grins, sipping his drink through the straw. 'Based on the smile on your face alone, I'd say you're good with the "beautiful" thing. You've got a gig with Cassie tonight, right?'

I nod. 'Piano bar duel.'

'Invite him.'

'Don't you think Barrel Room's a little romantic for a friend date?'

'Only if you plan on doing him on top of one of those pianos.'

I laugh. 'I'm not insane *publicly*... and I don't think that's what he wants. He never mentioned starting back up our old shenanigans. We agreed on friends.'

'Wasn't impressed, was he?' Dyl says jokingly. 'Bring River. He's a definite romance killer.'

'He is, isn't he?' I say, nodding.

Before answering Brooks's text, I call Riv. I might as well play it safe; otherwise, I will end up in that bathroom with my new old friend, and I'm hoping to give him a better impression of me than I have in the past. For reasons I am currently unsure of.

'What up, loser?' Riv answers the same way he greets every caller, minus his parents.

'*Hola*, cock dog. You have plans tonight, so dress like a normal human being and not a boy-band member, please.'

He laughs into the phone. '*Cock dog?* A little offensive but funny. I approve. What plans do I got?'

'We're hanging out.'

For a moment, he's so quiet I wonder if he's hung up. 'Do we not already do that enough?'

I'm almost offended, but he's not entirely wrong. 'Stop pretending you don't like it.'

'If I like it depends on where we're going and if you're paying?'

'Barrel Room, and sure, I'll pay for three drinks *and* drive. Now, are you in?'

'Free booze? Hell yeah, I'm in. Ya shoulda opened with that, and this convo could've been much shorter. What time?'

'I'm leaving at seven.'

My phone beeps in my ear with another incoming call. I pull the phone from my head to see who it is. Hols. 'Gotta go, Riv. See ya tonight.' I hang up and switch calls. 'Hey, Hols. What's up?'

'The wedding dress I want...' she says with a heavy sigh.

'You're gonna have to narrow it down, considering you're mulling over many.'

In the last month, we've been to three dress appointments, all at different stores, and she left each one 'absolutely in love' with dresses so similar I can't tell them apart. Now she's got the task of narrowing it down to one.

'The Hayley Paige ballgown is haunting me.'

'I can see why; it's gorgeous. I'm in as long as the maid of honor dress doesn't need to be a cupcake dress to match. Let's stop by the shop soon, and you can try it on again.'

'I knew you'd be cool with it! Mom thought for sure my indecisiveness would annoy you.'

'Never...'

'Liar,' she says with a chuckle, knowing me well. 'Meet Mom and me at the shop Thursday night at five. I already made the appointment. I'll even buy you dinner after.'

'Free dinner with my BFF? I can't wait.'

No way can I tell her what I'm doing tonight. She'll insert herself too early, and it'll be a nightmare. We chat for a few about basically nothing, as we usually do, then I hang up and flip back to Brooks's text.

'Alright,' I say to Dylan, who's scrolling through his phone as he eats and listens to my conversations. 'I'm asking Brooks to my gig tonight. If this goes all tits up, I'm blaming you.'

'I bet it goes exactly how you seeing him play at the bar went. He'll be completely charmed by your talent. Do you want me to text Cass and ask her to go easy on you?'

I cock my head. 'No. She and I duel all the time. There are no winners in piano. But you can text her and ask her to stop by your place after.'

He laughs like I'm kidding. 'That's never going to

happen. However, there are bigger tips if you play best, which you better count on if you're paying for River to drink. Let me know if you need someone to help coax him home.'

As I type a text to Brooks inviting him to my gig tonight, that fluttery feeling is back, but this time it feels like a beehive in my chest. I need to move slowly with this man, or I am for sure going to get stung.

9

MERCY

The Barrel Room is cool. It's in Old Town Portland, just a couple blocks from the river. Dylan and I each play here once a month, sometimes we duel, but typically it's us against someone else, sometimes even randoms, who surprise me with their talent. The bar's in a super-old building with brick walls, barrels for tables, a long bar on one side of the room opposite two baby grands facing one another. Perfect for piano dueling.

'Don't embarrass me,' I say to River as we walk in.

'Right back at ya, spunk monkey,' he says, holding the door for me. He might be the most annoying man ever, but he does have manners. Mostly.

I glare over at him. 'Where do you come up with these names?'

'I can't give away my secrets; then you'd win. Why am I here anyway? You need a fake date or something?' He follows me into the bar as I walk towards the pianos.

'Hey, Mercy!' Jonny, the bartender, lifts a hand to greet me.

'Hi!' I chirp like this is the best thing I've done all day. Then I glance at River. 'If I ever needed a fake date, *you* wouldn't be who got that call. You're the annoying little brother who keeps things light and breaks up the tension.'

He scrunches his face like I've offended him. 'Tension between who?'

I sit my bag on the piano bench. God, I have to tell him why he's here. I turn to face him. 'I invited a guy tonight.'

'I'm *not* having a three-way with you two. Unless you get me drunk, then maybe...'

I groan. 'There's not enough alcohol in the world to tempt me of that. We're just hanging out, but I'm nervous because he calls me beautiful and treats me, I dunno, *nice*? There's something different about him, and I can't pinpoint it. You're here to help me not act like a complete idiot and drag him to the bathroom to do... ya know, Mercy things,' I say with a lift of a shoulder.

River's now laughing, running his hand through his hair that surprisingly isn't in the man-bun yet. 'Wow, I suspected one day your softer side would show, and you'd fall for some guy, but to happen so young, I'm shocked. I'm also surprised you're going the opposite of your usual "wanna fuck" dudes. May I ask why?'

'No, you may not.'

'Why?' he asks anyway.

I glare. 'I said you couldn't ask.'

'That one was more "why can't I?"'

'Oh, well, that's easy. You don't need to know. Are we good now? Just hang out at the bar, and after Cass and I finish, help me make friendly conversation with him.'

'I can't believe you called me to make you look good. That was a risky move, bonerd.'

I roll my eyes. 'I called so you would prevent me from doing him in the bathroom. Not once did I think, *Bring River; he'll make you look good.* Seriously, Riv. No names. Please. Pretend you're normal.' I dramatically clasp my hands in front of my chest, my performance gene displaying Edie style.

'Normal?' He chuckles. 'No thanks,' he says,

walking backward from me towards the bar. 'Since my services aren't needed yet, I'm just going to sit over here and drink. Sound good?'

'Three,' I remind him, holding up three fingers.

Going out with River is always like babysitting a mouthy drunk teenager. How did I forget this? I avoid going out with him at all costs because of it. But he was the only one I could turn to tonight. I'm not ready to bring the others into this, so I'm depending on River to make tonight better and *not* humiliating. What on earth is wrong with me? Godspeed, either way, I suppose.

'Sure,' he says with a nod. '*You'll* only buy three. I promise.'

I don't like the sound of that.

'Good evening, Mercy,' Cassie says as she approaches her piano.

I love Cass because she's the opposite of me and reminds me of my best friend, Hollyn. She's sunshiney, looks like a blonde adult Shirley Temple, and always has a smile on her pretty face. She's played the piano since she was four. Her mom was a pianist for her local church and taught lessons her whole life. Now, after her twenty-seven trips around the sun, I'd say Cassie is one of the top players in the city.

'Hey, Cass.' I look over her colorful Zooey-Deschanel-style outfit and nod. 'You look adorable, as usual. How's things?'

For the first time, she lets out a grumble. 'I don't know...'

Well, that's not like her.

'Is, uh, something wrong?' She's never upset. I'm intrigued.

'Not really, just that I hate men. Do you ever feel like that?'

I glance over at River, now laughing with the bartender and one of the bouncers, as two of the three of them do shots. 'Only every day of my life,' I answer flatly, sitting at the piano and stretching my fingers. 'What happened?'

'Last night I went on a date, only he never showed, so I sat there for an hour drinking champagne and eating the free bread before finally ordering and acting like I was alone on purpose. It was so humiliating.'

'What's humiliating about that? You got to eat a meal without pretending to give a shit about some guy's fantasy football team. *Trust* me, it's always best to learn they're assholes early on,' I say. 'I know from experience. That said, I'm sorry. Some boys suck, but I have good news for you.'

'What?' She glances up from her piano.

'Dylan asked me to tell you to call him later.'

He will kill me for this and I'm cool with that. Cassie needs a listening ear, and Lord knows Dylan needs to sweet-talk a woman. The desperation of him needing a girlfriend is starting to show in weird ways. For instance, he recently bought his cat, Mozart, a tiny bed that resembles a human bed and it sits right next to his real adult-sized bed. He always wants to hang out lately, but I just don't have the energy. Our relationship works best when he's dating someone. Plus, I know he likes her 'cause I've never seen a man blush so quickly at the sound of a woman's name. So, if he won't make a move, I'll do it for him.

Immediate heart-eyes as her face lights up. 'He *did*?' Her voice raises with curiosity.

'Yep. He said you two hadn't talked in a while, and he wanted to catch up.'

She beams. 'Wow, I didn't expect that. Thanks for relaying the message. What a cutie he is.'

'Isn't he?' I gush with her. 'It's totally my pleasure,' I say, as the bar starts to buzz with people. 'Shall we do this?'

'Let's...' she says, playing a riff that grabs the attention of patrons.

Cassie and I sort of have this planned out. It's not as 'duel-ish' as one might suspect. She plays a song, and I add to it, and vice versa. The crowd thinks we're doing a bit but really, we've got a set we've practiced endlessly over the years.

Midway through our performance, I'm glad I took the piano facing the front door because I see the moment Brooks Hudson walks in. He looks good. Like *really* good and he's not wearing anything special. Just his usual jeans, T-shirt and ball cap. This hat is a white Under Armour. I wonder how many he has 'cause I've seen three now.

I watch as he glances around – probably looking for me. He readjusts his ball cap while momentarily confused, then approaches the bar and orders a drink. I should've guessed he'd be the guy to play it casually cool after wondering if I'd stood him up. Once he chooses a barstool half a dozen away from River, he turns to look at the entertainment, and our eyes meet, only I'm coming up on a super-complicated part of this piece and I can't do more than smile then focus. But I sense his gaze on me, and it feels like when you're so excited about something happening tomorrow that you can't sleep.

At the end, Cassie and I say our goodbyes. I almost asked her to stay for a drink, and then I remembered I've got River with me, and if he steals her out from under Dylan – who doesn't even know he has her – he

(Dylan) will kill me. And considering River's drinking, I was quick to agree that she shouldn't stay for a drink but rather get home because she's got an early funeral to play tomorrow. Though I reminded her to give Dyl a call before she goes to bed, so I'm sure I'll hear about that. But that's a problem for future Mercy.

'Wow,' Brooks says after I've approached him at the bar. 'That was—' his smile is contagious as I wait for his words '—absolutely amazing.'

I wave a hand like anyone could do it. 'It was nothing.'

'Are you kidding? It was everything and then some. I didn't expect the prodigy thing to be true, but Julio wasn't lying.'

I roll my eyes playfully. At this moment, River approaches with two shots in his hand. 'Well done, Chopinette. I got you a shot of tequila to celebrate your only talent. When's your new fuckboy get here?'

'Ugh, Riv,' I groan as I take the shot he's shoving my way.

Brooks grins as he lifts a single hand into the air. 'Hi,' he says. 'Pretty sure I'm the fuckboy you're referring to. I didn't realize she'd labeled us so sweetly.' Thankfully, he's obviously kidding.

River's eyes go wide as he glances between the two of us. He inspects Brooks for a hint too long to be normal, then forces a smile. 'Oops. Cool tattoos, man,' he says, lifting his chin.

I motion his way, only a little embarrassed by him so far. 'This is my roommate, River. He insisted he come.'

Riv lifts a single eyebrow my way. 'Yeah,' he says, playing along. 'I just can't get enough of her and that damn piano she keeps me up with day and night.' He downs his shot, setting the empty glass on the bar next to him.

Jesus. Why didn't I just bring Dylan? He's so much less obnoxious. Oh, right, because I thought it would be weird for Brooks to see me with him again. Like something is going on between us. Instead, my bright idea was to bring this fool?

Mercy! Brooks is just a guy. Just an ordinary, handsome, super-hot man who has heard some pretty intimate noises from you. Ugh, why does my head always go there?

What I was trying to say was that I want Brooks to know I'm single. Why? It confuses me because I'm terrified of losing people, have never pined over anyone, and we agreed to be just friends. But my loins don't want to be friends with him; they want more. My heart is somewhere in the middle, perking up at the sight of him but not trusting my head to make the right decision – and the only way to find out why is to get to know him.

'I thought she was incredible,' Brooks says to River.

'Oh, she is,' Riv agrees. 'Also loud as fuck when you sleep on the wall opposite her prized grand piano.'

Brooks follows our conversation visibly, a grin on his face the whole time. 'You have a grand piano in your apartment?'

'Takes up half the damn living room,' River complains like we're an old married couple, and by the look on Brooks's face, I'd say he's noticed.

'River's one of my oldest friends. He's more annoying younger brother than roommate.' I defend why I even know this man, but with each word, Brooks looks more amused. He seems to be enjoying this mess I've created.

'I do have a grand piano in my apartment, though. It is one of my prized possessions. I splurge on one thing, usually...' I display my foot, clad in my leopard-print Louboutin stilettos that cost more than I'm willing to admit. Brooks nods with approval at the sight of them. 'But when I saw someone on Facebook Marketplace with an 1865 Collard & Collard grand piano practically giving it away—'

'Pfft, giving, right... for *thousands* of dollars.' Riv throws in the truth.

'—I couldn't resist.'

'How many instruments do you play?' Brooks asks curiously.

'Five,' I reply before doing the shot River's forcing on me. 'My room looks like a music store.'

'Looks like you guys are good here,' River says. He leans into me but doesn't lower his voice at all. 'Call me if ya need me, and don't do any yankin' of his bacon if ya know what I mean...'

'Oh my God, go away,' I beg. As he walks away, Brooks and I watch him. Me hoping he doesn't turn around and come back and Brooks like he's trying to figure out what just happened.

'He's, uh...' He points in River's direction.

'The most annoying boy in all the land?' I finish his sentence. 'Yes.'

He chuckles. I'm glad someone is enjoying this because I've just realized the fluttering in my chest is back, and yet again, he's not got a guitar hanging around his neck. *Kick in soon, tequila; I need you.*

'Your complicated job is at rest this evening?' I ask as I slide onto the barstool next to him like I'm not as nervous as I am.

'I go in at midnight tonight, but things are on track

for now. Unfortunately, that means I can't drink with you. But can I buy you one? Or maybe another shot?' He eyes the empty glass I've set on the bar in front of me.

'Pick your poison, handsome. I'll drink whatever.'

I hear the words as they roll off my tongue. My usual Mae West man-hunting impersonation has surfaced, and that sounded flirty as hell. Shit, did I just call him handsome? What am I doing? Flirting? That's the opposite of what I'm supposed to be doing.

I glance over at him. Based on the smile growing on his face I'd say yes it happened, and no, he didn't hate it.

He orders himself water, and for me, he goes with a Bellini. The last guy who bought me a drink (that wasn't River just now) ordered a Buttery Nipple. There's nothing subtle about that. Brooks seems too grown-up and classy to act like my usual you're-only-temporary type. And I like it?

'You play five instruments fluently?' Brooks asks.

I nod. 'I started young on the ukulele, then moved to the violin, and it spiraled from there. I wanted to play all the instruments because music cleared the fog in my head. Do you only play the guitar?'

'No, I'm also a master of "Chopsticks" on the piano,' he says proudly.

I laugh. 'Maybe we should duel?'

'I'd like that, but let's leave the pianos out of it,' he says with a wink.

Thank God River's here. I glance down the bar at him and notice he's legit keeping an eye on me like I asked. Whew. There's no way he'll let my loins do the talking, so words better come from somewhere else fast.

'How was your day?'

Could I ask a more platonic question? Here he is flirting with me, and I'm asking about his day like I'm his fifties wife with dinner on the table.

'Good. It's getting better by the minute, if I'm honest.' He taps his water to my drink like he's toasting the evening.

'Are you always this flirty?' I ask, putting it out there. Might as well acknowledge it before we start talking about the weather in sexual innuendos.

'Not even a little bit. You seem to bring it out in me. Since we agreed on honesty last time we met up, I'm going to lay this on the table even though I probably shouldn't.' He pauses, looking me in the eyes and taking a deep breath. 'I don't think I can forget our past and focus on just being friends, can you?' He leans into me as he speaks, then moves back into his space and side-eyes me. His golden-brown eyes filled with specks of honey-colored gold sparkle under the lighting. I suddenly remember why he was addicting. Smoldering looks like this one are hard to say no to.

'Let's just say, pretty much every night since I ran into you at Oz's, I fall asleep replaying our past and wondering why things ended. Does that answer your question?'

'It does indeed,' he says. 'Douchebag move on my part. My life blew up. I apologize. Since we're on the same page now, how should we play this more-than-friends thing out?'

'Well, that depends on whether you're interested in just the benefits side or something more?'

'I'm interested in getting to know you.'

'But how?' I ask, sipping my Bellini. Oh, sweet sparkling peaches, this is good.

'With your clothes on, hopefully. Remember the fate thing we touched on recently?'

'Yeah...'

'My ex is a big believer – me not so much. But then came you, and things seem to be falling into place without either of us trying.' He pauses, smiling at me nervously. It's cute as hell. 'What I'm trying to say is, I've also been staring at my ceiling, thinking of the past, and I wonder if our timing was off before?'

My heart flatlines, then with the sudden appearance of his hand on my lower back as he leans into me, it jolts back to life, and the fluttering invades my chest again. Did he just say our timing was off?

'Would you be totally against me asking you out?' He talks directly into my ear – his voice is low and growly but in the best way, sending an unexpected chill down my spine.

'Out?' Somehow the one word comes out wobbly, like I'm speaking a foreign language.

'Go on a date with me, Mercy. You know you want to.'

Damn it, my answer to this, without a doubt, would usually be no. But he's right. I want to. I also want to play with him. Make him think my answer is no. You know, play hard to get.

Instead, my mouth says, 'I do want to.'

'Really?'

What? He seemed so sure of himself before. Now he's surprised I said yes.

'Don't act so shocked. I let ya see me naked.'

He grins wide. 'Yes, you have.'

'I can see you picturing it, and I hate to burst your bubble, but I feel like I should warn you I don't usually *date*. The whole heartless thing.'

'Then you've befriended the perfect person because I'm a pro. I'll teach you.' He glances at the time on his phone and frowns. 'Unfortunately, I've got to get ready for work. But I'll text you the details. Sound good?'

'Sounds great. You know you could have skipped tonight if you were busy?'

'Nah,' he says. 'There's no way my heart would have let me skip tonight.' He rests his hand on my thigh, and I suck in my breath involuntarily. Did him touching me feel like this before? All tingly and wonderful? 'I'm glad I came tonight because now I've got something perfect to think about while I work.'

My mind comes back once his hand has been removed from my thigh. 'You're going to think of me on shift – sounds dirty; I like it.'

He stands from his barstool, hands the bartender a twenty, then kisses my cheek. 'I like how you say anything you want. Talk soon?'

'Yeah,' I say half breathlessly, like he just had his tongue in my mouth. 'We'll talk soon.' I try to pull it together but don't sound as casually flirtatious as I want. More take-me-now flirty.

Once he's gone, like a can of Raid has fallen over me, the butterflies die off quickly.

'Dumped ya already, huh? Rough,' River says, startling me that he's so close. 'Barkeep! Two shots of tequila, stat!' He waves his empty shot glass in the air.

'Will you stop calling bartenders "barkeep"? It's the twenty-first century, you lunatic. We're not hanging out with Billy the Kid in the Old West.'

'But it would be cool if we were.'

I roll my eyes. 'He asked me out,' I say, finishing the Bellini in one swallow. 'Like on a date.'

Riv looks towards the front door, then back at me. 'Why are you still here, then?'

'Not *tonight*. Later.'

'Oh, booty call, gotcha.'

I shake my head until he gets it.

'You mean like on an actual date where you plan it out, go into public with your manners on high, and not just visit his apartment under the dark of night and exit before sunrise?'

'You're giving me a headache with all the eye-rolling I need to do around you. But yes, exactly like that.'

'Huh,' Riv mumbles as he sits on the stool Brooks was just on. 'Someone wants to date you. I want to say I knew this day would come but—'

'I don't know how to date, Riv,' I interrupt him.

'*What?* You go out with guys all the time.'

'And never give them my real name or number. They're just giant meat puppets that I use to make myself feel important when my heart and head tell me I'm not. What I do is not date. How do I do this?'

'Show up and don't be weird? And maybe pay for your half? I always appreciate it when women don't expect me to pay.'

'You appreciate when no one expects you to pay,' I remind him.

'True.'

I down the shot the bartender just set in front of me then bury my face into my hands. 'Why is this happening? Since when do I want to date a man? I thought I never wanted this, and now I'm dreaming of happy-ever-afters, while my estranged father haunts me from prison via a possible demonic letter that's living in my purse.'

'You still haven't read that thing?' Riv asks, surprise on his face. 'Are you serious?' He sets his empty shot glass in front of him. 'You *actually* like this guy?'

I lift a single shoulder. 'I think I do.'

10

BROOKS

I'm at the station on a paperwork day when my phone rings, and I realize I left it sitting on Andrews's desk across from me when I went for my thirteenth cup of coffee. Being in the office is rough, but coffee helps me get through it.

'Yeah?' Andrews answers before I can get to it. 'Who? He's here but call him on his phone, would ya? I ain't his secretary.' Momentarily he listens to the caller on the other end before pulling the phone from his head and looking it over with a scowl. 'Hang on,' he barks to the caller with his usually grumpy growl. 'Stop leaving your shit on my desk, Hudson.' He lobs the phone my way where, luckily, I catch it.

'Sorry, Dad, it won't happen again,' I joke.

He hates paperwork days more than I do, but I've got a secret weapon to turn his mood around. I open my bottom desk drawer, pull out a six-pack of raspberry-filled powdered Hostess donuts and slide them his way as a peace offering. His eyes meet mine, the permanent scowl still on his face and, without losing eye contact, he snatches the donuts from me.

'Hello?' I say into my phone.

'He seems like a real sweetheart. I bet he's loads of fun at parties,' the voice says. 'Hi, it's Mercy.' Her voice sends an instant smile to my face.

I spin in my chair so I'm facing away from Andrews. It's been a few days since I saw her. I didn't expect her to call me out of the blue like this. We've been texting for days, so it's not a total surprise to hear from her, but the last thing I need is Andrews giving me shit about this later. Our desks are shoved together, so I have to stare at his mean old mug anytime we're here. He loves to listen in on my calls and interrogate me later.

'Mercy, uh – what's up?'

'Truthfully, this is as stupid as it gets, but I wanted to call and say thank you for coming the other night. So many times in my life, I've looked around the room as I performed and had no one there for me. It meant a lot. And for the drink. I think Bellinis might be my new fave.'

'There's nothing stupid about that.'

'Well, that's because I haven't finished yet. Also, you haven't told me when or where this upcoming date is, and I'm making it a *much* bigger deal in my head than it needs to be, so I'm incredibly nervous. Can you do that soon?'

I bite my lips together to rein in the growing grin. 'You're nervous about going on a date with me?'

She chuckles. 'You weren't supposed to know that. But since I'm freaking out over this, yes, I'm a little nervous.'

'And you need me to hurry up and officially plan this so you can relax?'

'Plus, decide what to wear. I am a woman, so that's complicated as it is.'

'You are unlike any woman I've ever dated.'

'But... you secretly like it?' she asks.

'It's no secret. If I turn around right now, my partner will see the stupid grin on my face. I'll have to explain, and I'd rather not.' In the background, I hear what sounds like a toilet flush. 'Where are you?'

'A funeral for a man I don't know, but to make this call, I snuck away to the bathroom 'cause I had to pee, and I figured two birds, one stone. Is it too soon for me to be peeing on the phone with you?'

I burst out a laugh. 'Mercy, Mercy, Mercy.'

'Ooh,' she says, the sound of a faucet in the background. 'That's way better than "Lemon, Lemon, Lemon".'

'You'll distract me at work with memories like those,' I say, partially under my breath.

'You're at work? By the way, what do you do? I still don't know.'

'That sounds like a date conversation to me.'

'This top-secret job better be good, or I'll be disappointed. I'm expecting something big.'

'I'm a stripper,' I tell her. 'One of those Chippendale guys.'

'Oh yeah? You guys do shows at noon?'

I should have known she'd see through that one. We talk for a few more minutes until Andrews starts repeating my responses in a high-pitched giggly voice between inhaling donuts, and I realize he's heard too much, and I'll never live this down.

'It's like watching Samanthia talk to her boyfriend. Who's the girl?' he asks, batting his eyes after I set my phone on my desk.

Samanthia is his sixteen-year-old daughter. Offensive.

Andrews is a big guy. Thick graying hair. A flavor-saver of a mustache usually sporting some kind of donut paraphernalia. He's in his late sixties and looks it. He's always been a say-it-like-it-is guy, but now he's also that old man in the store, loudly complaining about the selection of pastries they're carrying.

'Just a woman I know, and that's the only question I'm answering.'

'A woman you know or a woman you *know*...?' He waggles his eyebrows, grinning like the dirty old man he can be.

'I said no more questions.'

'Is she pretty?'

'Very.'

He chuckles. 'God, you're easy,' he says. 'No more questions, then you immediately answer one.' He's leaning back in his chair, a napkin unfolded and tucked into the top of his shirt while he scarfs down the last donut from the box I distracted him with.

'Hudson!' Seiver yells it from his office.

Andrews laughs. It amuses him greatly that I'm the lead now. The being yelled at for ridiculous reasons while he listens in is what he's waited his whole career for. Someone else is the lead, and he's the 'partner'.

I drop my head, wondering what Seiver will spit poison over this time.

'Yeah?' I ask, now standing in his doorway.

'Sit down,' he orders.

I take my time, flip my hat on backward and settle in the chair facing his desk until I'm comfortable, and when I finally make eye contact, he's got his arms crossed over his chest and a glare that might set me on fire.

'Ya comfy there, muffin?'

I nod proudly. I feel like it's my job to annoy him a little bit. This career is stressful as fuck, so if I can lighten the mood, I'm going to.

'Please tell me you don't work with your hat like that? You look like you're having a mid-life crisis.'

Thoroughly offended, I flip it forward again. 'Did you need to say something, or is this just have-a-go-at-Brooks hour?'

'I've got shit to say.'

'Then say it.'

Seiver rolls his eyes. 'I got a guy at the state pen who says he's gathered some information we might be interested in about one of your cases. I promised myself I'd never deal with this man again, so I'm giving it to you.'

'What case?'

'A guy that rivals Dominic. He's been in for a while, so he may have inside information. I've dealt with him before, and I've no doubt he's up to his eyeballs in shady prison shit. He claims he knows about the head guy you're looking for, and he'll talk, *with* conditions.'

'What conditions?'

'This is the part where you do your job and go find out,' he snaps, tossing a manila envelope containing the prisoner info inside.

'You want me to go right now when I'm ten minutes from being off the clock?'

'Bring Andrews with ya, so ya don't get lonely,' he hollers, picking up the desk phone, signaling our meeting is over.

'God damn it,' Andrews grumbles from the other room, having overheard the whole conversation. 'On pot roast night?'

Food. It's his only language. I hesitantly walk around him to my side of the desk and sit down. I take my hat off and toss it on my desk along with the envelope. 'Looks like we've got to do something on paperwork day. It's no pot roast, but what do you think of Burger King?'

'I think you're buying,' he growls, grabbing his stuff from the desk.

As he drives, I text Mercy with our official first date info. *Final-ly*, she texts back with a wink emoji. And it's set. A proper date on the calendar with a woman I can't get out of my head. May the breakup gods leave me be for once.

11

MERCY

'What is this I hear about a letter from Nick?' Edie asks as he bursts through my apartment door. He seems to think the key I gave him is for whenever he's here. No knocking or emergency necessary – just come right in.

'Who told you about that?' I ask as I head into my room to prep for dinner with Brooks Hudson. Our first official date. He said it's casual, less pressure, but sweet Jesus, I'm nervous.

Ed follows me, stopping at my doorframe. A stupid smirk fills his face as he lifts a single shoulder while crossing his arms over his chest. 'I know all, remember?'

'Damn it, River.'

Ed shakes his head.

'Dylan?'

He smirks.

'It's creepy when you remind me you've got people watching me all over the city. You do realize I'm thirty now, right?'

'Thirty going on fifteen, yes, I'm aware. Spill it, little sister, or I'll have Carlos start charging you at the restaurant.'

'So, I got this letter,' I say immediately, making him laugh. 'What? I'm poor.' I grab my bag, digging through it for the letter.

'You're poor because you can't quit buying shoes,' Ed reminds me, side-eyeing the custom shoe storage I had built in my closet. Floor-to-ceiling shoes arranged by color. It's so beautiful I take selfies with it. My Instagram is pretty much a shrine to music and shoes.

I find the letter crumpled at the bottom of my purse. I haven't looked at it since the day I shoved it in here after it spilled out onto the sidewalk in front of Brooks. I pull it out, the loose change living on top of it falling to the bottom of my purse with a jingle.

Edie inspects it once I've handed it to him. 'I've never seen the man's handwriting,' he says. 'It reminds me of yours.'

'No.' I point at him aggressively. 'Nothing about Nick reminds you of me. Got it?'

He nods once, flipping the envelope over, furrowing his brow as his eyes meet mine. 'You didn't open it?'

'Truthfully, I'm trying to pretend it doesn't exist.'

'Still haunts you, doesn't it?' He carries the letter into my room, sitting at the end of my bed. Obviously, he's not leaving till we discuss this, and considering I have plans, I better explain quickly.

'Yes, it haunts me like a banshee on a mission. I'm about to buy a fire-proof safe to keep it in because River's convinced it's cursed and will burn down the building. Maybe I should get a rosary too? Do those work?'

'Work at what?' Ed asks.

'Breaking curses? Warding off evil? I dunno.'

'Can a letter be evil?'

'Anything could be evil. Do you never watch *Ghost Adventures*? Zak Bagans has an entire museum of it.'

Ed shakes his head. 'No, I never watch Zak Bagans and his museum of evil. That's your thing. You're seriously not even curious about what it says?'

'Not really. The judge asked if he had anything to say to me during the trial when I was nine, and he couldn't even be bothered to speak the word "no".

Daddy dearest just shook his head. It's been decades, Ed; what could he possibly have to say that shouldn't have been said a long-ass time ago?'

'Sugar—' Ed says gently.

I lift a single hand. 'Don't "sugar" me with this one, Edie. You can't fix this with pretty words. There's no way for you to relate. You can't make it hurt less. You don't have the memories I have of that man or that night. Whatever way he's arranged those words will hurt worse than a bad period. Something else you know nothing about.'

He slumps his shoulders like he's disappointed, staring at the letter in his hands. 'I know I can't fix this, Merc. You're right. I didn't have the early childhood you did. I never knew Nick. But I can help you deal with it. Do you want me to read it?'

I grab it from him, shoving it back into my purse. 'I said I'm not ready yet.'

Someone walking into the apartment catches my attention. I drop my head when I see him. Damn it. Why must people continually stop by to check on me? I'm a full-grown woman, for crying out loud.

'Dylan,' Ed greets him enthusiastically, leaving my bed and heading his way.

'Did you come over to see what kind of damage

running your mouth about the letter did?' I ask when our eyes meet.

'You won't talk about it; I was worried,' Dylan says defensively.

'Why does everyone I know worry about me like I'm incapable of taking care of myself? I've made it this far, and that's saying a lot.'

'Love, we worry about you because you can. But you do it silently, and we're trying to prevent a massive future blow that takes out the sister I once knew,' Ed says as he turns to me, the fatherly voice he's so perfected over the years front and center. 'Our worry is born out of love, darling.'

'Fuck love. It's the most painful four-letter word on the planet, yet people long for it. I don't get it.'

Both Dylan and Ed's eyes are wide. Edie moves his attention to Dylan, apparently not in the mood to talk me off another anti-love rant. 'How are you, sweets?'

'Doing well,' Dylan says. 'Still trying to figure out how you two are related.'

'Hey...' I object.

'I'm your brother,' Ed reminds me. 'You can live your life however you want. Do whatever makes you happy. I support you. Despite constantly fighting it, I think your heart exists, and it's lonely, Merc. Lonely because you refuse to let anyone in. Read the letter; maybe it'll help heal what he injured.'

I glare at both of them. 'You two think I'm lonely?'

They both nod.

'Then I have great news. I'm meeting someone in forty minutes, so if you both would get the hell out of here, maybe I'd have a chance of looking decent when I get there.'

'You have a date?' they ask in unison, glancing between one another wide-eyed.

I'm not ready to label it as a date yet. 'I'm meeting a friend for dinner.'

'Hollyn?' Ed asks.

'I have more than one friend.'

'River!' Dyl yells over his shoulder.

'Yeah?' Riv hollers back from his room.

'You going to dinner with Mercy in a few?'

'Only if she's paying...'

I cock my head with a sigh. 'It's not River.'

'Well, love, besides Carlos, everyone you'd consider a friend is either in this apartment or has been ruled out. Who are you meeting?'

'Again, I'm going to remind you, boys, I'm *thirty*.'

Right then, Dylan's jaw drops open. 'Tattoos?'

Ed's eyes practically bulge out of his head. 'What

does "tattoos" mean?' he asks, his head following our conversation.

'He came to your gig the other night?'

'What gig?' Ed asks.

'Yes, he did. And he informed me he didn't want to be just friends and asked me to dinner tonight. It's casual so let's not make it a bigger deal than it is.'

'*He who?*' Ed bolsters as his head flips back to me.

I roll my eyes. 'Have I ever told you guys you're a tad over-involved? Like helicopter parents, but I'm a grown woman.'

'Trust me, doll. We all know you're grown based on your birth certificate. The problem is, you love making bad decisions, and if I can save you from that, I most certainly will because that's what a good helicopter parent does. Don't make me go all Beverly Goldberg on you.'

'Queen Edie has spoken,' I say with a playful roll of my eyes.

Calling Ed a queen only makes him beam with pride. He doesn't wear a crown or anything. Usually, I mean, I wouldn't put it past him. He's got an entire bedroom he's turned into a closet full of sparkly gowns and size twelve stilettos, as his kind of queen is more drag than royalty. You'd never know it by how he's dressed now, in jeans and a T-shirt. Still, five nights a week, Ed struts his stuff across a stage at the drag club he owns – The RoseWood – where he sports the most elaborate costumes ever, with a face full of make-up, high-dollar wigs, his junk taped to his backside, wearing sparkling jewelry I'm not allowed to touch, while a gang of scantily clad side queens drop it like it's hot behind him. It's my favorite place in the world.

My phone dings from my dresser where I laid it with an incoming text. All of our eyes move to it.

'Touch it, and you both die,' I warn.

Ed rolls his eyes.

'Is that him?' Dyl asks.

'That's none of your business.'

'*Him?* This is the boy you're meeting up with shortly?' Edie asks, now wholly invested in the conversation.

I shoot him a glare. 'He's not a boy.'

'Oh, God,' Ed groans, dramatically pulling his hand to his chest. 'What kind of man-boy are we talking about here?'

'The kind I've previously known in a way you'd be disappointed in,' I say, flashing him a coy smile. Usually, this will stop the conversation.

Edie lets out a long, exhausted sigh. 'I'd act surprised, but...' He shakes his head, glancing at Dylan.

'I'd explain, but not only do I not want to, but I don't know how. I like him,' I say, pulling outfit options from my closet and tossing them onto my bed. 'But I'm trying to stay calm. Breezy, ya know? We're having dinner at a food truck pod. It's nothing fancy.'

Ed's gaze follows each piece of clothing, and he picks out the things he doesn't like as they hit the bed.

'Nothing fancy?' he asks, lifting a very revealing scoop-neck tank I've optioned. He tosses it to the chair in the corner of my room with his other vetoes. 'This seems like a date?'

I lift my shoulder like I've no idea. 'We agreed to be friends.' I stop digging through my closet and glance out at Ed. 'That was the plan at first, at least. Then it turned into him admitting he wanted to get to know the other side of me.'

'The clothed side?' Ed asks.

I lift a shoulder. 'Yep. He's nice and polite, handsome and funny, and I *want* to go.' The words even taste funny. 'Are you happy? Your insistence that I'm lonely and need love has worked, and I'm putting myself out there. If the whole thing's a failure, it's both your fault.'

'Honey?' Ed asks, his eyes wide. I glance over at him. 'I think your heart might be digging its way out of the shallow grave you've got it in.'

'Not a conversation I want to have right now. I've only got thirty minutes before I have to go, so if you could focus on *why* you came over and not my love life, that'd be great. My lips are sealed on my personal life.'

'Are you going to read the letter?' Ed asks firmly.

'Probably not.'

'Mercy...'

'If I ever read it, I'll let ya know. But until I have some undeniable sign, it's living in the bottom of my purse. Now, both of you, go home. How am I supposed to choose the perfect shoes with an audience? I need to concentrate.' I herd them towards the front door like a border collie and promise I'll update them later. I won't. But it gets them out the door long enough for me to lock the deadbolt neither of them has a key for.

12

BROOKS

'Why are you pacing?' Oz asks.

That's right: Ozie has come on my date with me. I dropped Ali off with my brother, and since he lives across the street, he insisted he come. He didn't exactly pick up on my hint that I was grabbing a bite alone – but not. He just heard 'food' and got into my truck. Then he laughed when I told him I was meeting a woman.

'I'm not pacing,' I say, stopping to force it to be true.

'You're going to freak this girl out if you prove how terrible at relationships you are on date one. Relax, would you? You're making me anxious. She'll never touch your naughty spot with this aura.'

I roll my eyes. 'You better start thinking on your words before they leave your lips, or when we leave here, you're gonna pay.'

'Oh *noooo...*' he says, faking a shiver as he acts terrified. 'She a dog?'

'*What?*'

'That why you tried to drive off without me? She's a total bow-wow? I can't say I'm shocked; you've pretty well dated all the hot ones available, and everyone's dumped you. It was definitely time to lower your standards.'

I rub my hand over my face, readjusting my hat. And here she thought her friend River was embarrassing. Oz is about to win that award. This is going to be a nightmare.

An older Honda pulls up along the curb across the road. Both Ozie's and my eyes are on the woman who's just stepped out. Mercy.

'Holy shit,' Oz says under his breath. 'Too bad you just lowered your standards 'cause this girl is on fire.' He does a chef's kiss to drive his point home.

'You realize you're married, right?'

'Marriage doesn't make you blind, son. I mean, Jesus, Brooksy, how am I not supposed to see her when I have eyes?'

'Do not call me Brooksy, and roll your tongue

back into your mouth, would ya? Don't look at her like that. You're going to humiliate me, so shut up right now.'

'I'm not even talking. I'll behave when your lady gets here; for now, boom chicka-bow-wow.'

I shove him away from me for some space, so it maybe looks like I'm here alone, then turn towards Mercy as she crosses the street, lifting a single hand. One smile from her and my heart immediately speeds.

'Wait?!' Oz's hand is suddenly on my shoulder, squeezing tightly. 'That's her? No fucking way! The smokin' hot girl?'

'Those are the things I want you *not* to say...' I say under my breath, shoving his hand from my shoulder.

'She's outta your league.' He coughs the words into his hand.

Mercy's on the sidewalk at this point, looking at Oz like he has a third eye. Despite him using the age-old invisible-to-everyone-but-the-one-you-want-to-hear coughing trick, she picked up on every word he just hacked.

'Hi,' she says with an unsure smile, a single confused eyebrow lifted as her eyes dart between Ozie and me.

'Hey, gorgeous.'

Ozie snickers into his fist, causing her to glance his way, then back to me, confused.

I sigh heavily, fidgeting with my hat. 'This is Oz. He couldn't take a hint that he wasn't wanted tonight, so here we are. For reasons I'm currently unsure of, we're best friends, and if he doesn't settle down, he's paying for everything.'

'No-go, *compadre*,' Oz says, slapping me on the back. 'Forgot my wallet.'

'Convenient...' I say, slightly annoyed.

He shrugs.

This is not a new forgetful moment. He figures his friends drink for free at his bar, so we pay for every-thing else. His wallet is often forgotten.

'It's cool,' Mercy says. 'I made you suffer through River, so I suppose I can handle one night with Tommy Lee tagging along.' She glances at Oz, who frowns at being compared to a guy he can't stand. 'But consider your words, Tommy-boy, 'cause I have no feelings.'

'Damn,' he bellows. 'Smokin' *and* bitchy. You hit the goldmine, my friend. Feisty women are the most fun. Especially in bed. Why do you think I married Angel?'

This is already a disaster, but Mercy has a goofy grin, so maybe it's not as terrible as I suspect. Oz can be an icebreaker, and I'll look like a saint compared to him, which can't be bad.

'I understand if you want to cancel,' I say apologetically.

'It's cool. I'm fluent in tag-along.'

Oz stands silently with his jaw dropped open in offense. 'Tag-along?' he asks under his breath.

'Shall we?' I ask, extending an elbow her way. She hesitantly slides her hand into the crook of my arm, walking by my side towards the food truck pod entrance.

Ozie trails behind us. Eight food trucks are parked side by side in a fenced area, with covered picnic tables along one side, outside heaters, string lights illuminating the dining space, and even TVs mounted in the seating area.

'You've been here before?' she asks as she inspects the place.

'A lot.'

'What's your fave?'

'Shawarma Express, the Mediterranean place. Gyros to die for.'

'I'm going Korean barbecue,' Oz says. 'Gimme twenty bucks.'

Like an annoyed parent whose child is demanding

mall money, I pull a twenty from my wallet and hand it to him.

'Later.' He walks away from us towards his favorite truck, leaving us in peace for a moment.

'Seriously, I'm sorry.' I glance at Mercy as I shove my wallet back into my pocket. 'I didn't intend to bring him.'

'It's cool,' she says. 'We have needy friends. It's just one more thing we have in common.'

'That's a way to look at it.'

She grins as she inspects the menu attached to the top of the trailer we're now in front of. 'My therapist says I need to stop filling internal holes with penises, so it's perfect to have a third wheel to ensure things don't get away from us.'

I don't know whether to laugh or not. Stop filling holes with penises? Her therapist? I love that she just threw that in with no embarrassment but is that something they've seriously said? I'm not used to this much upfront honesty, and I want to let her keep talking to know everything about her, but she's staring at me with a coy smile that I can't look away from.

'Did that not scare the hell out of you?' she asks.

'In no way do I know you well enough to judge you. I'm not scared. If anything, you going to therapy says you're one of the more stable humans. You saw a problem and got help. Life can be rough, so I think that's admirable. More people should do it.'

'Do you say that out of experience?' she asks.

'I see a lot of stuff I shouldn't daily. I have one of those app therapy things on my phone. My therapist's name is Gino. He helps bring me back to earth after an adrenaline-rush moment.'

'An adrenaline-rush moment. Are you a stunt-man?' she guesses.

'Not a stuntman.'

'Bank robber?'

I laugh out loud, shaking my head as I pay for our dinner. 'I'm a rule-follower. I try to be a good example. I've never even had a speeding ticket,' I say proudly.

'Oh,' she says with a chuckle. 'Well, I'm sure you'll get a special room in heaven for that.'

'My dad will be glad to hear it. He's still trying to secure my spot with the magic man in the sky.'

'Why?'

'Securing spots in heaven and saving lost souls is his job.'

She looks me up and down, her eyes steadily on my tattoos. 'You're a preacher's kid?'

I nod. 'Fair warning, it was as much fun as you've heard. I wasn't as good at the rule-following back then. My brother and I made it our mission to push those rules hard and often. We had a stereotype to uphold.'

'You got the tattoos to piss your folks off, then?' Her eyes move over my skin, inspecting my tattoos.

'No, but I can't say that wasn't a bit of a selling point. My parents and I aren't on the best terms. In their eyes, I haven't made choices they approve of. They're still waiting for me to get my life on track.'

She scrunches her face. 'I can't say I have a lot of parenting experience, but it sounds like they're waiting for you to get your life on *their* track?'

I'm seriously impressed with how she reads between the lines. We jibe easily. I remember that from before.

'You're a smart woman.' I wave a finger her way.

It takes us a few minutes to get our food, and we choose a table a few spots away from where Ozie is currently yelling at a game on TV. He's not a sports guy, so I'm not sure what he's doing, but I'll ask questions later.

Mercy glances up from her food. 'You didn't seem very preacher's kid five years ago.'

'Now you know why my parents are petitioning heaven to get me in,' I say with a chuckle. 'I was in a jacked-up place five years ago...'

'I wasn't complaining,' she says, taking a bite of

her gyro. 'I quite enjoyed Drake Ramoray, if I'm honest. He was up for anything.'

Heat rises from my neck to my ears. Her talking about our past distracts me from everyday topics of conversation as memories of it roll through my head.

'Come on, Kansas! Pull your head outta yer ass!!' Ozie grabs our attention as he yells at the TV angrily while punching a fist through the air. I glance up at the game. Neither team playing is from Kansas.

'Your friend's weird,' she says.

'Yes, he is. But I've known him since I was nine, so he's like the weird uncle you can't disown at family events. You get used to him.'

'Weird uncle, as in the perv who asks you to sit on his lap every time he sits down or the guy who wears his wife's swimsuit into the pool at the family barbecue to get a laugh?'

'Thankfully, the latter. You nailed it with the Tommy Lee joke but throw in a touch of Jack Black, and you'd have pinned him exactly.'

She stares over at him, her brows pinched together, before looking back at me. 'Interesting. And he supervises all your outings?'

'He's here to ensure I don't ask you to go steady.'

Mercy's eyes widen. I'm going to have to explain myself.

'My friends are under the impression that I'm terrible at relationships because I want to be in one too badly. They say I don't know how to go slow. I want to label things too early, hence me getting dumped a lot.'

'Is that true?'

'Maybe a little,' I admit sheepishly. 'Being single is lonely sometimes, don't you think?'

'Yeah. Though you should know I'm scared to death of both the L and R words.' She glances up at me, lifting a shoulder. 'Part of that whole complicated past thing I mentioned.'

'You're afraid of leeks *and* radishes? That's weird.' I wink. 'Love and...'

'Relationships.'

'Have you never had a serious relationship, or is it something else that stops you?'

'Good ole childhood trauma. I've lost a lot in my life. Relationships scare the hell out of me because those are the worst kind of losses. When it ends, it's like a death.'

'I think they scare everyone.'

'For me, it feels like jumping off a bridge and then realizing my bungee wasn't yet secured.'

'Ouch,' I say, but inside, I want to know what created this fear. 'If you ever want to talk about it, I've heard I'm a good listener?' I lean my elbows on the tabletop between us, waiting on her answer. She is absolutely gorgeous. Ozie wasn't wrong when he said she was out of my league. That said, I'm trying out for the team anyway.

She cocks her head, taking a moment to choose her words. 'I appreciate that.'

Little by little, she's softening for me. Opening up. I love her wit and spitfire ways, but I'm also really liking this other side of her. The part where she looks at me like she's not sure she should say it, but she's taking a chance.

She sips her drink, her eyes on me. 'I just don't get it,' she says, setting it on the table. 'You're handsome. Polite. Single. Pretty good in bed, if I remember right. *And* you have a job. You're the perfect man for nearly every woman in the world. Why do women keep dumping you?'

'I—'

'Marry him,' Oz interrupts me as he makes his way to our table, sitting so close to her that she leans away. 'Seriously, you got him laughing; he was nervous as hell you weren't going to show, so I know he likes you. The guy's desperate for someone to love, and he'd be *good* at the doting boyfriend. He's the coolest guy I know, and he's got a crazy dangerous job where he's basically a damn superhero. A total catch.

His daughter adores him. Even his ex-wife still likes hi—'

'Oz,' I say his name sternly. I realize he's trying to talk me up here, but I haven't exactly told her everything about myself yet.

'Yeah?' He glances over at me.

'You're not helping.'

'You have a daughter?' Mercy asks curiously.

She heard that. One if the things I was going to *wait* to tell her, and Ozie threw it out there on date number one. Alijah is why most people dump me.

'*Ohh...*' Oz says, now getting why I want him to shut his trap with a grimace. 'Forgot about the baggage.'

Mercy's eyes are still on me, so I nod. 'I hadn't told you yet because I wanted you to know me as a man and not as a single father. But he's right. I do have a daughter. She's six, which is why I was so absent-minded when I knew you before. I'd just divorced and found out shortly after that my ex was pregnant. The next thing I knew, the baby was here, and it was a bit of a roller coaster. You made me feel like a single guy with a possibility at life again.'

'She's six?' Mercy asks, the look on her face an emotion I'm not yet familiar with in her.

'She'll be seven on Halloween.'

The look on her face is blank. I fiddle with my hat. *Please don't let this be the last time I see this woman.*

'A lot of women leave at this point. Someone else's kid is usually too much for them.'

'Well, you didn't just ask me to go steady or suggest I be her new mommy. So, you have a daughter. I was once someone's daughter. It's totally cool.'

13

MERCY

'You said you were cool with him having a kid?' Hollyn asks from the dressing room. *'Are you?'* She peeks out of the curtain.

'I am the opposite of cool with it. But what was I supposed to say? He didn't ask me to play the part of stepmom – no mention of her showing up on our next outing. I was just coming to terms with the fact that I like the guy. Now I find out he has a child? I can't handle that.'

'You can handle it because you're an adult, and you're not dating his daughter,' Penny, Hollyn's mother – who is now in possession of a few wedding gowns – says as she approaches the dressing room I'm standing outside. 'Hols, try these too. I feel like they're just you.'

'Mom,' Hols groans, pulling back the curtain and balking at the stack of dresses in her arms. 'I'm here to choose between three dresses. Not add more to my list.'

'Just *try* them,' Penny insists, shoving them her way before turning to me, her arms now crossed over her chest. 'Mercy, do you like this guy?'

'In a way that confuses the hell out of me…' I lean my head against the wall I'm standing in front of with a thunk.

Penny's been my stand-in mother since Hollyn deemed me her BFF in the first grade. I was that kid who ate the 'special' lunches the cafeteria ladies made for the children whose lunch tabs were never paid. Hollyn is so soft-hearted that she asked her mom to start making a second lunch for her new friend, and instantly we bonded. Like an unclaimed cat who wanders into your yard, I chose them as family decades ago, and I don't regret it.

'As I hear it, he's a man who "needs someone to love"? I'd assume that means he's looking for long-term and serious. Do you plan to screw him until he falls for you, then disappear on him? Like Dylan.'

'I didn't disappear on Dylan. I see him every single

day. We just weren't right together romantically. It was a mutual decision,' I defend myself as I yank the curtain back and glare at Hollyn, who's grimacing as she listens to our words in her safe little closet-sized changing room. Penny repeated precisely what I told her on the phone last night, word for word.

'What?' Hollyn asks in a sheepish tone. She's standing in only a slip and heels, looking guiltier than I've ever seen her. 'I'm sorry. It was either talk about my life or your drama, and yours is more interesting at the minute.'

I sigh heavily, dropping the curtain closed.

'He makes her all fluttery inside, and she can't stop thinking about him,' she throws in as soon as she's invisible again.

'Remind me to stop telling you things.'

She laughs to herself. 'She'd find out. She always does.'

Penny's perfectly manicured eyebrows are halfway up her forehead when I glance her way.

'What?' I ask.

'He makes you *feel* something? Even when you're not in bed with him?'

Penny's never been the sweet, cookies-baking-in-the-oven, always-says-the-right-thing mom. She's like me, saying what she wants and not giving two shits about who it might offend. Perhaps that came with her being in the spotlight as a pop star when she was a teen. She had to find a way to stand up to people in the industry who wanted to turn her into something she didn't want to become. She's authentically herself, a hint of eighties style included.

I scrunch my face. 'I'm not answering that.'

'I'm trying to see the whole picture, so I know what motherly advice to give.'

'Fine.' I toss my hands into the air. 'Yes. Somehow the man's presence creates this fluttery foreign feeling in my chest – *even when* we're not in bed.'

'A fluttery feeling in your chest? Like a heartbeat?' Penny says sarcastically.

I laugh under my breath. 'I don't know. I've never had one before.'

She rolls her eyes the same way Hollyn would if I said something she knew was untrue.

'Ask her about the letter from Nick.' Hols spills one more thing I've told her as she opens the curtain, the saleswoman now helping her walk with the dress she's got on.

'Seriously, you're about to need to hire a maid of honor,' I threaten.

I want to be mad that she's told her mom every detail, but I'm temporarily speechless as she walks to the pedestal. Hollyn in a wedding dress. She's wanted this for so long. Suddenly my vision goes blurry. I blink a few times to clear it, but it stubbornly stays. Am I near tears at the sight of my best friend in a wedding dress? No. Way.

Hols's gaze meets mine in the mirror. 'Are you... *crying*?'

'No,' I snap with a sniffle as I wipe away tears before more surface.

Penny sits beside me, throwing an arm around me like a true mother. 'I thought you didn't want all this?' She waves around the bridal shop.

'I don't,' I say. 'But my insomnia has me believing otherwise ever since I ran into Brooks Hudson. I mean, I agreed to *date* him.'

Both Penny and Hollyn's jaws drop.

I nod. 'At first, we agreed on just friends, and even then, his presence was so overwhelming that I asked River to supervise.'

'Why?' they ask in unison, their faces full of confusion.

'Because of the whole no-strings-attached thing we had before. I want to do him, yet I don't want it to turn back into booty calls because I want to know him. Clothed. But that leads to this.' I wave around the room. 'And there's no way it'll end here because once he hears the details of my past, he'll want me as far from his kid as a restraining order can command. I'm the daughter of a murderer, for fuck's sake!'

'Mercy, sweetie.' Penny touches my knee. 'You are not your father. Yes, you had a traumatic past that is now tormenting you from behind bars with words – for the record, know this pisses me off – but part of letting all that go is working through it, and you've worked hard to do just that. It sounds like maybe the dam has broken, and now you need to figure out what to do with whatever spilled out.'

'Oh, well, that should be simple enough, right? I've only been trying to figure it out my entire life.'

'Your answer could be in the letter,' she says.

'I can't read it. Ugh.' I drop my head into my hands. 'Why must I face all this for a guy?'

'You're doing this for you. Healing is what you've worked towards, what you want.'

'Now your heart has found something it wants too,' Hols says, a crooked, lovesick grin on her face.

I blink, staring at her blankly, unsure how to feel about that. 'Until now, my heart has felt very wormhole-y, sucking the life out of me, never allowing me to feel more than I can handle. I feel like I'm in a cab with a driver who speaks zero English, and we have to hand-motion our way through a conversation. Is this how—'

'Relationships start?' Hols says quietly. 'Yeah. I mean, not usually with the murdering father sending you cryptic letters from a prison cell in the background, but yeah. I think you might have actual feelings for this guy.'

'But I don't even know him! That's impossible.'

'You've slept with him how many times?' Penny asks. 'Obviously, you *know* the guy,' she says without my answer. 'Now you want to know more than just his penis. What could it hurt?'

'Uh, my already-destroyed heart?'

Penny rolls her eyes. 'We all go through heartbreak, Mercy. I'm not a psychologist, nor do I claim to be one, but I am a woman who lived a chaotic, confusing life, and to get through it, I had to face some hard truths about myself. Sometimes, the trauma we lug around with us, we didn't pack ourselves. It's given to us like a backpack full of boulders.'

'My boulders feel more like bombs.'

'I could bet Nick is your biggest boulder, and he's behind all this confusion. Kicking karma in the teeth by allowing that hurt to heal would be a blast right to that asshole. Read the letter; it might help.'

That sounds scary as fuck. Who goes head to head

with karma? People who don't believe. I told Brooks I didn't believe in that stuff, and I don't. Fate hasn't blessed me in any way, shape or form, besides maybe the musical prodigy thing and the fact that I'm not terrifying children on the street with my looks. Otherwise, a complete dumpster fire consumed much of me at a very young age. Maybe his letter *will* help me heal that little girl inside.

'Having a makeshift mother complicates things,' I say with frustration.

'A stubborn as hell bonus daughter isn't easy either,' Penny snaps back.

'So, I'm just supposed to take this buzzing in my chest as my sign to get to know Brooks Hudson – *romantically* – and let him into my life even though this could all blow up and damage me more than I already am? Because when I say it out loud, I hear "run away".'

'Everything in your life so far has been about running away. Surviving. Maybe start living instead?'

That was so truthful it hurt. I glance at Hollyn. 'Your mom's being mean to me.'

She laughs. 'Be thankful she's not asking you about the sex.'

Penny lifts a curious eyebrow.

'I'm not about to kiss and tell with my best friend's

mother. But for the record – it was never just fine.' I say the last part under my breath, causing Penny to smile wide. She once told us if the sex was just 'fine', he's not the one.

'Then what are you worried about? I bet the man problem will be fine on cruise control until you figure out the dad problem.'

'She's worried about liking him so much she'll want to stand on this pedestal one day,' Hols tells her.

'That's absolutely not true. I refuse to let myself want any of this because I can never have it. I have no mother to come ooh and ahh over me in a big white dress. No father to walk me down the aisle and threaten my fiancé's life if he ever hurts me. No extended family to cheer when we exit. I'm close to like eight people. That doesn't exactly fill up the bride's seating at a wedding. I'd be humiliated.' My words slow as I speak, realizing all these things hurt to say out loud. I've thought them a thousand times, but to say them out loud. Ouch. 'Once you all get married and start families, it'll be just me. Your weird single friend spending holidays alone eating my frozen dinner while I curse *It's a Wonderful Life*.'

My breathing speeds. I like being on my own, don't get me wrong, but am I seriously destined to spend an entire lifetime alone? Because if I don't figure this out, that's where I'm headed. River's words the day I got the letter – *could be a curse* – play through my head, making the panic move through me a little faster than before. Fucking hell, I feel cursed!

'You won't have *no one*—' Hollyn reassures me.

'River was right,' I say in a panicky voice, not letting her finish her thought.

'About what?' she asks like she refuses ever to believe that possibility.

'He said the letter might be cursed. It had to have been. *Look at me!* I just teared up seeing Hollyn in a wedding dress! I'm suddenly mourning a life I thought I never wanted. I *want* to date a man, and I'm considering reading words written by actual evil. River was right about something! That's like being hit by lightning odds!' I shove my hands into my chest dramatically, trying to hold back whatever this is.

Just breathe, Mercy.

I stand from my chair, pacing back and forth between Penny and Hollyn. 'That asshole hexed me from prison with a single letter! He's going to ruin my life forever from behind bars! Why didn't anyone tell me that his life sentence was actually for me?! Have I just wasted years trying to forget my childhood only to realize that no matter how much therapy I do, it's never going away unless I face it?' I glance between

Hollyn and Penny's now blank faces. 'Please have an answer,' I plead, tears surfacing quicker than I can blink them away.

There's no denying I have feelings right now. Panicky, traumatized feelings that require medication to control slide down my cheeks via tears. The shop assistant helping us looks concerned.

'Here,' Hollyn says, handing me Penny's newly topped-up glass of champagne and rooting through my purse, looking for the magic pill that will slow my heart to barely beating again. She hands me the tablet, and I swallow it with the champagne.

'Should you drink on medication?' the saleswoman asks, holding up a *please stop* hand that I ignore, downing the entire glass without a breath.

'She'll be fine,' Hols says to the woman as Penny approaches me.

'Mercy,' Penny says, slowly guiding me back to a chair with an arm around my waist. 'Honey, let's take a moment to breathe, alright?'

She sits next to me, her hands on her knees as she breathes in deeply, eventually rolling a hand in front of me, insinuating to follow her lead. I do the same, my heart rate slowing breath by breath. When I re-open my eyes, Hollyn's on the pedestal in front of the mirrors in a new dress.

'This one's so much better. Simple but elegant. Like you,' Penny says to Hols.

'Simple?' she moans. 'I wanted beautiful and elegant.'

'Brooks calls me beautiful,' I say to no one in particular.

'What?' Penny asks.

'Brooks Hudson,' I say with a kind of drunk giggle. 'He says "Hey, beautiful," whenever he greets me.'

Hollyn grins. 'Tell us about him while I overthink this dress.'

'He's super handsome, six-two-ish, medium build, short sandy blond hair, mesmerizing light brown eyes, stubble and many tattoos.'

'Oh, the bad boy. I should've guessed.'

'I don't think he's a bad boy. He seems... sweet? And most importantly, normal.'

Penny laughs. 'You're attracted to normal? That's relieving, as your stand-in mother. So now that you're calmer, do you still want to date this man even though getting close to the opposite sex terrifies you?'

I nod without overthinking it. 'I think I deserve to know why I feel like this around him.'

Penny and Hollyn's heads snap to each other, their eyes wide.

'That's a good sign,' Hollyn says. 'When do you see him again?'

'I dunno. He hasn't asked me out again yet.'

'Then ask him.'

'I tried that, and River ended up with us. I have no clue how to do this.'

'You've never been on a romantic date with a man where you made deals with God for him just to hold your hand?' Penny asks, her jaw now agape.

'Nope. If I want something, I'm not afraid to make a move. I can't even remember the last time I held hands with a guy in a cutesy lovey-dovey way. I think it might have been Matt Hawthorne in the sixth grade. He was the first and only boy to give me goosebumps.'

'What stopped the goosebumps with him?' Penny asks.

'Mostly him kissing Shelbi Trumpet.' Her name leaves my lips like poison. As if I still have some unresolved grudge years later. 'They were under the baseball bleachers where he asked me to meet him. I thought it would be this big romantic first kiss. I sincerely thought this twelve-year-old boy loved me because he said the words. But apparently, he had scheduled his afternoon with ladies, and I was just part of his sixth-grade harem. When I figured it out, something inside me broke. Like I felt it. Right then, I knew men would always let me down. No one would ever really want me because there would always be someone better. So, I figured Matt had the right idea, and I took up his way of life, using and ditching dudes when I needed them.'

Hollyn and Penny have the same expression on their faces – like they want to hug me. This is why I don't talk about feelings and hope my panic attacks happen at home, where I won't get chatty as the meds kick in.

'I'm long past it. Just – that's when I gave up on love.'

My meds are evening out, and I'm feeling more level-headed, so I'm suddenly aware that not only have I outed all this shit I thought I'd buried deep, but I'm humiliated that I did. I honestly thought I had this all under control. I've worked hard to build these walls, and now feelings are rushing through me as they spill through new cracks.

'Let this guy in, Mercy,' Penny says gently. 'If for nothing else than to prove to yourself that you can. You have to take chances to get past self-doubt; otherwise, you'll sit home and live the life that just scared the crap out of you.'

'Please, can we stop making sense and go back to

admiring Hollyn in a wedding dress? I've felt about as much as I want to for one day.'

We do. None of us mentions it again, and we switch to this being Hollyn's day, not mine. Somehow, I make it through the afternoon in one piece feeling only the tiniest bit guilty that I'm planning to sneak into the building across the street when I get home and use their hot tub to destress. I need to relax before that backpack full of boulder bombs explodes.

14

BROOKS

'That was some crazy shit I saw on the news earlier. Were you there?' Tyler asks through the phone.

'I was,' I say as I walk down the hall towards the elevator.

'Did things go as planned?'

'Pretty much.'

I can't talk about details for most of my job, but that doesn't stop Ty from pretending it's Christmas Eve and attempting to guess what's in every present with his name on it. It can be annoying. We did a drug raid tonight, and even though it went well, it made the news. They usually do, but I'd still rather they didn't.

'I can't believe they put you in charge of life-or-death situations. Clearly, you're way more serious at work.'

'It's much easier to arrest someone when they know you're serious. My mind's in one place at work because if I mess up, maybe I die. Maybe someone else dies? I'm trying to prevent that.'

'Such a superhero you are,' Ty says, clearly not meaning it. 'That's deep, though. I can't say death is involved in my housebound life here.'

The elevator dings closed.

'Where ya headed?' he asks, clearly bored out of his mind.

Emily has a great job with the state, and Ty was recently laid off, so to save money, he's become a stay-at-home dad. This means both mine and Emily's phones ring off the hook as he finds someone above the age of six to talk to. I get it.

'Jacuzzi. I'm tense. And since it has a fancy name, it doesn't feel the same as brewing testicle tea in my upstairs bathtub.'

Ty laughs. 'Testicle tea. Gross. I bet Oz is a bath guy. There are an awful lot of candles in that master bathroom.'

'What a nice image to relax to. Oz in the bathtub. Disgusting. This is a fantastic conversation, by the way. Mind-numbing is what I needed right now, so I guess thank you? I can hardly tell you're home with a child all day.'

He huffs into the phone. 'I hope you get stuck in that hot tub with a slurring, fat lonely old guy in a Speedo a size too small who needs to talk about his day.'

'Another alarming image. Thanks.'

'My pleasure,' Ty says proudly.

I shove open the door to the pool room in my apartment building, stopping in my tracks when I do. 'Speedo guy isn't here,' I say to Ty in a whisper. 'Someone else is. I gotta go.'

'Wait! Who—'

I end the call, him still yelling as I do.

Slowly I make my way to the Jacuzzi on the other side of the pool. To my surprise, Mercy Alexander is sitting inside, her head resting against the edge and her eyes closed. There's no way we also live in the same building. That would be just *weird* weird – Norah and her serendipity-believing-ways weird.

As my phone rings with Tyler calling me back, Mercy's eyes suddenly snap open, and she jumps when she sees me standing outside the hot tub staring at her. A smile creeps up on her face.

'I'm starting to feel like you're stalking me,' she says jokingly.

'Or you're stalking me, considering I live here.'

'You live here?' She points at the water as I strip off my shirt and toss it onto one of the loungers I'm standing near.

Don't think I haven't noticed her trying not to look, head tilted down, but her eyes are on me. I toss my phone onto my shirt, ignoring Ty's repeated call-backs, as I slip off my flip-flops slowly and take my time stepping in with her. Maybe she's seen it all before, but she's never looked at me like this. I like it.

'I don't live in the poolroom, no.' I point to the ceiling as I sit down a few seats away from her. 'Upstairs. Seventh floor.'

'You're one of these snooty-palooty, I-have-a-doorman apartment dwellers?'

I raise a single eyebrow. 'You're not?'

'I, uh...' She shakes her head with a guilty smile. 'I live across the street in the ancient three-story walk-up. My air conditioning works "when it wants to, and I shouldn't fight it", and that's quoting our maintenance man.'

Laughter bellows from me. I'm relaxing faster than I expected. 'How'd you get in the building without a keycard?'

'I have a keycard.'

'*How?*'

'Your back security guy, Ernesto. He's real easy to sweet talk, especially when you show up in a bikini and sarong. Anyway, he knows me as Sacha Black in apartment 4D. Your building keycards, thankfully, don't have photos.'

'Did you steal Sacha's card?' I ask, only the tiniest bit concerned, but for the most part, I'm just amused by the whole story.

'She dropped it, I found it, and one day I tried it, intending to turn it in, but, on my way to the front desk, I passed the sign directing the way to the pool/hot tub/sauna, and I thought, *What could one dip hurt before I turn the card in?* One dip turned into two, which turned into three, and here we are a month later, and no one has noticed. So, I kept coming back. Until now, no one's asked any questions. I plan to be super mature about it when I get caught while lying my ass off. "Oh, I'm not Sacha? Prove it!"' she snaps out like she's been rehearsing. 'Then when they leave to get the real Sacha, I drop the card, sneak out the back, and pray karma – or the cops – don't come knocking,' she says with a lift of a shoulder as if this story makes total sense.

I can feel the disbelieving but entirely impressed smirk on my face. 'Wow. Beautiful and a little bit criminal-minded. Be still, my heart,' I joke. 'What if I told you your confession was recorded and given to a cop?'

She glances around the otherwise empty room, her eyes finally settling on me as her jaw drops open. '*That's* the superhero job? No way. People hate cops.'

'Ouch.'

'Seriously. You're a cop?'

I nod. 'Can I trust you?' I ask under my breath, moving a seat closer to her.

'Shouldn't I be asking that, considering you've got the room bugged?'

'*I* don't have the room bugged; the building has security cameras.' I point to the one aimed our way.

'Ah, then we better not have sex in this hot tub,' she says, moving a seat closer to me, running a single finger down my arm under the water. 'Ernesto might be a gossip, and you wouldn't want the whole building to know Sacha got down and dirty with the cop on floor seven. What if she's married?'

'She is,' I say. 'The video would clear my name pretty quickly, though...' Her subtle *take me now* cues cloud my vision, and without really thinking about it, I slide an arm around her waist, pull her onto my lap and kiss her unexpectedly. Her hands in my hair send goosebumps over my skin. After a breath-taking moment, I break the kiss with a smirk. 'We're not doing this here.'

'What?! Then why did you kiss me like that? And since when do cops wear their guns into the hot tub?'

I laugh. 'That's not a gun, which I know you know because you're grinding your pelvis into it.'

Pink fills her cheeks. 'That answers one question...'

'I can't quit thinking about kissing you like that, and your not-so-shy clues led me to believe you wanted it. Now it's out of our system. We can commence the slow-roll dating.'

She laughs as she floats away from me, sitting across the tub, her feet on mine.

'Are you saying you respect me too much to do me in a public hot tub with CCTV probably capturing the whole thing and Ernesto eventually releasing it onto Pornhub's "amateurs" section?'

'Amateurs?' I say, pretending I'm offended.

'You gonna arrest me for breaking and entering?'

I smile. 'You only entered – *with* a valid keycard as far as I know. I also don't work the patrol side of things, so unless you're mixed up in some pretty shady shit, I would not be the officer arresting you.'

'You're not a patrol cop?' she asks curiously. 'What department do you work for?'

'I'm a detective with the drug and organized crime unit with the Portland Police.'

She sucks in a breath that sounds a little like a gasp, her face shocked by my words. Shit. Having a daughter didn't send her running, but maybe my job will. It has before.

'You work on murders and drug stuff?'

'Mostly.'

Her bottom lip is firmly between her teeth while she thinks this through. 'Do you know someone named Travis Seiver?' she asks, wide-eyed.

I nod. 'Seiver's my boss. You know him?'

'I met him once a long time ago. Things were chaotic, and he saved me in a moment that changed me forever,' she says meekly, a tone I've never heard from her. Her complicated past may be more complex than I expected.

'Do you want to talk about it?'

'Not even a little bit,' she says. 'I'm just here to relax. Had a rough day.'

'Need to talk about that?'

'No. Way,' she says with a laugh as she sinks into the water, leaning her head against the edge of the hot tub and closing her eyes again. 'Not only was my day

emotionally exhausting, but sprinkle in some humili-
ation, and it's now playing through my mind like I'm
at an IMAX theater and can't get out.'

'A naked-in-public nightmare?'

'Pretty much.' Her foot brushes my calf, so I grab
it, gently massaging it with my thumbs.

'What are you doing?' she asks, pulling it from me
with a sudden stare.

'You said you had a rough day, so I was going to
rub your feet while we sit in a hot tub. Is that not
alright?'

She thinks about this and finally rests her right
foot in my hands again.

'I once dated a woman who did reflexology massage at a spa,' I say as I try to remember what she
taught me. 'I'm convinced it works because she nearly
had me in tears one night, but afterward, holy hell... it
was heaven. Maybe you can tell me how good I a—'

'Ohh,' she interrupts me with a long moan,
leaning her head against the side of the hot tub again.
'Good, good, yes, you're very good. Outstanding, actually. I think I'm into this, so if you could tell your ex
"thanks"...'

'If I ever see her again, I'll let her know.'

Her eyes are closed, and she's completely ignoring
my words. 'Holy. Magical. Man. In. The. Sky. This is

better than sex. Besides the place I get my pedicures, no one's ever voluntarily rubbed my feet. Lisa doesn't have a soft touch; she's strictly business. And...' She lifts her head, making eye contact, a coy smile on her face. 'She isn't nearly as pretty as you.'

I feel myself blush like I'm thirteen years old with a crush. I drop my chin, focusing on my hands on her foot instead of her admiring me the way she is.

'Are you here 'cause you had a bad day too?' she asks suddenly. 'Or was this on your calendar – foot massage for random woman in the hot tub at nine?'

'I don't normally come down here,' I say. 'So no, it's not a part of my scheduled day. My night was adrenaline-filled, and I'm too wound up to sleep. I thought this might help.'

Her spiky personality settles, and she goes soft again. 'Need to talk about it?'

I shake my head. 'It was nothing. Just work stuff.'

'So, we're both stressed...' she says. 'Or at least were... this foot rub is doing wonders.'

'What else could do wonders, I wonder?' I say flirtatiously.

She opens one eye, lifting an eyebrow like she's sure she knows where I'm going with this, and she's all in. 'I can think of *one* thing,' she says flirtatiously. 'We could try it. I mean, we're both adults. Hell, we're in our thirties!'

'We can do anything we want,' I say casually.

'Exactly.'

'What do you want, Mercy?' I ask, now rubbing her second foot the same way she liked before.

She drops her head back to the side again, this time with a heavy sigh. 'I had a massive panic attack today over things too big to get into right now, but it made me realize I *want* to date you, kid, cop and all. The thing is, I've never really dated anyone seriously, and I've got some heavy stuff going on in my personal life right now that might scare the hell out of you.'

'Not much scares me.'

Her gaze meets mine, precisely how I've wanted someone to look at me. After a beat, she stands from her seat. She's wearing a skimpy green and white zebra-print bikini, and it's melting my brain. My God, why on earth would I ghost this woman?

'Ready?' She extends a hand my way.

'For what?'

'The obvious.'

'Which is?' I play along, knowing exactly what she's hinting at based on the tone of her voice alone.

'We're sleeping together to destress, and since you're too much of a gentleman to throw me down here and do it live for security to watch, we're going to your apartment.'

'Mercy, I...'

She rests a hand on my shoulder, looking at me in a way I almost can't refuse. 'I liked that side of you too. We're adults; let's mix the two – isn't that what we were talking about earlier?'

'Yeah, but I told you, I always move too fast, and things fade quickly. I was hoping this might not turn out like that.'

'But that kiss?'

I laugh. 'That was Doctor Drake Ramoray kissing Lemon Rockefeller. I knew you wanted it too, and we might as well get it out of our system so we can leave our alter egos in the past and start fresh.'

I stand from the tub with her, the two of us drying off, her wrapping the towel around her chest as she slips on a pair of white Birkenstocks. I get dressed and extend my elbow, which she takes, then swiftly guide her outside the building.

'What are we doing? I thought we were going up-stairs?' she protests as we walk across the street to-wards her building.

The city streets are softly lit, vibrantly colored blooms and trailing greenery hang from baskets attached to streetlights, and it's starting to smell like summer.

'I'm not exactly dressed for an outing,' she says as we walk.

I stop on the sidewalk in front of the building I assume is hers, turning her way. 'I like you, Mercy. A lot. I mess this up often, so I'm doing things right this time.'

She grins shyly. 'I like you too. But I also liked the version of you from before too. Can't we mix Brooks and Drake?'

With that, I kiss her softly, my hand on her face. She reaches up and grabs my wrist, a tiny gasp leaving her lips before she pulls me closer. Instead of the desperate kiss we shared in the hot tub this one is sweet, soft, and slow. Almost as if it's our first. When she pulls away, she looks a mix of confusion and swept off her feet.

'Was that Drake or—'

'That was Brooks. And I have to say, Mercy is a hell of a kisser. You're going to be hard to say no to, but I've gotta be up early, so I'll text you date two details soon.' I back away from her slowly.

She stands on the sidewalk, her jaw hanging open, but a grin shines through. 'That's it? You're just going to kiss me like that and then go home?' she hollers, zero worry about someone else hearing her.

'It's the anticipation that makes you want to see me again. Now you're going to think about me all night,' I say from across the street with a sly smile. 'Goodnight, Mercy.'

15

MERCY

I'm leaving the bathroom after showering, my head still in the clouds after last night. Brooks was right; I thought about him and that last kiss all night, and now I can't wait to see him again.

'Hot coffee!' Dylan warns as we nearly collide.

Momentarily I'm terrified I'm about to need emergency services when he dumps scalding hot coffee down the front of my nearly naked self. But he steps back quick enough I'm saved from burning my boobs. Thank God, they're one of my best features.

'What are you doing here?' I practically yell.

'I brought you a coffee and one of those Gouda breakfast sandwich things you like. I tried to call last night, but you never answered. I was worried.'

'Oh,' I say, completely confused.

I never even checked my phone after sharing a hot tub with Brooks Hudson. I just went to bed and dreamed of that fairy-tale life I pretend I don't want, and somehow he was in it.

Wait a second. Dylan was so worried he brought me coffee and breakfast and delivered it before the shop even opens.

'You're hand-delivering coffee and breakfast? *Why?*' I inspect the tray in his hand, spotting my name on one of the cups.

He lifts a single eyebrow, pulling the food and drink tray away from me. 'You can have this if you answer the next question truthfully.'

'Oh-kaaayyyy...'

'Did you tell Cassie to call me because I wanted to "catch up"?'

'Uh...' Shit. I forgot about that. She must've finally done it. 'Perhaps.'

'Mercy,' he moans, reluctantly extending the food my way. I take my reward from the tray and head to my room.

'What? Tell me honestly that you didn't enjoy it.'

He shakes his head. 'I asked her out.'

'Good. Finally.'

'She suggested we double date.'

I stop in my tracks and turn towards him suddenly.

'With you.'

'*No.*'

He cocks his head. 'I already said yes.'

'Dyl! I don't want to double date with you. I barely know what I'm doing as it is.'

'I figured, so we can help each other out.'

'How?'

'By making sure neither of us embarrasses ourselves. By the way, I'm actually here because I had a funeral this morning, but they canceled.'

'Canceled? Wasn't dead after all?' I ask. Funerals don't usually cancel. Dead is dead.

'Nope. I guess nobody liked him? Family's words, not mine. So instead of paying for a goodbye party no one would attend, they're using the money on a family vacation.'

'Brutal. Sounds like a future episode of *Dateline*,' I say, walking towards my room with him hot on my heels.

Holy shit. It sounds like it could be me. One day I'll die, and all my friends will have moved on. Will anyone turn up for my funeral? Or will I be buried in a grave with a small tag that reads my name and dates of life I never used out of fear while the people I thought loved me head to Cancún to spend the week celebrating my death?

'Hello?' Dylan waves a hand in front of my face, returning me from my brand new day-mare.

I will not die alone. I'm kicking karma in the teeth, just like Penny suggested, starting right now.

'I need to get ready for my not-canceled funeral. But I appreciate this.' I lift the food and drink before slowly closing my bedroom door with my foot, hoping he gets the hint.

'I'll tag along,' Dylan says, not allowing the door to close on him.

'While I get dressed?' I snap. 'I think not.'

'To the funeral...' he says loudly but slowly like I'm a complete dumbass. 'Check your messages once in a while, will you? Your clients originally requested a trio, but I'd overbooked. Now I'm free, why not give them what they initially wanted? I couldn't get a hold of you last night to tell you, so I figured I'd stop by this morning and fill you in – and also inform you of your upcoming double date all in one fell swoop. I'm going to get ready. Meet me at my car in thirty.'

* * *

'Why are you depressing me with heart-wrenching ballads?' Dylan jabs off his stereo.

'It's inspiration music.'

Dyl lifts a single dark eyebrow, glancing over at me as he drives. '"Make it Rain" is inspiration? For what? Revenge?'

'Man-hating music.'

'Oh, God. I take it things aren't going well with the new guy?'

'No. Things are going great, actually. It's more "father" man-hating music. I'm trying to get pissed enough to read the letter. I think facing it might be the only way to move on.'

'Honestly, I sort of assumed you'd avoid that thing for life. But that's a good idea. Face it head-on,' he says, a fist in the air. 'Especially since it could be him telling you he's out on parole. The last thing you need is him showing up at your door.'

I hadn't even considered that. 'He could do that? They just let murderers out on parole without telling the daughter whose life he destroyed?'

'I don't know. Our justice system is flawed, Merc. It's a definite possibility.'

Dylan pulls up to our venue, and Cassie stands at the front doors, smiling as she waves our way. She plays piano today while I play the violin, and Dylan is on cello. Dyl lifts a hand after putting the car in park, his cheeks pinking at the sight of her.

'Hi, Dylan!' She bounces over to him when we exit, stopping at his side of the car. 'How's things?' she asks, touching his arm flirtatiously. 'You look great.' She glances my way, flashing me an innocent smile. 'As do you, Mercy.'

'Well, thank you, Cass.'

'Do you need any help?' she asks, focusing on Dylan.

'Sure,' he says, handing Cass a box of equipment as I grab my violin case from the back seat.

After ten minutes of watching Dylan sweat and stutter in an attempt to make conversation like he's talked to a woman before, I start to play. There are no guests here yet, so I can play anything I want, and sticking with my kick-karma-in-the-teeth mood, I go with 'Make it Rain'. Dylan shoots me a look, but Cassie distracts him – leaving me to my feelings. Revenge. I *wish* I could get revenge. I'm just not sure how to do that when Nick's behind bars.

Cassie and Dylan finish setting up, her subtly flirting the entire time, but I see it clearly. When the three of us are seated, I lean into him.

'Well, that almost wasn't painful to watch,' I whisper.

'Ugh, it was exceedingly awkward,' he whispers back, now busy with his cello.

'I was picturing playing at your wedding and what those vows might be like. Please don't make me.'

'Will you stop?' he whispers but with a 'tone'.

'But you like her, right?'

'Why else would I have asked her out?'

I blow air from my puffed-up cheeks like I've no clue. 'Where's all that Rico Suave crap you tried on me?'

'What?' he asks loudly, earning Cassie's attention, so he lifts his chin and flashes her a smile. 'I do *not* have a Rico Suave side.' He lowers his voice. 'A woman's never fawned over me like she does. I don't know what to do with it.'

'Uh, enjoy it? Give it back to her. It's not that hard.'

'Says Miss Anti-romance...'

'I'll have you know I'm learning the same lesson you are right now. We are apparently on the same path.'

'You think *we're* on the same path?' he asks like it's impossible, which is a little offensive.

'Yes, in fact, I humiliated myself in front of a man just last night.'

'How?'

'Remember that keycard to the building across the

street I found over a month ago? I never returned it like I said I did. I use it every week to sneak in and use the hot tub, claiming to security I'm a resident.'

'That's more criminal than embarrassing.'

'Brooks lives there and caught me. Not only that, I admitted it, and it turns out he's a cop.'

Dylan chuckles a little louder than necessary, earning the attention of a few early guests. 'Is that where you were last night? *Jail?*' he says, lowering his voice.

'Yeah, yeah, it's so funny. I'm a moron.'

'God, you need as much help with this as I do,' he says.

I catch movement from the back of the room as the funeral director gives us the sign to start playing as she ushers in mourners. Perfect timing.

'I guess I'll ask Brooks if he opposes a double date,' I say, lifting my violin to my chin. 'It's not like we haven't already brought a third wheel each time. It can't possibly get any weirder.'

16

BROOKS

I worked later than usual today, so I had to drop Ali with Norah. I hate doing that on my days. I feel like I get so little time with her as it is.

'I said you could wait until morning,' Norah says, her fluffy no-sex-for-Levi-tonight robe wrapped around her tightly as she ushers me inside. 'She's already in bed.'

'My days keep getting interrupted by sickness and work. You know I hate disappointing her.'

'She's asleep, Brooks. She won't even know.'

'Oh yeah?' I lift my phone, dialing the number to the cellphone Ali has that she's only allowed to speak to Mommy and Daddy on, flipping it to speaker so Norah can listen in. Instantly she answers.

'Daddy! You coming?'

'I'm here, baby. Get your stuff.' I waggle my eyebrows Norah's way.

'Yay!' Ali's squeal can be heard from her second-story room above us.

'She's been calling me for an hour,' I inform Norah as I hang up. 'If I didn't show, she'd have been let down, and I just can't do that to her.'

'We're human, Brooks. You *will* let her down at some point, and she'll learn to deal with that.'

'But if I can prevent it, I'm going to.'

'Daddy's here! Daddy's here! Daddy's here!' We can hear her above us jumping around her room, talking to her toys as she gets her things together.

Norah drops her head with a laugh. 'Sometimes I wonder if she loves you more than me.'

'She doesn't. You're Mommy, I'm Daddy, and we're the kid's entire world. She loves us equally.'

'If you say so. But you could have waited until morning. I was trying to help ensure you weren't completely exhausted after the insane hours you work but since you seem good with it...'

'Totally good with it. Quick question, though.'

She grimaces, crossing her arms over her chest.

'I've been busy and have a date coming up, and I want it to be romantic.'

'I'm listening.' She perks up visibly. Gossip. She adores it.

'Got any good restaurants you'd recommend?'

'Maybe. Is this, by chance, your dream girl?'

'She was your dream girl and possibly...'

'Daddy!' Ali squeals from the top of the stairs. She practically jogs down them, her purple travel suitcase rolling behind her, bumping down the stairs with an armload of toys in her other hand.

'Text me some places,' I say to Norah under my breath. 'Ali girl!' I match Alijah's excitement, kneeling to catch her as she runs into my now open arms. 'Ready to go home with Daddy?'

'Yeah!' she says with a giggle.

I pick up the suitcase and the kid, nodding for Norah to get the door. 'See ya.'

'Do you want fancy or casual?' she asks, following us to the porch.

I strap Ali into her booster seat, load the suitcase and army of naked Barbies in her arms, then walk around to the driver's side, stopping to face Norah, only ten feet from me.

'Send both but keep whatever visions you have to yourself. It'll only make me more nervous.'

Norah cocks her head, a slight smile growing. 'You're nervous? That's cute.'

'Don't get any ideas, Nor. Just send me some recs, would ya?'

'I'll do it in the morning. Bye, sweetie!' She waves to Alijah, who gleefully waves back. If anything can make you feel like a good parent, it's your kid being as excited to go home with Daddy as Ali is.

It takes us a couple of hours to get settled at my place, and as always, she refuses to sleep in her bed on night one, so she's curled up asleep on the other side of my kingsize while I read through the case Seiver's shoved off onto me.

When Andrews and I visited this guy, he requested I call him Sir Nicky. I laughed. Then promptly said no. His actual name is Nicholas Trent Alexander. He's sentenced to fifty years, with the possibility for parole after twenty-five, charged with one count of manslaughter, one count of attempted murder with a deadly weapon, possession of drugs with intent to sell, child endangerment – Jesus.

There was a kid involved in all this? My chest hurts at the thought of it. The worst cases for me include children. I glance at Ali, sleeping peacefully, probably innocently dreaming about butterflies and Barbie dolls. I don't know what I'd do if someone ever hurt her.

I turn my attention back to the file. The next page

is a laundry list of more minor charges going back years. This guy was a criminal from birth, it seems. Juvie. County. State. He's served time in them all. He's also been disciplined while in every one for violations against other inmates. He was no peach to talk to, either. The moment I walked into the meeting room, I got that this-is-a-nasty-guy gut feeling. Only a few prisoners have done that to me. His brand of arrogance made me want to punch him. I didn't, but I pictured it. He didn't put off the vibe that he's a prisoner reformed either, so what could be so important he wants to rat someone out for early parole twenty-two years into his sentence?

I glance at the notes I wrote while I met with him. He never said why he wanted this. Something about making amends, but with who? That's probably what I need to find out.

The ringing of my phone startles Ali and me, but I grab it quick enough she doesn't stir much. I lay my hand on her back to settle her as I answer.

'Yeah?' I answer quietly.

'Hi,' she says. 'Is this a bad time?'

'Well, hello, beautiful.' I lean back against my headboard, a smile on my face involuntarily. 'No, not a bad time at all. I'm just working from home.'

'Do you ever stop working?'

'Crime has no downtime, so rarely. What are you up to?'

'I can't sleep. It's one of those nightly problems I usually solve with a Netflix or Hulu binge, but I'm in between shows right now. Got any suggestions?'

'Honestly, I work when I can't sleep, so I don't watch much TV. What are you into?'

'Mostly funny, ghostly, ridiculous – I just finished *Supernatural* for the third time.'

'I've seen that one. Let me ask, are you a Dean or a Sam fan?'

'Depends on the situation. To save my life, Dean. To romance me off my feet, Sam,' she says, sounding quite confident of her answer.

'You've thought of this before?' I ask with a chuckle.

'Every viewer has thought of it. The cast of this show is so beautiful it makes me feel ugly.'

'Completely impossible, Mercy. You're gorgeous.'

'Can I say something sappy?'

'Please do.'

'You make me *feel* gorgeous. So, thank you for that.'

'It's my pleasure. I hope to do that as often as possible. Did you see there's a new *Supernatural* spin-off? *The Winchesters*. You could try that.'

'There *is*?! How do you know this if you don't watch TV?' she asks, the sound of a keyboard clicking in the background. 'Also, I'm blowing by the sweet part of that because if you could hear a person blush right now, it'd be filling the phone like static.'

'I like the sound of that. I heard about it from Norah, my ex. She was talking about it recently.'

'Are you two close?'

Talking about Norah seems risky, but I want to know everything about Mercy, and that means I need to let her into my world too. 'Yeah, I mean we have to be to raise our daughter together. It wasn't easy at first, but things are smooth sailing six years later.'

'What's that like?'

'What? Divorce?'

'No, being someone's dad. Is it weird? It must be nerve-wracking to be responsible for a tiny human. What if you screw her up?'

I laugh, running my hand over my head nervously. 'I try not to focus on that part and take it day by day.'

'Good idea. Oh my God, you're right. I found it – *The Winchesters*. Want to watch with me?'

'Over the phone?'

I haven't done that since I was a teen, and Norah was on vacation with her family in Texas one summer. She insisted we watch a movie together because she missed me. Just the idea of doing this with Mercy fills me with that teens-in-love excitement.

'It's way better than working late into the night. Give your head a break and let someone else chase the monsters for a while.'

She doesn't need to ask me twice. I toss the file onto my bedstand and grab my remote, following her instructions on watching this with her. We chatter about the show, and she pops the question midway through.

'So, are you ever gonna text me details for our second date, or do I need to follow my friend's advice and plan it myself?'

I've been so busy lately it's taking me forever to do this stuff and I think it's making her feel like I'm unsure. She's talked about me to her friends, though. I think that's a good thing.

'It seems like you like me...'

'Perhaps,' she says playfully. 'Honestly, I'm drawn to you in a way I don't understand, or I'd explain it.'

'Same as me, then.'

'Can you explain it?'

'I can't. But I know I like it.'

She sighs into the phone. 'Me too.'

'This would probably be a good time to ask you on that date officially, wouldn't it?'

'Yes, it would.'

'Mercy... would you like to go on a second date with me?'

'I dunno,' she says playfully. 'Kidding, my answer is absolutely yes, but I do have a slight problem.'

Uh-oh. 'What?'

'My friend asked a woman on a double date and expects me to be one half of the other couple. It's weird, I know it is, but so far, our dates have included our most obnoxious friends. Are you up for a double date with one of my less annoying friends? My business partner and co-worker?'

'Someday, our strange connection and story will captivate a room. That said, let's add to it. Sure, I'm up for a double date. I'll text you details tomorrow, but this time we're not meeting; I'm picking you up like a gentleman. We're following all the proper dating rules from here on out.'

'If you insist,' she says with a laugh, but I can hear in her voice she's intrigued.

17

MERCY

'That's the one,' I say, dabbing a tissue to my weeping eyes. 'It's so you.'

Hollyn and I are back at the bridal shop, this time without Penny but with River.

'Are you... *crying*?' he asks, inspecting me from the chair next to me. 'I thought your heart was made of stone?'

'Merc has had feelings lately,' Hollyn tells him.

She's really pushing our secret-keeping boundaries. I shoot her a glare. 'Don't out me to your brother; we live together – he'll torment me over it daily.'

'You have feelings?' River asks coyly.

'*And* PMS. Mix those two, and this is what you get.'

'Yikes. I'll mark the calendar, so I'm prepared for the future.'

'Prepared for what?'

'Hiding from you during shark week.'

I roll my eyes. 'You're not good with crying women. You hide from PMS-ing women. What kind of women do you like?'

'Horny, mostly.' He lifts a single shoulder.

'Gross.'

'Do you like this dress, Riv?' Hollyn asks, completely ignoring his previous words.

'Not even a little,' he says, not worried a bit about hurting her feelings. 'You look like one of those Barbie birthday cakes. I bet Dax would prefer something sexier. Which is weird to say to your sister, but I promised him I wouldn't allow a princess look.'

'He hates the idea of a princess gown?'

'Yep, but he's on board with a sexy-as-fuck queen... where do I find those dresses?' He stands, wandering the shop and looking through racks of dresses for a revealing dress his sister can marry his best friend in.

'He said that?' Hols swoons hard, then comes to reality. 'Riv, there's zero way you'll pick a dress I'd ever wear,' she says, now watching him as he lifts dresses for her approval. 'It's the most important dress of my life,' she reminds him as she repeatedly shakes her head with each one until he pulls one out, making her gasp.

'It looks good on the hanger,' I say, knowing there's no way she's going to fall in love with a dress her brother picked.

Hols's eyes meet mine. 'I kind of want to try it on.'

'Ma'am?' River yells, glancing around for the woman previously helping us. 'Hello? Miss? Does anyone work here?'

'Yes, sir.' She appears beside him.

'She'd like to try this on, please, and *we* would like the complimentary champagne.' He motions between him and me. 'Booze will help stop the tears,' he says to me like it's some magic cure-all he's discovered.

'I can fetch the champagne; yes, however, that's not the dress style Miss Matthews requested.'

'Exactly,' River says. 'Her style sucks, so we're going in a new direction.'

'Says the guy wearing teal leopard-print skinny jeans, yellow Converse, and currently looks like a missing member of the once famous – now forgotten – LMFAO...' I mumble.

'My style does not suck,' Hols protests.

'Nor does mine,' River says with a glare.

'I'd never considered sexy for my wedding day, but

I bet Dax would like that more than fluffy cotton-candy girl.'

'And your father will be thrilled.' I laugh.

'He's giving her away. What the hell does he care what she wears?' River asks, his annoying little brother persona shoving through.

As Hollyn changes into the dress River's picked – and he downs a glass of champagne in one swallow – I wander the bridesmaid dress section. Hollyn hasn't settled on a style yet. Maybe I can influence her, so I don't have to wear some frilly dress I'll burn afterward. I start in the black dress section. You can't go wrong in black.

Black with ruffles *and* bows. Pass. I flip to the following dress.

Black and from the Kardashian line. Mega-pass.

Black and fluffy tulle. Vomit-pass.

Black and vintage-y. Stop.

I pull out a dress that's very date night as opposed to black tie wedding. It's a little bit Audrey Hepburn with a hint of Marilyn Monroe. Totally me, and I have a date tomorrow night. Pretty sure that requires new clothing.

I sneak into a dressing room and strip quickly, trying on the dress before I'm discovered. If I'm going on an actual date while following these supposed dating rules – I don't know – I'm dressing up; I don't care where we're going.

Oh my God, it's perfect. I suck in my breath as I turn in every direction, and with each glance, I fall in love with it a little more. Perhaps I'll be overdressed, but who cares. Hols has to see this. I step out of the dressing room at the same time she does.

'Ho-ly sexy wedding dress, Batman,' I say, looking her up and down. 'It looks better on you than the hanger!'

The dress River picked is beautiful. It's a super-feminine ivory-colored silhouette, fitted through the bodice and hips, with the appearance of boning, delicate rose lace, and upper arm straps. It's totally her. Romantic and gorgeous.

'Right back at ya,' she says, inspecting what I'm wearing. 'Maid of honor dress?'

'I was thinking date-night dress...'

'Date two?' Hollyn asks excitedly.

I nod, worried that even confirming the words out loud might jinx me.

'When is it?'

'Tomorrow night.'

'Buy. It,' she says, now walking to the pedestal with the saleswoman.

One more look at it in the mirror, and it's sold.

'Welcome to my collection,' I say as I peel it off and get dressed again. 'I have the perfect shoes for you.'

I exit the dressing room, date dress in hand, and see Hollyn mesmerized by her mirror reflection. Tears start to flow, and the sales lady hands her a tissue. I think this might be the one.

'Oh, my God, River was right,' Hols cries.

'Again...?' I glance his way, my brow furrowed.

He glares in return. 'You two act so surprised, but I'm always right. You just refuse to see it.' He steps in front of his sister with a wide grin. '*This* is the dress, not that cupcake princess thing.'

My phone rings while River circles Hollyn, telling her what he knows Dax will like, respectfully, because she is his sister.

'Hello?'

'Hey,' Dylan says. 'I have that gig in Seattle tomorrow morning, so I'm leaving now. You busy?'

'Now?'

'Tonight.'

'I had big plans of scrolling the internet and laughing at the idiocy on Reddit, maybe watching another episode of *The Winchesters*, but other than that and annoying River, no big plans.'

'Good, I need you to feed Mozart. Dinner tonight.

Breakfast tomorrow morning. Seven and seven. And scoop the litter box.'

Mozart is Dylan's spoiled rotten cat, and he's on a strict feeding schedule 'cause he's fat as fuck. He's also an asshole and a half.

'I'm not shoveling that cat's shit. I'll feed him, but if he bites me again, he's getting the emergency dry food at the back of the cabinet.'

'Don't abuse my cat,' he snaps. 'Follow my cat care instructions on the fridge only. Please, Merc. Are you sure you'll be alright running the shop on your own tomorrow?'

'I'm not going to abuse your cat, you freak. Well, verbally, maybe. Must I remind you that I'm not fifteen and at my first-ever job?'

'Sometimes I wonder...'

'Well, stop wondering and remember we own this shop together, so yeah, pretty sure I can handle a day without you. I've got lessons all day. It'll be nice. No one will be barking orders at me from the back room or making me feel bad for taking an hour-long break. Just make it back in time for our weird date.'

'I'm looking forward to nothing more,' he says sarcastically.

'This is the one,' Hollyn says as I hang up, still

dabbing the tears from her eyes. 'What do you think, Merc?'

I stand and join River in front of her. The saleswoman adds a veil to her blonde head, and suddenly, it's real. River and I glance at one another. If I didn't know any better, I'd also think I saw a glistening of tears in his eyes. Our best friends are getting married – to each other.

'I was wrong before; this is the one. I love it,' I say, grabbing a tissue from the box as River rolls his eyes.

'Girls and their endless tears. Ring it up!' he says to the saleswoman. 'I got to get out of here before I turn into one of you weepy losers.'

* * *

I go to Dylan's apartment at seven on the dot as ordered. His apartment is cozy. A brown leather sofa sits against one wall. His grandmother's painting of an ocean hangs on the wall above it. One side is sunny and whimsical, and the other shows a storm approaching from a distance. I love this painting because it reminds me of Dylan and me. Each of us represented on the same canvas.

A black vintage chest is in front of his couch as his coffee table. Music books are perfectly stacked by size in the center with a houseplant he's successfully kept alive perched on top. A large bowed lamp, the light glowing through a black fabric shade, is positioned over a black side chair that looks straight from a cigar bar in the fifties.

He's one of those people who doesn't own a TV; anything he watches is on the screen of his laptop. So instead of the room being centered around a television, he has a wall of bookshelves full of antique books, music and instruments. I glance at the photos he's chosen to display. Him at his brother's college graduation. A picture of him in high school at his parents' lake house. A family photo at Christmas. Even one of him and me backstage at a *La La Land* show.

'Mozart.' I call the cat's name as I enter the kitchen, digging through his cabinets for food. God forbid this creature eat dry kibble. He feeds him expensive canned food in bowls with his name inscribed on the front. If that says anything, it's that Dylan *needs* a girlfriend.

Something brushing against my ankles earns my attention, and I notice Satan has snuck up on me.

'Hey, asshole,' I greet him, causing him to look up and notice I am not Dylan. He jumps onto the counter near me, staring as I prepare his meal. 'I'm not mashing it with a fork like he does. You get it can shaped, and if that's not good enough, well fuck you.'

Fuck you is the exact look on this cat's fuzzy face. He's one of those angry-looking flat-faced cats. Gray, fluffy and just cute enough that you want to touch him, but if you do, he'll maul you because he thinks he's king of this apartment. I know from experience.

I toss the can and lid into Dyl's trash and slowly slide the bowl across the counter to Mozart, who sniffs it but doesn't dig in, just glares.

'Well? He's going to call me in an hour and verify I haven't starved you to death, so eat.'

His eyes move to the bowl on the floor, nearly empty of its water. I grab it, dump the contents into the sink then open Dylan's fridge to grab a bottle of water. Yes, bottled water only is on his cat care list. Ooh, he also has wine. That's not on his list, but I pull it out as well, grab a mug from his open cabinets, and pour myself a cup as I water the feline.

'You deserve toilet water at most,' I say as I set it next to the food. Mozart hisses in return, then dips his paw into the water dish and licks it off like a spoiled-rotten princess.

As I wait for him to feed himself, I wander the apartment, running my fingers along the top of Dylan's baby grand piano, the focal point of the living room. I sit down on the bench and lift the cover from the keys. I've played this piano a hundred times, but it feels brand new tonight.

I glance at the cat, who's still drinking water from his paw. His gaze is on me, though.

'Do you need mood music to eat? Because I've not got all night slow, poke.' Yes, I do. Who am I kidding?

My fingers meander over the keys as I start 'Mia & Sebastian's Theme' from *La La Land*. The photo of Dylan and me reminds me of it. It's a movie I own on DVD and digitally in my Amazon Prime account, so it's available anytime I need a reminder that life can be both beautiful and painful all at once, and that's completely normal.

I haven't played this song in so long, but it returns quickly. The fluttery feeling I had as I watched the movie for the first time races through my chest when the song gets dramatic. In the film, this song happens at my favorite parts. One is when Mia sees Sebastian playing and falls in love with him at first sight. A feeling not returned immediately and utterly foreign to me. Love at first sight? I mean, come on. There's no possible way that's a thing, right? I didn't think so. But the scene rolling through my mind isn't Mia and Sebastian this time; it's Brooks at the bar that night when he suddenly came back into my life. It's the night he watched me play the piano. It's every night I've seen him since we saw one another. I stop playing mid-song. Holy shit-oli. Brooks gives me this same fluttery feeling. Huh. What the hell do I do with this realization? I have no idea, so I play it again to verify.

This time I close my eyes so as not to think of anything but the music because that will settle this sudden flutter epiphany I've just had. But only one thing fills my head while I play, and it's unexplainable.

When the song's over, I glance back at the cat. Finally, he's eating. I sip the wine from my mug, the dark screen of my phone sitting on the music rack staring back at me.

'Should I call him, Mozart? Or wait for him to call me?'

He doesn't answer, so without allowing myself to overthink, I grab my phone and call.

'Hi, beautiful,' he answers, the same way he always does, and I swear, just like Mr Grinch, I feel my heart grow a size.

'Hey, you busy?'

'Daddy!' I hear a soft little voice in the background, giggling through the word 'daddy', making me smile.

'Right now, I'm being bullied into playing Barbie's best friend. What's her name?' he asks away from the phone. His daughter says something I can't make out. 'Tiana,' he says. 'That's right. She's named after her favorite Disney princess.'

Listening to him play with his daughter makes my chest bubble in the best way. Like champagne spilling over. He. Is. Adorable.

'He-llo?' he says playfully.

'Sorry. I uh – you're playing Barbies with your daughter?'

'I am. Tiana and Barbie are getting ready to go on a double date. How should I play my couple?' The phone jostles as he talks away from it again. 'Lijah, what's my guy's name?'

'Umm, Brooks!' she says with a giggle.

'I'm playing myself, apparently.'

'Is it awkward that I'd like to hear how this goes?' I ask, enjoying every second. 'But I can totally let you go too.'

'No, please stay. I'm wearing a tutu over my pants and a tiara instead of a ball cap, and your voice reminds me that I'm not as girly as I feel right now. Plus, it's the perfect time to teach you some dating rules.'

'You're seriously going to teach me how to date?'

'Tiana and Brooks will teach you how to date.' Brooks lowers his voice. 'By the way, the Brooks in my hand is stark naked from the waist down, and I've no idea where his pants went but be warned, I will not be arriving to our date Winnie-the-Pooh style.'

This makes me laugh. 'So, it's not a naked date, then?'

'Sadly, not this time, no.'

'When might that part appear in these dating rules?'

'Uh... after date three, I'd say.'

'And we're on?'

'Date two. Which consists of an evening of fun and romance, possibly a little quirkiness considering we're doubling up, and a handsy goodnight kiss.'

'No kissing yet!' his daughter yells. 'It's got to be romantical!' she demands.

'Jeez, sorry,' he says to her. 'You run Barbie world like a prison, girl.'

'No way,' the little girl says.

'Brooks, were your dolls kissing?'

'They were, but the Barbie warden has spoken; it's got to be romantical first!' he commands with a chuckle.

Oh my God. I have to get off the phone before I totally fall for this guy. Why am I attracted to this? The man is wearing a tutu, a tiara, and playing Barbies with his six-year-old daughter, and my insides are melting for him.

'I think I'm going to let you two go. I feel like I'm imposing.'

'Merc, you're not,' he says, his voice now more than serious.

'Seriously, you're adorable as hell right now, and before my heart prematurely wakes from its decades-long slumber, I gotta go.'

I can almost hear him smile through the phone. 'I'll see you tomorrow night?'

'Yes. Don't forget your pants,' I say with a laugh, reluctantly hanging up the phone and dropping onto Dylan's couch to stare at the ceiling. What is this man doing to me? I lift an arm and stare at it.

'Goosebumps?' I say out loud. 'Well, that's new.'

18

BROOKS

I dropped Ali at my brother's for the evening to hang out with Sophie. She's beyond excited, and I'm edgy, jittery and a complete basket case as I attempt to rein in my nerves for tonight.

Mercy was stressed over something earlier and said she needed some light conversation to ease her nerves, so I spent some time making her laugh via text. At one point, she casually mentioned she was PMS-ing and apologized in advance for her possible irritability, so instead of flowers, I picked up a four-pack of chocolate cupcakes.

I've been standing at her door for a couple of minutes, pacing the hall, hoping to breathe these nerves away. I'm not usually this anxiety-ridden over a date.

But there's something about Mercy. Every time I talk to her, she opens up a little more, and I fall in like with another part of her.

Knock. Knock. Knock – knock.

I hear a bit of commotion on the other side.

'River! Why must you always act like a child?!' Mercy shouts, her voice slightly muffled by the closed door.

'Get back, Jerkface McQuaken,' a male voice says. 'It's my job to make sure he's not a psycho.'

There's a thud, then the door suddenly swings open to two faces. One I've been daydreaming about, the other – not so much.

'What up?' River asks, lifting his chin as he casually leans against the door frame in front of Mercy.

I bite my lips together at the sight of her. I swear, whenever I see her, she's prettier. Black dress. Black heels. Her hair swept behind one ear. She grins, giving me a silent compliment like I am her. Once I remember we're not alone, I lift a hand to greet River, still standing beside her.

'Sorry, *Dude, Where's My Car* here needed to see who was at our door because, apparently, he's expecting someone?' she says more to him than me. 'This is River, the same man who embarrassed me at the piano bar that night.'

If this is the level of awkwardness tonight brings, I'm all in because this is entertaining.

'You gonna introduce him this time?' River asks, crossing his arms over his chest.

'Since I have to,' she says with slight irritation.

These two have to be related somehow. This feels very sibling rivalry.

'Riv, this is Brooks, a man I actually enjoy spending time with, so don't say anything that will force me to turn this date into a body-burying adventure.' She glances at me, a coy smile on her face. 'You'd help me bury a body, right?'

I lift a shoulder. 'I might have some questions... but ultimately, if your reasoning is good, possibly?'

Riv scrunches his face, looking from me to Brooks, now throwing a thumb my way. 'She's kinda scary. You sure you want this one?'

'Yeah, oddly enough, this is enticing me more,' I say.

'Huh,' River grunts. 'Weird one, are ya? Alright.' He inspects me from head to toe. 'No flowers?' he asks, disappointment in his voice. 'Dude, weak. I know a guy. He'll give you a great deal.'

'She didn't seem like a flower kind of girl, so I brought these instead.' I lift the pink bakery box lid.

Mercy's jaw drops through a giant smile. 'You brought me cupcakes?'

'To appease the PMS demon lingering in your shadows right now.'

When we were texting earlier, I asked what she was wearing tonight, and she very plainly said she was lying in her underwear with a heating pad on her aching belly. *Why must we be punished for not creating life monthly?* she'd asked.

'That is...' She stops talking as she takes the box from me. 'I don't even know what this is. A man has never brought me chocolate to ease my period pains before.'

'You might be smarter than I thought,' River says. 'Shark week,' he says with a shiver. 'Yikes.'

I nod, acknowledging that he may not be wrong but that I know better than to say it out loud.

'Put these in the kitchen, then go away,' Mercy says to him, shoving the bakery box his way, then stepping into the hallway and closing the door behind her.

River pulls open the door again. 'Have her home by midnight, or she'll turn into a frog, vampire or something equally freaky.'

I laugh as she grabs the door handle, yanking the door closed on him.

'Sorry,' she apologizes. 'Every day with River is like

a day in high school that I'm repeating for all eternity. It's exhausting.'

As we walk down the stairs towards the building exit, I can't help but let my eyes wander. 'You look beautiful.'

'Why, thank you. As do you,' she says flirtatiously, glancing at my pants (which I am wearing, by the way). 'Thanks for the cupcakes. I didn't expect that. It was very thoughtful.'

'As Barbie Brooks said, romance and fun are in store for you this evening.' I stop at my truck, pulling the door open for her.

When I glance back at her, she's staring at my vehicle with a wide smile. 'This is new and nifty from our time previously spent. A vintage cherried-out Bronco? Can we even fit in the back seat of this thing?' she asks, referring to that time we did it like teenagers in the back seat of my previous truck.

'I can't wait to find out,' I say with a wink.

She rolls her eyes playfully. 'I should've guessed your car would be as cool as you seem.'

'This thing falls in line right after my daughter by way of importance.' I pat the roof like it's my pet. 'I saved from high school to buy her.'

'Her?'

'The more you get to know me, the weirder I'm

going to get, so I'd just accept it now,' I say, motioning for her to get into the truck.

'Ditto, handsome. Prepare yourself,' she says, finally getting into the passenger seat.

Twenty minutes later, we walk into a South American-inspired restaurant called Lechon. Wood floors, brick walls, dark leather booths, loads of vintage mirrors and wicker hanging on the walls, and even a tropical fish tank sits to the side. Colorful vintage rugs hang from the balcony that overlooks rows of long group tables. It's very boho hipster cool in here. Norah suggested this place, and since my mind was running circles without sentences over tonight, I agreed and even let her make the reservation.

As the hostess shows us to our table, I see *that* has backfired. I should have known letting Norah make the reservation was a bad idea. There she sits, with Levi, a couple of tables away from us. I shake my head while pretending I don't know them as we pass. She and I will have words later.

Focus on this being fun, Brooks. Ignore your psycho ex-wife and make it fun.

We approach a table where a couple is seated and quietly sipping their wine. This must be her friend Dylan and his date.

'You're here,' Dylan says with enthusiasm. He

stands, motioning for us to sit opposite him and his date. It must not be going well if he's this excited for others to join him.

'I'll go get us drinks – you two good?' I ask Mercy's friends while motioning to Norah behind my back to meet me at the bar with whatever hand gesture works. Currently, it's my middle finger pointing towards the bar. 'Any requests?' I glance at Mercy.

'Surprise me.'

It takes her a minute but, eventually, Norah shows up and casually sits on a barstool a couple away from me.

'What in the hell are you doing?' I ask, the man between us looking over at me suddenly.

'Having a beer, man,' he answers, lifting it from the bar.

'Not you,' I say, glancing over him. 'Her.'

'After I made your reservation, it sounded good, so I made one for us, and they only had this time slot available.' The innocence in her voice kind of pisses me off.

'Why don't I believe you?'

She laughs. 'I just wanted to see the two of you to-gether. I really think I'm right about this. She's your one.'

Random man's head follows our conversation as he sips his beer.

'Who's the other couple?' she asks, glancing back at our table.

'That's her business partner and one of her friends, Dylan, and his date, Cassie.'

'It was total awkward silence between them until you two showed up. Is that why this is a double date?'

'Probably.'

'You look nice,' she says, looking me over.

I'm wearing black. Black dress shirt with the sleeves rolled to my elbows because I can't stand constrictive sleeves buttoned at the wrist, black jeans and black boots. No baseball cap tonight. If my mom beat anything into my head growing up, it's manners.

'Do *no* play the part of the ex-wife,' I demand.

She pulls her head back. 'That's the only part I know. Unless you prefer I act like your current wife? That's a role I know well, and with the way you're annoying me right now, that seems most plausible.'

Some mix of laughter and moaning leaves my lips, causing Norah to lift an eyebrow.

'I'm nervous, alright? I hate the first few weeks of dating. It's so much pressure. So, if you could make it easier and act like someone I don't know, that'd be awesome.'

'You think I'm going to walk over to your table and embarrass you? No. I'm just here to observe.'

'That's called stalking.'

'Put your work personality away, please. If something goes awry and you need a distraction, "Oh, looks who's here, my ex. Family emergency." It's perfect.'

'What could go awry?' I say sarcastically.

'I don't know; you're the one getting dumped all the time. After tonight I'll be able to tell you why. I'll also be able to say for sure if my dream was right. Now, stop being mad. I know you're mad.'

There's that intuitive thing I hate. She knows, er... *feels*, everything. The amount of times she's blurted out exactly what I'm thinking is mind-blowing. If we need to talk about something, she'll call before I even have the chance. I hate that she's always right too. I sigh heavily before requesting drinks for Mercy and me.

Relax, Brooks. You like this woman. I run a hand nervously over my head.

'Dial down the mind-reading tonight, would ya?'

'I'm not a mind-reader. I'm an emotional, intuitive empath.'

'OK, well, pretend you're not. Act normal. Like you've never met me. I don't want to be embarrassed.

Stay at your table, and if you make this weird, I swear – Nor, I'll never tell you anything about my personal life again.'

'You're so sensitive tonight,' she says, standing from her stool with a fresh glass of wine. 'Relax. She already likes you.'

'Yeah?' I ask, this time hoping her 'intuition' is spot on.

'I promise. You've got nothing to worry about. Now you go first, and I'll pretend I've never seen you before.'

'And I will relish every second of that.'

Norah glares as I walk away.

At the table, introductions are made. 'Brooks, this is Dylan, my business partner. And this is Cassie. She's the pianist I was dueling the other night.'

'Right,' I say, shaking hands with each before sitting down.

'Wow,' Cassie says, her eyes on my tattoos. 'What beautiful tattoos you have. Did they hurt?'

'At times, yes.'

'I've never been brave enough. What's it like?' she asks, wanting to know the answer.

'Um, it feels kind of sunburn-y.'

'How odd! I'd never thought that.' Her gaze moves to Mercy. 'Do you have any tattoos, Merc?'

She nods. 'A couple of small ones.'

A tattoo show-and-tell game fills a bit of time between ordering and our food arriving. Cassie and Mercy are discussing some performance they are coming up on, and Dylan's gaze lands on me.

'How're things going?' he asks, glancing Mercy's way and then back to me.

'Good, I think?'

'You're a cop?'

'Yep. You're a musician?'

He nods. 'Symphony, lessons, gig work. We both do it. I'm willing to admit she is more talented than I, even plays more instruments than me.' He sips his beer. 'I saw you play, and you're good too.'

'It's just a hobby.'

'As a fellow hobbyist guitarist, you're incredible. I've paid to see bands with guitarists not as talented as you. Did she tell you we have a recording studio?'

'No,' I say. They have a recording studio in their shop? That's impressive.

He pulls a business card from his wallet, handing it my way.

'We're not at work, Dyl,' Mercy says suddenly.

'When you run your own business, you're always at work,' he says to her.

'Ignore him,' she says to me. 'Tell us about you two; how did this happen?' she says to Cassie.

Dylan smirks Mercy's way. Nervously, he leans into the blonde and says something into her ear under his breath that makes her smile. She leans into him and looks pleased to be here for the first time tonight.

'Like you don't know how it happened,' Cassie says to her with a giggle.

I think I'd forgotten how awkward double dates can be. Every talkable subject has evaded my mouth, and I'm small-talking with the rest of them while we eat. Soon enough, Mercy takes it upon herself to break the silence and starts telling funny stories about her and Dylan's performances. It makes me relax, and she leans into me as she speaks. I like her close to me. Her perfume wafts my way. It's sweet yet spicy, just like her. I wouldn't choose to be anywhere else right now, even if we start talking about current events.

19

MERCY

I think things are going alright, considering I have no idea what to talk about on a double date. Do we talk about Dylan and Cassie, me and Brooks? Are embarrassing stories allowed to break the tension? Or do we continue small-talking until we're discussing the latest news topics?

My phone buzzes in my purse, and I'm sure I'm not the only one hearing it. Brooks glances my way curiously as I ignore whoever it is.

The small talk and awkward silences were getting weird, so now I'm doing most of the talking. Brooks listens intently like he's genuinely interested in every word I speak. It's lovely. He even asks follow-up questions to learn more about me. Usually, when men find out I'm a classical musician, they see me as some hoity-toity violinist who listens to Bach on the weekends and plays Vivaldi as folks eat an eight-course meal. They don't expect my sometimes-harsh mouth. But Brooks seems to enjoy it.

I think having Dylan and Cassie here is helping. It's giving us more to talk about; since I'm not great at talking about myself, work stories are easy.

'You play AC/DC on cello and violin?' Brooks asks, glancing between Dylan and me.

I nod, distracted by the buzzing once again coming from my purse. Who is this, and why are they blowing up my phone?

'And they are more than amazing,' Cassie raves. 'Watching them perform as Violated is just as hypnotically beautiful as watching them perform with the symphony.'

'Even when we're playing Eminem?' Dyl asks.

'Yes.' Cass laughs, touching his arm flirtatiously. 'Even then.'

Dylan even appears to be relaxing and enjoying the evening. Am I the only one who's still nervous as hell and hoping no one outs something humiliating about me that I'm not ready for Brooks to know yet?

I've been steering the convo towards music and away from family, personal lives, etc., but I can't do that forever. Eventually, Brooks will ask the questions I'm afraid of. I need to figure out how to answer them.

I catch him looking at me with an impressed smile. 'I knew you were talented, but I'm not sure I've witnessed the prodigy yet, it seems.'

'Maybe I'll invite you next time,' I say, setting my napkin on the table as my phone buzzes in my purse again. Whoever is calling is about to get an earful from me. First, I need to make sure it's not some kind of emergency. 'I'm just going to run to the ladies' room.'

Both Dylan and Brooks stand as I leave the table. I need some air, and since disappearing outside to check my phone would seem like I'm fleeing the scene, bathroom air is as fresh as I'm going to get.

I'm staring at my phone, googling the unknown number, when a woman approaches me.

'I saw you earlier; your shoes caught my attention.'

We both glance down at my feet, clad in Dolce & Gabbana black suede multi-strap heels. One of my favorite pairs.

'Thank you. I've got kind of a shoe fixation.'

She smiles sweetly, and it reminds me of someone. But I don't know who.

'I didn't really notice your shoes, though they are gorgeous. Truth be told, I'm intuitive and felt drawn to you enough to corner you in the bathroom and tell you that I get vibes from people, and yours is so interesting. Do you believe in fate?'

I meander around this woman to the paper towels. Sure, she looks normal with wavy brown hair and bright blue eyes, but she's 'feeling my vibe', so I think I'm way off.

'I don't,' I say. 'Fate has bitten me more times than I can count. Now I do my best not to tempt it.'

'Heartbreak at a young age can create that fear of living.'

'Fear?' I ask, suddenly intrigued.

'Abandonment. Insecurity. Not trusting others or even yourself. What was their name?'

'I'm sorry?' I ask, completely confused.

'The person who broke your heart and gave you trust issues. Was it family or a relationship?'

How in the hell does she know this?

'It was, uh, family,' I say meekly, tossing the paper towel in the trash.

'Not trying to pry,' she says softly. 'But it would help if you confronted them. Tell them how you feel. Admit what their actions did to you and ask for an explanation. Whether they have one or not, speaking your feelings may help you find peace and heal that childhood trauma.' She points to my chest.

I'm staring at this woman, my brows stitched together with confusion. Not talking about a stranger's childhood trauma should be a given at any social event. Yet this woman just guessed mine.

'Do I know you?'

'No,' the woman says confidently with a friendly chuckle. She sets her bag on the counter and fishes around for something. When she pulls out a set of tarot cards, I laugh nervously. 'Do you mind?' she asks, shuffling the cards quickly. 'This will make things clearer for you.'

Considering she's pushing through without my answer, I don't think she'd care if I said no. This is happening. My only out is to just exit, but I sort of want to know what she's about to say.

I awkwardly watch as she lets a couple of cards slip from the deck onto the counter. She sets the deck down and breathes in deeply before flipping the first card. She's concentrating hard on reading me, so I can only imagine the words about to leave this woman's lips. Slowly she flips the card, glancing at it before I can see it. She smiles softly.

'Death?' God, that would be just my luck.

She shakes her head. 'Nine of Swords reversed. It can be good – eventually. Trauma from your past is currently haunting you in a way you don't know how to deal with. Push forward with the healing. Deep down, you know what you need to do. It's scary, yes, but if you confide in the right person – someone possibly new to your life – you'll find clarity and peace.'

'What the hell does that mean?'

She flips the second card, ignoring my concern. 'Eight of Swords reversed. Huh. Anxiety and fear plague you at times. You try to hide it from the world, but it's always lingering. Recently a block you've had has unexpectedly opened, and you've been traveling a path you're unfamiliar with. Might it have to do with a new man in your life? An older man? Possibly two men? That part's not very clear. It all feels very... devil in the details. You may have to make difficult decisions as those blocks continue to open when you're with him. Healing can follow – if you let it. Want my advice?'

'Why stop freaking me out now?' I ask.

'Follow your heart – dead as it seems – it knows exactly what you need to do.' With that, she packs up her magic cards, checks her reflection then walks out the door.

'Thank you?' I ask after the door closes.

A new man? An old man? Two men? Devil in the details? Anxiety? Trauma? The woman is a psychic looking at my life without a crystal ball. That was so spot on it hurt. I was holding my breath as she spoke because there was no way she would know any of that if she didn't have some natural spiritual gift. Hollyn and I once went to a palm reader downtown, and she predicted my life would be long, happy and full of laughter and children. Obviously, that was complete shit. But this stranger just touched on pretty much all things haunting me like a fucking poltergeist; she just skipped the details.

I burst into a stall – not having to pee, just needing to escape from my escape. I stand, my head pressed against the metal door now closed in front of me, as I try to settle my insides.

Just breathe, Mercy. She didn't read your mind; she read a tarot card that happened to match your current inner turmoil. It's a magic trick. Anyone could fit the profile she laid out.

God, I hate magic. If there's one thing that freaks me out, that's it. It doesn't matter if it's Criss Angel or a tween with a magic kit at a birthday party; it all makes me cringe.

My phone buzzes in my hand again – the same

number as before. Finally, I can put a stop to whoever this is.

'What?'

There's silence for a second, and an automated voice speaks into my ear when I expect to hear creepy breathing. 'You have a call from prisoner – *Mercy; it's Dad, Nick* – to accept press—'

He says the words where his name should be, quick to fit it all in, and his sentence shocks me so much that I drop my phone onto the floor, and it skids out of the stall.

My heart seizes in my chest. *Dad?* Does he remember our eight short years together? He has no right to call himself Dad.

'Fuck. Me,' I say, opening the door to get my phone. I grab it, not caring that it just slid across the dirty bathroom floor. My thumbs tap out a text as fast as I can to Hollyn.

SO-fucking-S. I just got a collect call from Nick. IN PRISON. I am freaking out, Hols. AND some wacky woman just read my tarot against my will in the bathroom.

What? I thought you were on a date tonight?

I. Am. It happened ON the date. And she was spot on, Hols.

About what?

Well, it was pretty wordy, but when you put it all together, I took it to mean I need to face the evil in my purse and quite possibly the man himself to stop being scared.

Uh… call me?

Can't. Gotta go back out there before someone thinks I've drowned in the toilet. The next text you get from me will be either a head in the clouds Mercy or a very drunk one. May the odds for the former be in your favor.

LOL CALL ME when you get home.

I shove my phone into my purse.

'Pull yourself together, Merc,' I say to myself in the mirror. 'Tarot lady was just a run-of-the-mill whack job who violates people's ears in bathrooms. She probably wasn't actually reading your mind. As for Nick, you knew he was looking for you, so a phone call shouldn't be that surprising after he found your address.'

After rewashing my hands, I grab a paper towel and wrap my phone, shoving it into my purse. I'll sanitize it when I get home. And possibly change my number. Until then, I'm sure a more potent drink will help me get through this.

I sneak to the bar, my first shot of the night in my hand when Dylan interrupts me.

'What are you doing? Brooks is starting to worry you've bowed out with a family emergency you forgot to tell him about.'

I down the shot before setting the empty glass on the bar next to me and turning to face him. 'He is?' I glance towards our table and, sure enough, he's scrolling through his phone.

Dylan nods.

'Shit.' I turn back to the bartender. 'Another,' I say to him. He does what I ask and pours another shot of tequila that I down quickly.

'Should you be drinking like this while on a date?'

'I'm not driving, so why not?'

Dylan sits on the stool next to me. 'Merc, what's going on?'

Finally, I sit, dropping my head towards the floor with a heavy sigh. 'Nick called me.'

'When?'

'Tonight, it's why I went to the bathroom. Someone kept calling, and it was distracting.'

'What did he say?'

'Have you lost your mind? It was a collect call; I didn't accept it!'

Dylan furrows his brow. 'Maybe you should.'

'Why? The man is a piece of garbage. He killed someone over drugs and nearly killed a second person as he fled. *While* I watched, Dyl. He tore my innocence from me in a second. What could he possibly have to say that could fix any of that?'

He nods as if he understands. 'That's rough. Did you bring your medication, or is that what the tequila is for?'

I groan, dropping my head onto the bar in front of me with a thud. 'Did I bring my medication?' I repeat his words before sitting up again. 'That's great. Don't listen; just drug me. Medication is a mask, Dylan. It closes the curtains on the horror film looping through my head just long enough for me to catch my breath and realize I'm not still there. But it always comes back. Eventually, I'll have to face it. I'll have to face him. In person.'

A disbelieving laugh leaves his lips. 'Well, that's the worst idea you've ever had. You have two reasonable options that are way safer than meeting the man face to face. Read the letter,' he urges. 'Accept his call. Tell him to F off, then forget he ever existed.'

'Yeah, because it's that easy,' I say, lifting my empty shot glass. 'If I could do that, I wouldn't be sitting here attempting to drink away decades-old feelings instead of figuring out how to deal with them.'

I glance across the bar, noticing Brooks as he and Cassie walk our way. His hands are in his pockets, and it hits me again just how incredibly handsome he is, all dressed up for me. And I'm sitting at the bar fighting with my heart.

'We're going to head out, I think,' Dylan says as he stands from the stool as Cassie approaches. 'You good?'

I nod, feeling Brooks's eyes on me. Cassie and Dylan walk away as he takes Dylan's stool.

'Hey, gorgeous,' he says gently, resting his hand on the small of my back, sending a ripple of chills through me. 'Did I say something wrong?'

'No,' I blurt out a little too quickly, but he smiles. 'It's nothing you did.'

'Good. Can I help?'

'My complicated past just came to visit via a random bathroom tarot reader and a phone call that terrified me.'

Brooks lifts a single eyebrow, leaning back and glancing into the dining room. 'Is that so?'

'Was it uncomfortable? Yes. She's right, though; something *is* haunting me. Despite years of avoiding it, hoping it will go away, it won't. And I know how to deal with it; I just don't want to.' I glance over at him. His beautiful eyes are mesmerizing as he stares into my soul. Never have I been so scared yet so sure of the words I'm about to say and God I wish I knew why. 'I think you may be a part of it. Or at least able to help? I don't know.'

'What do you mean?'

For a second, I consider telling him he makes my cold, dead heart beat, which has never happened with anyone else. But I'm too overwhelmed with my past to focus on my future. Why is this when Nick chooses to get involved?

'This part of me drives people away. And I hesitate to let you in because I don't want you to leave yet. I kind of like you.'

'Kind of?' he says with a smirk.

'Are you beyond "kind of"?'

'Yes.' He nods, unable to hide his growing smile. 'Mercy, I think about you all the time. I just spent the last fifteen minutes terrified you'd ditched me. As loser-y as this may sound, the thought of that hurt.'

He touches his chest. 'Anytime you text me or call, I get excited, no matter what I'm in the middle of.'

'You get excited over me? But I'm crude and horny, and—'

He rests a hand on mine, stroking his thumb over my skin. 'And beautiful, funny, talented, and complicated enough that all I want to do is make you smile.'

'Trust me; you'll feel differently when you learn about my past.'

'I already like you, Mercy. It would take a lot to scare me. I want to hear all of your stories, good and bad. I want to know why I feel like I've known you forever. So, whenever you're ready to talk, I'm happy to listen. Until then, I planned a second location tonight, just us, because I knew this double date thing might be weird.'

'You planned a secret second location to this date to escape Dylan and Cassie?'

'I did.' He laughs. 'Is it wrong I want you to myself?'

I shake my head. That is sweet.

He wastes no time paying our tab, refuses to take my money, then leads me towards the exit. When he reaches down and takes my hand, the irritation settles, and the fluttering begins. My hand in his feels, well, incredible. Like I could walk on water. I lace my fingers through his as we exit, and he glances at me with a shy smile.

'Did I make tonight a total disaster?' I ask as we walk down the sidewalk towards his overly cool bright blue vintage Bronco.

He opens my door. 'Not at all.'

20

BROOKS

'Where are we headed for this surprise second location?' she asks.

'Fifty Licks.'

She laughs. 'Sounds like a dirty distraction. I'm in. Back seat?'

I drop my head with a laugh. Good God, I like this woman.

'Settle down, horndog. We're going slow, remember? Fifty Licks is an ice cream shop.'

Her cheeks turn bright pink. 'An ice cream shop?' She laughs.

'Yes, dessert comes after dinner.'

'Sorry, the tequila shots I did are settling in. Don't be surprised if I say even more obnoxious things than usual. Like this – hand-holding is allowed on date two?' She lifts our hands, displaying them as if I didn't know what my right hand was up to. ''Cause if we're at second base/second date, shouldn't you be doing this?' She plants my hand on her breast.

I laugh out loud. 'That's an interesting play,' I say, feeling super awkward driving down the road with my hand on her boob. That doesn't stop me from running my thumb over her clothed nipple and watching her reaction. Freeway lights flash through the truck, illuminating her right as she sucks in a breath, letting it out with a shy smile. I remember this part of her.

'If this is uncomfortable, I have the perfect second-base location,' she says. 'After Fifty Licks, we'll go there. I hope you're ready.'

'Should I worry?'

'Perhaps.'

Fifteen minutes later, we're settled in the shop with ice cream in front of us. She chose mint chocolate chip with a chocolate drizzle for the PMS – her words. I decided on chocolate with a caramel drizzle. I take the chance and return to our earlier conversation.

'Why do you think I can help with whatever haunts you?'

'Partly because nutjob tarot reader predicted

something about a new man and an old man in my life.'

I raise an eyebrow hoping to God I'm not the old man. 'Nutjob' is an understatement. I can't believe Norah did this and got inside Mercy's head. She and I will have words when this is over.

'You're a new man in my life and maybe you showed up at the right, or possibly very wrong, time. I'm not sure sure, *but* you work in law enforcement, so I'm going to assume you know a few things I don't. Maybe you could give me some advice?'

'Possibly. Are we talking laws, or what?'

She takes a deep breath, releasing it slowly. 'The prison system. Do you know anything about that?'

'A little, yes...'

She eats her ice cream silently, obviously deep in thought, before suddenly stabbing her spoon into it and setting the bowl on the table in front of her. She sits back in her chair, fidgeting with one of the rings on her fingers. Her emerald-green eyes meet mine. She's nervous about whatever she's thinking; I can see it all over her pretty face.

'Do they release people on parole without notifying victims or family?'

'Uh—' I'm confused but don't want her any more

anxious than she already visibly is. 'Yeah, sometimes. Why?'

She grabs her bowl and restlessly stirs her ice cream. Instead of the confidence she usually oozes, she seems scared. I want to know why. This can't all be because of Norah.

'I've no clue why I'm about to say this. For some reason, I want to talk to you.'

'I want to listen, so we're in luck.'

She nods, taking her time to find her words. 'My early childhood was complete shit. When I was eight, I was removed from my home during a chaotic and terrifying night and placed in foster care. At five in the morning, I walked into a stranger's home with a trash bag full of everything I cherished – which wasn't much. I don't know why they even bothered. Social services were eight years too late. The damage had already been done. After that, I moved around foster homes for years until the half-brother I barely knew, Edie, legally became my guardian when I was thirteen.'

Shit. That's heavy. She was yanked from her home in the middle of the night and felt like they had taken too long? Jesus. Something went terribly wrong in this woman's life.

'Is one of your parents in prison because of this

terrifying night?' I'm trying to read between the lines here like I would if I was on a case. Maybe that'll make it easier for her to talk about.

Mercy nods, looking at me like she's expecting me to bolt out the front door and abandon her right here in the ice cream shop.

'One's in prison, and the other left when I was one. She was only seventeen and wasn't prepared to have a baby with a junkie, so she left me behind because I was a bad reminder. I don't know that for sure or anything – just assuming based on the situation. I don't even remember her,' she says, forcing a playful crooked smile – a mask. Most people with this kind of trauma are experts at wearing the perfect cover for every occasion. No one would ever know they were struggling. But she just took hers off right in front of me.

'You scared yet?' she asks, a slight grin on her face as she attempts to lighten the mood.

I shake my head. 'I'm sorry you went through that. Is this the story Seiver plays into?'

'Yeah,' she says, surprised I remember she asked about him. 'Travis was one of the officers on scene that night. He did everything he could to protect me from seeing what went down outside my bedroom door.'

What in the hell happened to this woman? I need to know, but I don't want to push her.

'Seiver might make my life miserable at times, but from what I know, he was the best in his job. You were in good hands.'

She nods, eating ice cream again to distract herself; clearly, a lot is happening in her head.

'Every second of that night is burned into my brain for all eternity. The thunderstorm, the police lights, the 911 operator's calming voice, even the chaos. Sometimes it escapes through anxiety or panic attack at the worst possible times.'

The silence surrounding us feels delicate. I need to say the right thing here.

'What do you usually do to distract yourself?'

'Four things,' she says. 'One, medication. It's a must. It sometimes makes me feel a little drunk, but it levels out soon enough. I didn't realize I didn't bring any with me tonight, so I self-medicated at the bar earlier and am now on my way to loosey-goosey Mercy, as you'll probably witness at our third location of the night. Two, music. When I play, all the disarray in my head settles.'

'And the third?'

'You'll find out after this.'

'Tonight's third location can't be my bed, Mercy,' I say somewhat jokingly.

She laughs. 'That's the fourth – patience, grasshopper. Tonight you get to feel me up and kiss me goodnight, and that is all. Your rules.' She winks my way, putting a spoonful of ice cream in her mouth with the spoon upside down and removing it slowly, intently watching my reaction.

I never know what to expect from her. She lightens things every time I think we're moving into serious territory.

'If I have to line dance to settle your head or heart or whatever, I'm up for it. I want to help.'

'You'd line dance for me?'

'Would that make you feel better?'

'Maybe?' She grins. 'I want to tell you everything, but I can't do it all at once. It's way too much for even me.'

'That's alright. As I said, I'm here whenever you're ready.'

'Thank you.'

'Totally my pleasure.'

With that, she takes a deep breath, blows away her stress, and flashes me a mind-melting smile. 'Ready to feel me up?'

'You're making me incredibly nervous.' I take her

hand, following her out the front door of the ice cream shop.

* * *

'I can't believe I almost guessed it with the line-dancing comment. You go clubbing for number three?' I ask, now following her through the dark hall into a club called Genesis, where the music is so loud it vibrates through your entire body, and you must speak into one another's ears to be heard.

'Can you think through this?' she asks. 'The music consumes you, and you forget about everything else.'

'I think I exceed the age limit,' I say, glancing around the room at the twenty-somethings making out in private seating areas around the main dance floor. The place is dark, with strobe lights and scantily clad hipsters everywhere you look.

'You're not that old, grandpa. You hardly look a day over thirty-six.'

'Funny,' I say into her ear, now behind her, following closely, so I don't lose her. 'I haven't been to a club since I was in my twenties.'

'So, decades ago?' she says, suddenly turning towards me with a coy smile.

'Dec-ade. Singular, thank you very much.'

'Total technicality.'

Suddenly the music cuts, and she points to the DJ booth, the DJ pointing back. 'Portland royalty Lemon Rockefeller is in da houz. This one's for you, girl.'

'Royalty? They know you by your fake name here?' I yell over the music with a laugh.

'This club is hard to get into. I had to get on the list last minute, so I texted in a favor. In my defense, he's both a creeper *and* a musician – so he's totally my type.'

I glance up at the guy. He's young. Probably early twenties. Black over-gelled hair and one of those tank tops muscly dudes wore in the eighties. For those reasons alone, I hate him.

'I'll give him creepy.'

As I speak, she's guiding my hands to her waist, moving in closer and swaying to the song's beat. Feeling her against me is causing a buzzing in my brain, pushing out all other thoughts than just being here with her.

'See, you're a natural,' she says in my ear after I've finally given in and proven how long it's been since I've been in a club, but she doesn't seem to mind.

'That's you. I'm just following your lead.'

'Or...' she says, moving in closer. 'You're better than you think, and it's us? Plural.'

'You're killing me, woman.'

'It's intentional,' she says with a grin, sliding a hand over my shoulder and to the back of my neck, kissing me hard. I love that she does what she wants. She's not one of those women who waits for a man to make the first move. I kiss her back, and suddenly we're just one of the couples on the dance floor making out to a beat. I no longer feel old. I'm not worried about her not liking me. I'm just that soft-hearted single guy who's starting to hope she isn't truly anti-love.

21

MERCY

'Wanna come up?' I ask, knowing his answer before he even opens his mouth. A girl's gotta try. Did we spend the last hour pretending we were the only two in the club? Yep. He felt me up really well, and I wasn't disappointed. Now, I'm preparing to go home alone and overthink the entire night.

'I want to, yes, but I'm not going to,' he says coyly, lifting my hand to his lips. 'I've got my daughter this week. I knew you'd be hard to say no to, so to prevent myself from breaking my dating rules, I promised her I'd pick her up tonight. Can't let her down.'

His daughter. I almost forgot he's someone's dad. He doesn't want to let her down. Wow. That's a life I've never lived.

'I have her until Sunday night and don't usually date when it's my week. I made an exception for you.'

'You made an exception for me?'

'Don't act so surprised.'

'Can I tell you something?'

'Absolutely,' he says.

'I've never hoped a man would ask me on a third date, and right now, it's all I'm thinking about.'

'You really want to get into my pants, don't you?' he jokes.

'I've traced outlines of your tattoos with my tongue while I was in your pants.'

He drops his head, his cheeks turning a rosy color visible under the streetlight's glow.

'You're embarrassed by that?'

'No,' he says. 'You're just making it hard to leave here.'

'Is that the only thing?' I ask with a wink.

'Being this close to you makes me feel like I'm walking to the edge of the high dive board.'

'High dive or plank? Because most of my life is more walking the plank. Truthfully, though, both sound terrifying.'

'It's the opposite of that.' He reaches over, his thumb grazing my chin as he kisses me softly. I stand against the building for a moment, the bricks cool on my skin, as I desperately try to catch my breath through this goodnight kiss.

'Go on a third date with me?' he says after breaking the kiss.

'I couldn't say no right now if I wanted to,' I say, my lips buzzing from his kiss.

'Good. I'll call you.'

'You better,' I joke.

He insists I go inside before he walks to his building, so, reluctantly, I walk in alone. When I get to my floor, I dig through my purse for my key, but when I open the door, I hear the one sound I do not want to deal with tonight. Ugh, River. I close the door and press my ear against it to verify and hear precisely what I was hoping I wouldn't – Riv with a girl in his room.

'Damn it. I can't sleep in the next room while that's going on,' I say to myself.

I hesitate because my head is spinning, and I just wanted to go to bed and dream about Brooks Hudson. Instead, I feel the need to step up to my past tonight. But I can't do it alone, so take River's lucky night as a sign.

All those poltergeists I was afraid were attached to Nick are now suddenly in my head, causing havoc, knocking shit around and poking at the backs of my eyes, stinging in a way that hurts more than just my feelings as I walk through the dark city towards the train.

After missing my stop two times because I was busy staring at Nick's handwriting across the front of his letter and having to double back, I'm finally on Edie's side of town and making the few blocks' trek to his house. The night air is warm, but sporadic water droplets on my skin tell me it's about to pour a summer rain that I won't escape.

The closer I get to Ed's, the harder the rain falls. The earthy, musky, petrichor smell that comes with summer rain sinks into my lungs as I breathe it in deeply. It's one of my favorite smells, yet it terrifies me simultaneously. Thunder rolls across the sky, lightning crashing in the distance as I stop to stare up, closing my eyes and seeing the flash of red and blue light.

They're only in your head, Merc. Keep walking.

Edie stands when I walk in, probably because I look like a drowned rat. 'What in the hell happened to you?'

'I want to read the letter,' I say, yanking the wet envelope from my bag.

Forty minutes later, I've had a warm shower and

explained the situation between Brooks, Nick and the rando tarot reader. Edie has blow-dried the letter. I'm dressed in Carlos's gray sweats and one of Edie's T-shirts. We're sitting at their built-in dining table, the lights dimmed, and lavender-scented candles flicker between us. A plate of homemade chocolate chip cookies that Carlos heated in the oven sits in front of me, and I'm drinking sleepy-time tea at Ed's insistence.

'Ready?' Ed asks, tearing the end off the envelope, blowing into it and pulling out the letter.

'Does this feel a little séance-y?' Carlos asks, glancing at each of us for a response.

I nod. 'Like we're summoning a demon.'

'Eh, we can't have that. Wait here, I have the perfect thing,' Carlos says, standing from the table and disappearing into the back bedroom. When he returns, he's holding a three-foot-tall ornate golden cross that looks as if it has come straight from a Catholic church. He sits it in the middle of the table.

'Did you steal that from the Pope?' I ask curiously, inspecting the Goddy thing.

'No, *amor*. My father's great-uncle did. And not the Pope, just a regular ole Catholic priest. Now it's a family heirloom. Remind me to tell you the story—'

'Tell the story later, Car. We've got bigger fish to

fry tonight,' Ed says. 'Now that we've got the stolen cross for "good luck"—'

'I'm not done yet...' Carlos displays a small vintage bottle with a crucifix design on the front and clear liquid inside.

'If you're suggesting we get drunk, I'm in,' I say, reaching for the bottle.

'It's holy water, Merc, in case the demon-summoning thing comes true,' he says, motioning the sign of the cross on his body as he sets it in front of the stolen cross. 'We can't be too safe.'

'But we can be too insane,' Ed says. 'Are we armed against Satan enough to start, love?'

'I think so,' Carlos says, nodding as he inspects his table spread.

Ed's gaze shoots to me. 'Out loud, doll?'

'No,' I say with a shake of my head. 'Silently, then warn me how bad it is before you speak any of his words.'

He and Carlos look nervous as Ed holds the letter between them, the two reading it silently.

I chew on my freshly manicured fingernails while their eyes are on the paper, so nervous I could puke. What would happen if I took a swig of that holy water? Instant salvation or eternal damnation? It's too risky to find out.

Ed's eyebrows lift, then drop. Carlos's eyes grow wide. I grab a cookie to not chew my fingers off with anticipation. Finally, Ed sets the letter on the table between us.

'It's not great,' he says softly.

'Is he... dying?' I ask, hopeful.

'No.'

Damn.

'Did he apologize?'

He and Carlos shake their heads.

Asshole.

'Did he say *anything* about what happened?'

'No, love. The letter is more – about what you can do for him.'

'My mind is moving like a hurricane, Ed. You're going to need to spell it out for me.'

'How can we say this gently?' he asks Carlos.

'Sugar.' Carlos rests his hand on one of mine. 'Nick is the spoiled sour cream on a taco sitting in the Mexico sun who's up for early parole and hopes your place might become his safe house as no one in prison knows he has a daughter, and he's pissed some people off.'

My gaze moves to Edie, who grimaces, nodding his head to confirm it's true.

'He wants to *stay* with me? But he doesn't even

know me. We've had zero contact for twenty-two years.'

'He's the biggest tool in the she—'

'I want to see him,' I say, interrupting Ed's words, then covering my mouth with my hand at the shock of them.

The two of them exchange worried looks.

'Why?' Ed asks.

'He deserves to know what the demon he left me with has done.'

'Understandable, but you want to see his garbage face? Why not just answer one of his calls or write back?'

'Because something bigger is at play here, Ed. I need to *see* him to do this.'

'Then, I'll come with you.'

'No,' I say, grabbing another cookie from the tray. 'You can't fix things for me all the time. No more meddling. You promised.'

'You're not going to the prison alone,' he argues as a good father/brother would.

'I'm thirty, Ed. I can do anything I want. You have to stop seeing me as that terrified untrusting thirteen-year-old girl who asked why you were so weird the moment she stepped into your home, then spent a week ignoring you with the help of headphones you eventually cut the cord on to make me speak. I've grown up.'

Ed and Carlos exchange glances again. 'Have you, love?' Ed asks, concern all over his face.

'I'm desperately trying. Does that count?'

'Yes,' Carlos answers for Ed. 'Trying your best is all we ask.'

'Then I'll keep doing that.'

'When do you plan to have this little family re-union?' Ed asks, his concerned father mode still activated.

'I dunno yet,' I say, moving to the couch bed they've made for me. 'When I feel like I'm strong enough. It could be tomorrow or next year. I'll know when I'm standing in front of the man.'

22

BROOKS

'Hey.' Norah answers her phone like she's done absolutely nothing wrong. Nothing, my ass. Her random tarot reading freaked out Mercy, and if she thought I wouldn't guess who that random tarot-reading woman was, she's way off.

'What did you do?'

'I have no clue what you're talking about.'

'Norah,' I growl.

She moans to herself. 'It was for the greater good. She's confused and needed a push, so I pushed.'

I suck in a breath, blowing it out slowly, so I don't erupt at her. 'You nearly pushed her right off a metaphorical cliff.'

'Listen,' she says, trying to save herself from my

reaction. 'All I'm going to say is that whatever cliff she's standing at the edge of, she needs your help with it.'

'I don't know what that means...'

'It *means* work and your personal life will soon collide. Be on the lookout.'

I pull into Ty's driveway and turn off my truck, dropping my head against the steering wheel with a thud.

'Hello?'

'I'm not in the mood for your mind-reading riddles, Nor. You freaked her the hell out.'

'I'm sorry, but it was only because I'm right. She is *super* complicated, Brooks.'

'Exactly why I'm mad. I asked you to make a reservation, *not* show up to sabotage my date. What does Levi think of your extracurricular activities tonight?'

'He doesn't know all the details, and that's how I prefer it stay.'

'Your secret is safe with me *if* you stop inserting yourself into my dating life, Nor. I like this woman. Please don't screw this up for me.'

'I'm not screwing anything up. If anything, things will move smoothly now. She was looking for a sign; I gave her a sign. You're welcome.'

'You are so annoying at times.' Without saying

goodbye, I hang up the phone and make my way into Ty's house.

'Daddy!' Alijah yells as I walk in.

'Ali!' I say with enthusiasm, dropping onto Ty and Emily's couch.

Alijah crawls onto my lap, laying her head on my shoulder, her eyes partly glazed over with exhaustion as she stares at the Disney movie on Ty's giant TV. Sophie's asleep on the floor, Barbies and stuffed animals spread around their makeshift bed.

'It's only midnight,' Em says from the couch. 'I expected a text saying you'd be by tomorrow morning.'

'She reject ya after you whipped it out?' Ty asks. He's sprawled across the other side of their sectional, watching Elsa dance across the screen.

'Considering I like this woman, I whipped nothing out. Though my ex-wife did make an appearance.'

Ty mutes the television, his attention now entirely on me. 'Did freaky-deeky Norah scare the shit out of her?' he mumbles quietly, so Ali doesn't hear.

'That's a possibility,' I say. I run a hand over my head. I can't believe she did this. 'Can I tell you guys something weird?'

'Weirder than bringing your ex-wife on your date tonight?'

'I didn't *bring* her; she invited herself. That's not

what I'm talking about, though. A while back, she called me with a dream she had. A dream where I d-i-e-d.' I spell out the word because the last thing I want to do is worry Ali with a story about my possible pending death.

Ty lifts a single eyebrow. 'Oh boy, here we go. If Dad were here right now, he'd already have the exorcism kit out. Want me to call him?'

I roll my eyes, jumping at the sound of the front door suddenly opening.

'That was fast,' I say. 'Are you out fighting crime for Jesus now?' I ask, glancing over at who I assume is my father bursting in right on cue.

'Ha!' Oz says, slamming the door behind him and waving a single finger Ty and my way. 'Sneaking over in the middle of the night and hanging out without me? Jerks.'

Ali jumps awake at the sound of his bellowing accusing speech, glancing at Ozie with a frown. 'Oz,' she greets him with disappointment in her tone. I've never been prouder – half-asleep and still giving him a hard time. Exactly like I've taught her.

Oz grunts at Ali's response as if she's offended him.

Sometimes I forget these guys live on the same street we grew up on. Mom and Dad live at the end of the block. Oz inherited his dad's house after his passing, and Tyler bought the house across the street. Every inch of this neighborhood brings me memories, good and bad.

Tyler shushes us, sitting up, now interested in what I was going to say. He pats the seat next to him, inviting Ozie to stay. 'Norah predicted his d-e-a-t-h.'

Oz cocks his head, putting the letters together slowly. His eyes go wide when he gets it. '*No*,' he says with a gasp, sitting beside Ty, ready to listen. 'She hex ya? What'd you do? Was it the date thing tonight? 'Cause, dude, *never* tell your obsessed ex you're going on a date. That's weird, man.'

'Why do I hang out with you two?'

Ty and Oz look at one another proudly. "Cause we're Oz-some,' Ty says, bringing a wide grin to Oz's face.

With a roll of my eyes, I continue. 'Back to Norah's dream, a woman appeared, apparently distraught over losing me.'

'Unexpected twist right from the go,' Oz says. 'I'm intrigued – continue.'

'Dark hair, emerald-green eyes, stiletto heels. Nor swears this woman is my soulmate.'

'What's a soulmate?' Ali asks, her words slow and soft.

God, I thought she was asleep. 'It's, uh – the word for a make-believe person you really like,' I say, my brain moving about as fast as hers.

'Like Elsa?'

'I'd soulmate the hell out of Elsa,' Ty says with a laugh, earning a glare from Emily.

'What's that mean?' Ali asks innocently.

'It means Uncle Ty is an idiot,' I say to her softly, rubbing her back to lull her back to sleep and away from our conversation. Once she settles like she's falling asleep again, I continue our conversation. 'Norah thinks Mercy is that woman.'

Both Ty and Oz's faces sober.

'I hate to be the bearer of bad news, brother, but most of the stupid shit that spews from her lips comes true. She told Emily she was pregnant a month before we knew. Are you sure you don't want to hear her when she's predicting your soulmate *and* d-e-a-t-h? Those two seem important.'

I glance at Alijah, asleep again and hopefully not listening to my brother's mouth.

'She predicted your pregnancy?' I ask Emily, trusting her way more than Tyler.

'We did fertility treatments to get Sophie,' she reminds me. 'No way did I suspect a surprise accidental pregnancy six years later. I'd made my peace with an only child.'

I'm rethinking everything Norah just said. Work and my love life are going to collide. She could be correct, but how? Suddenly it hits me. Fucking hell.

'I gotta go,' I say, lifting Ali off the couch and not waiting another second to see if I'm right.

Twenty minutes later, Alijah and I are home, and she's asleep as I carry her from my truck to our apartment. I gently lay her in bed and tuck her in, leaving the door open so I can hear her. I shower, change and get into my bed, spotting the file I was working on recently still lying on my bedstand table where I'd left it. I grab it, looking through, flipping to the page I stopped at.

Nicholas Alexander – arrested in 2000 on murder charges. A drug deal went bad. An eight-year-old child was one of two witnesses.

Mercy's last name is Alexander. She has a father in prison. Nick's in prison. And according to him, he wants out on early parole to make amends. Is she who that's with?

Holy fuck. My heart is racing in my chest as I grab my phone and dial Seiver's number, realizing after it's ringing that it's nearly two in the morning.

'This better be important,' he says groggily.

'Why do you refuse to deal with Nick Alexander?'

'What?' Seiver says, now sounding a hint more awake.

'My new informant. Nicholas Alexander. What's the deal? Why'd you give me his case if it was originally yours?'

'Because he's a piece of shit whose dirty deeds have stuck with me. I'll never forget that sweet little girl's face.'

Sweet little girl. No.

'What was her name?' I ask nervously.

'You think I can remember when rudely woken from a dead sleep?' he asks with a groan. 'I dunno. It was something weird – it starts with an M. Macey? Mazie?'

'*Mercy?*'

'That's it! Mercy Alexander. I found her crying in her closet, playing the ukulele, scared to death. Family services took forever, so she was picked up at McDonald's, where I'd bought her a milkshake. She kept asking me why her daddy would do this. It was heartbreaking. Why in the hell are you calling me this late about this?'

My heart sinks through my chest, making me nauseous. How many Mercy Alexanders could there possibly be in Portland? I stand from my bed and walk across my room, glancing towards her building.

'Hello?' Seiver barks into the phone. 'Hudson, if you hang up on me—'

I end the call, pulling up Mercy and my text thread. I can't just ask or force her to talk. But there's no way Nick Alexander isn't her father. This is precisely what Norah was talking about. Damn it. This could blow up in my face. I can't let that happen.

You up?

My eyes are glued to my phone while I wait to see the text bubble of her typing. *Respond. Please, Mercy.* After ten minutes of staring at the screen, I glance out my windows towards her building again. The third floor is completely dark. Fuck. I have to figure this out before she discovers I'm investigating her father.

23

MERCY

The sun shines through the blinds, hitting me in the face way earlier than I hoped to wake up.

'Holy tequila shots,' I groan, feeling those almost immediately. I pull the blanket over my head, but something falls, hitting me in the head. 'Ow.' My phone.

'Want some coffee, sugar?'

I jump, shoving the blanket off, glancing towards Ed's voice. 'Why are you up at—' I fumble with my phone, finally turning it on. 'Nine... forty-two?' I sit up. Rechecking my phone. 'No.'

'Something wrong?'

'I have a gig in one hour.' I jump out of bed, slipping on my heels from last night and grabbing my bag. 'Can you drive me home?'

Ed's eyes move over the T-shirt that belongs on his back and sweats that belong on Carlos, mixed with my black stilettos, and he bursts out laughing.

'Yeah, I can't have you walking home like that. I've got a reputation to uphold, honey.' He grabs his keys from their designated key hook and leads the way to his car. He parks along the curb when we pull up to my apartment. 'You better call me before you go to that prison. Understood?'

'We'll see, Dad.' I get out of his car, shutting the door behind me but hearing the purr of the window winding down.

'Mercy.' He says my name sternly.

I turn, flashing him a smile that I'm hoping screams, *don't worry, I'll live.*

'Thank you for the ride and the weird séance letter-reading girls' night. I promise to call you if I come upon a part of life I can't handle.' I dodge into the building, running up the stairs, thankful for once in my life to see River exiting the apartment.

'Don't lock the door!' I call, sliding into him, unable to stop in these shoes.

'What in the hell are you wearing?' he asks, catching me before I crash into him.

'I'm late. I'm late. I'm late.'

'For a very important date? Please tell me you don't usually go into public like this?'

'I stayed the night at Ed's. My night was, uh – rough.'

'Date didn't go well?' he asks with a smirk, following me towards my room as I kick off my shoes, nearly knocking a lamp over in the process.

'Um – parts were amazing. Others – not so much.' I stop at my door, turning towards River. 'I'll see ya later.' I shut the door on him. Racing to my closet to get dressed, only to discover I've started my fucking period. As if today could go any worse.

Thirty minutes later, I'm sitting in my car, my violin strapped into the passenger seat.

'Come on!' I yell, turning the key again but getting nothing. 'Damn it!' I pop the hood and get out, propping it up like I know what I'm looking for. Really I'm just hoping someone who knows cars will notice, stop and fix whatever is wrong, then send me on my way.

'Excuse me, ma'am?' A truck slows.

It worked. I mean, it may have been the fact that I was bent over my car in a skirt, but someone stopped.

'Hi, do you know—' When I turn and see who my knight in shining armor is, my jaw drops. 'Anything about cars...?' I finish my sentence, my heart beating at his crooked smile.

He parks a few spots up and across the street, walking to me with a grin. 'I know a little,' he says. 'What's going on?' Brooks stops in front of me, looking me up and down. 'Wow, so you just always look good?' He kisses my cheek before looking at my car engine.

'I'm late to play a soul into the afterlife, and my car won't start.'

He touches a few things in my engine before letting my hood drop. 'I can give you a lift.'

I don't have time to think this through, so I say yes and hop into his truck with my violin in my lap. I check my phone and see three new text messages, all from Dylan. Shit. I bet he's about to lose it because I haven't checked in. He has a particular process of ensuring the business runs smoothly, and irritation follows when I don't do my part.

I hit his contact. 'I need to make a call really quick.'

'Love Notes, this is Dylan.'

'Dyl, my car wouldn't start, but I am on my way to the Whitman funeral. Brooks is giving me a lift.'

'Long night?' he asks with a chuckle. 'You realize you're supposed to be there in fifteen minutes, right?'

'Yep, he's driving at the speed of light.' I turn away

from Brooks to ask about Dylan's night. 'Was your night not long, or did you drop her at home immediately after dinner?'

'I'm not a kiss-and-tell kind of man.'

'Yes, you are. But fine. I'll wait until I get back to the shop to find out what happened.'

'Go to your gig. You're not getting details. Ever.'

After I hang up, Brooks glances my way.

'I know a mechanic. I can arrange for him to pick up your car. He won't rip you off.'

'You'd do that?'

'Absolutely. I'll call him this afternoon. How'd the rest of your night go?'

'Oh, um... well, I went home to find River inside with a woman. I can't sleep through that, so I wandered the city for a while, the words of that tarot reader last night playing through my head repeatedly. Then I got caught in a thunderstorm while I walked to my brother's. There we, or *he*, read a letter my incarcerated father sent me after twenty-two years of no contact.'

'He wrote you a letter?' he asks in disbelief.

'Yep. He also shocked me with a collect call from prison. Somehow the guy found my address *and* number. How's that possible?' I look around his car, noticing the empty booster seat in the back. 'I thought you had your daughter this week?'

'She hangs out with Norah's little brother when I have to work. I dropped her off with him about fifteen minutes ago. They're going to the zoo.'

'You're working right now? Are you going to get in trouble for driving me to my gig?'

'No, I'm off right now, but I'm the lead on a growing case, so I'm on call until I start swing shift tomorrow. I was going home to sleep today, but you needing help seemed more important.'

'I'm keeping you from sleeping?'

'I can sleep anytime. I can't often woo a woman as beautiful as you.' He reaches over and touches my hand. 'Truth be told, I was hoping to run into you.'

My entire body settles with his touch. It could also be that the meds I took when I first realized how late I was earlier are kicking in too. Either way, I'm calm, and something about his presence is helping.

'I didn't expect you to distract me by being bent over the front of your car, but here we are.'

'Is that a complaint?'

'Not even a little bit,' he says with a chuckle. 'I'm excited to see you play again. Does the song match the life lived?'

'What, like "Stairway to Heaven" or "Highway to

Hell"? That would be perfect. But no. The most popular choice is "Ave Maria". I could play it on both piano and violin in my sleep.'

'How long have you been playing?'

'I was five when I started.'

'*Five?* The prodigy thing is true, then?'

'No,' I say, shaking my head. 'You're bound to get better when you play six to eight hours a day to escape the outside and inside of your head. I seriously practiced every spare moment I had. When I was a teenager, I got my first electric violin and would go to the Saturday market and busk. Those were my first gigs outside the school band. I felt like a rock star, and the tips were awesome.'

'My first gig was the high school talent show my sophomore year.'

'Really?' I ask with a grin. 'Did you win?'

'Did I win? You've seen me play,' he says with a wink. 'I'm kidding. Yes, we did win that year and every year after. My parents were horrified as they watched. I think they hoped we might play a hymn of some sort.'

'What did you play?'

'Uh, Rage Against the Machine.' He glances at me guiltily, yet he's obviously proud.

I burst out laughing. 'So, the opposite of a hymn. Please tell me it wasn't—'

'"Killing In the Name"?' He shakes his head. 'Almost. Then we realized how long Ty and I would be grounded, so instead, we dialed it back and went with "Renegades of Funk". Mostly because "funk" sounds like "fuck". Teenage boys, you know? We pushed those rules hard. And my parents reciprocated with long stints in solitary.'

'Solitary?'

'That's what we called groundings. If chores were the punishment, it was child labor. We were hellions.'

'I'm starting to see why the petition for heaven is necessary,' I joke. 'But look at you now, putting away drug dealers and murderers. You're out there making a difference in the world. I won't pretend I understand anything about parents or parenting, considering I didn't have any, but I'd think they'd be proud.'

'They're more tolerant than anything else. Mom calls me once a week to ensure I'm still alive; otherwise, she refuses to talk about my job. My parents aren't bad people. Just a tad "live the life we say, and all will be alright". And since I didn't want that life, they see a guy running with criminals all day, who has a child out of wedlock, hasn't been to church in years and has relations with women before I've put a ring on their finger. I'm the ultimate disappointment. My mother has even called my boss to tell him I'm too soft-hearted to deal with the people I am – and that she disagrees with me carrying a loaded firearm. "It's so dangerous. What if there's an accident?"' He mimics her with a single eyebrow lifted. 'My dad... well, he sneaks boxes of mini bibles into my truck every time I'm there, suggesting I hand them out to the criminals I come across. He also puts Bible verses in my sun-shades so I'll find them "right when I need them".'

I immediately flip down my sun visor, and a handful of paper strips with handwritten Bible verses fall into my lap.

'He's been putting them in the passenger side too?' Brooks asks, shocked. 'Holy hell, I bet those are for my dates.' He shakes his head in disbelief, readjusting his hat, which looked just fine from my seat. I think that's his nervous tic: fidgeting with the hat he nearly always wears.

Only the chapter and lines are written, so I pull out my phone and look one of the verses up.

Brooks's world was so different from mine. At their insistence, I go to midnight Mass on Christmas Eve with Ed and Carlos, and that's pretty much it. I do a blanket 'forgive me for the sins I've committed and ones I'm about to', and hope for the best.

'Ephesians 5:22.' I read what I've found through a Google search. '"Wives, submit yourselves to your husband as you do the Lord".'

I scrunch my face and glance over at him. 'I say the Lord's name a lot when I "submit",' I say, using air quotes. 'I'm guessing that's not what they mean?'

He shakes his head, an overly amused grin on his face. 'Sounds like you need a petition as well.'

'Oh, I'm going straight to hell, no questions asked, and I'm cool with it.'

Brooks laughs. 'Maybe I could request the room next to yours?'

'Perhaps we could *never* get married, have all the sex – but not for reproduction purposes – and then we could book a double room in the underworld's sin city?'

'*Or*, if you need some points with the big guy upstairs next time my dad gives me a box of bibles, I'll let you donate them to the homeless shelter for me.'

'You donate the bibles to the homeless?' I ask with a laugh. 'That seems right. Every time I drive by a homeless person, I think, you know what they *really* need? Something to read.'

Brooks bellows a laugh. 'Are you picking on me?'

'I'm just saying, try a bag of cheeseburgers next time, and you'd have eyes all over the city.'

I like the way he sincerely thinks my ridiculousness is funny.

'This it?' he asks, pulling into the parking lot of an ornate church where this service takes place.

'Yeah. Word to the wise: if I were you, I'd stay near the back; otherwise, you might end up "Bradley, the deceased's second cousin twice removed, here to pay your respects 'cause y'all go way back, but you can't remember anyone's name..." I've been there; it's uncomfortable.'

'Excellent advice. I would hate to bullshit my way through a conversation while standing in a church after just bad-mouthing the head guy. It'll be a miracle if we don't get struck by lightning as we walk in.'

Lucky for us, lightning doesn't strike – just the waft of carnations and incense hits us in the face as we walk in. The church's pianist, Genevieve, an older woman with gray hair piled on top of her head, greets me.

'I'll be back,' I say to Brooks, setting my bag on the back pew near him, then I follow Gen to the front of the sanctuary.

My partner for the morning starts to play after the priest's prayer. When I glance out at the mourners, I spot Brooks at the back of the room, standing against the wall, his hat in his hands and his eyes on me. I'm afraid to see his reaction to witnessing me play violin for the first time, so I close my eyes with my first note, focusing only on the song.

Genevieve and I have played this one dozens of times together, so it's almost like having Dylan next to me, reading my mind.

I open my eyes midway through the performance and instantly meet Brooks's gaze. He looks as mesmerized by me as I was by him that first night I saw him on guitar. No one has ever looked at me like this. It makes me warm and fuzzy inside. He steps forward, his hands on the back of the pew in front of him. When he finally notices me looking back at him, he smiles proudly. 'Wow,' he mouths, making me grin in return.

24

BROOKS

One hundred percent. That's how in love I just fell with this woman. I knew I was falling but didn't realize how far until right now. The way we click, her allowing herself to be vulnerable with me, how gorgeous she is, our brief history, I'm not sure which sealed the deal, but the second she started playing, lightning did strike. It resembled one of Norah's you-just-know moments, and I have no clue what to do with it now, but I like it.

I've got to figure this Nick thing out. I can't work with her estranged father. This could all take a turn for the worse and end with me being dumped again. For the first time, that terrifies me.

Mercy's phone is sitting on her purse and lights up

as I glance down at her things. I recognize the number on the screen. It's one of the phones at the prison. Nick's calling her *now*. I'd call and tell him to stop, but that's not how the prison works. If I answer her phone and say it, that'll blow up on me and not help Mercy. I can't get involved on her end. I have to talk to Seiver.

After the funeral, I drop Mercy off at her place, acting as if I got a work call that needs tending to. In reality, I'm pulling myself off the Alexander case. Seiver doesn't know yet, but considering I'm currently walking through the station towards his office, he will soon.

'What in the hell are you doing here? You bitch when I call you on your off time, then you come in when you're off to bother me. Why are you so complicated, Hudson?'

'I can't take Nick's case.'

He lowers the coffee cup that is nearly to his lips. 'Why?'

'Because I'm dating his daughter.'

'What?'

'Mercy Alexander, Travis. I know her. *Well*. I didn't know Nick was her father when you gave me his file. Now that I've figured it out, I can't do that to her. I can't work with a man who ruined her life so he can get parole. She's likely who he wants to make amends with, and I get the feeling that isn't something she wants.'

'You're dating Mercy Alexander?' he asks, still stuck on that. He sets his mug on his desk, sloshing coffee onto a stack of papers. 'Little eight-year-old Mercy? You're *dating* her?' he says in a near whisper.

'She's, uh... *thirty* now, but yes. We've been out a couple of times and talk daily.'

Travis drops his head into his hands with a groan. 'This happening is like lottery odds.'

'Maybe I'll buy a ticket on my way home.'

'You should.' He rubs his face with his hand. 'Shit. I swore to myself I'd never help that man.'

'To be clear, you'd be helping Mercy, not Nick.'

'What do you have on him so far?'

'Not much,' I say hesitantly. 'He's written and has been calling Mercy. I don't know what he wants to say, but you could find out. Then we try and convince her to testify against his parole. Besides our victims' families – who haven't been involved at all – she's the only one who can do it.'

'Will she do that?'

I lift my shoulders. 'That's what you need to find out.' I throw the words he's often used on me back at him, and by the look on his face, he doesn't enjoy that. 'I can't do it, Travis. She's only started to open up to me because he's harassing her after decades of zero contact. I haven't even told her I know yet.'

'Good. Pretend like you know nothing. I'll take care of Nick. You get to know her story and check in with me. When's his hearing?'

'He gave me some good info on Dominic's crew, so I got him a date two weeks away – *if* the tip pans out. You know how often that happens.'

'Fuck! Why must you be so good at your job?' He slams his fist on the desk, earning the attention of my co-workers in the bullpen. 'Sweet-talk her into telling you everything.'

'As much as I appreciate you giving me *one* compliment in the last decade, I can't deceive her by pretending I don't already know her entire story. I read the whole file last night.'

'Pretend you didn't and get her to talk, then read that letter.'

'I can't let her get hurt through this, Seiv. Not by me, you *or* Nick. *She's* my priority here.'

'Fell pretty hard, did ya?' he asks with a chuckle.

I nod.

'Then this should be no problem. I'll take the lead. You just casually collect information undercover like you always do.'

Precisely the words I was afraid he'd say.

25

MERCY

This time I'm on the pedestal while Dax and Hollyn sit a few feet from me, inspecting every detail of dress number four. I told Hols I'd happily comply with trying on five dresses, but that was it. I'm not spending all day here modeling every possibility.

'I think I like the last one best,' Hols says to Dax.

'They pretty much all look the same to me. I think our biggest choice is long or short,' Dax says.

'Not short, tea length – it's a wedding, not a prom,' Ed says, sitting next to Hols, his legs crossed and a champagne glass in his fingertips. 'This isn't it, sweetheart. If you go with the last one, it'll give the wedding a black-tie vintage-glam vibe. You can do so much with that. I see a softly lit room with a sea of candles.

Your maid of honor isn't upstaging the bride, and it'll be classically beautiful in a way your wedding photos won't look dated over the years. Plus, I can imagine this one wearing the last dress on gigs, and every time she puts it on, she'll think of your special day.'

Way to suck her in, Ed. Hollyn's gaze and mine meet in the mirror. 'He could sell a bad wig to a bald man and give him the confidence of George Costanza in a rug,' I say.

Ed laughs, nodding his head. 'I could, sugar. That last dress is the winner.'

'This is why I brought you,' Hols says enthusiastically. 'Put the last one back on,' she says to me.

'Thank God,' I say, glancing down at the dress I'm still in. 'I thought you were going to make me walk down the aisle looking like Morticia Addams.'

'Ohh.' Ed swoons, resting a hand on his chest. 'Morticia Addams! Halloween? *The Addams Family*? I'll be Morticia, Carls can be Gomez, and you can be Wednesday.'

I step down off the stool towards the dressing room. 'Maybe?'

'You're still doing a family costume for Halloween?' Hollyn asks. 'But you're seeing someone. Wouldn't you go for a couples' costume instead?'

'A couples' costume?' I ask like the words are entirely foreign. 'That sounds super lame.'

'We're doing a couples' costume.' She motions between her and Dax.

'Super lame for everyone else, I mean!' I attempt to save it, but it's too late by the look on her face. 'Why are we talking about Halloween when it's months away?'

'Because Edie brought it up, and you have a boyfriend now,' Hols rambles.

I shake my head. 'He's not my boyfriend. We're only on date number three. Plus, I haven't heard from him in a few days, so I don't even know when this date is happening.'

'I don't know the guy, but I've heard he's got a job that might keep him busy?' Dax suggests.

Hollyn nods, agreeing with him like he's the most intelligent person on the planet. Ugh. Love.

'Thank you, Captain Obvious. His work schedule changed. Maybe he's changed it on purpose? To avoid me.'

'Oh boy,' Ed says, downing his champagne with one swallow.

'He's not ghosting you,' Hols says reassuringly. 'He'd be an absolute idiot.'

'Well, duh, but must I remind you my "dating" pool consists primarily of idiots.'

'When you have a type...' Dax says with a smirk. I shoot him a glare.

'He's not like that. At least, I didn't think he was. Maybe things changed when I told him about my past?'

'So, he knows your past,' Ed says as if it's no big deal, taking the skirt in my hands – to prevent me from tripping over it – and coaxing me towards the dressing room. 'Everyone has a past, Merc.'

I step into the dressing room, making sure the entire black lacy skirt makes it inside with me.

Before Ed closes the door, he leans in, his fatherly face on full display. 'You're afraid to get hurt, so you're self-sabotaging again. Stop believing you're not enough because you absolutely are for the right person. So, you like him. Hell, you might even love him, and if I know you, that scares the crap out of you. Why not face those feelings head-on? But do *not* convince yourself he's disappearing from your life because he knows parts of your past. Be patient, give him a chance and see if he's got it in him?'

'Was that the long way of saying you think *I* should call *him*?'

Ed laughs. 'It sure was. Call while you change before I drink this entire bottle of champagne. I have a show tonight. You know how I am when I'm tipsy. I get all loosey-goosey with my words, and next thing you know, my set becomes a one-woman show.'

'The kind where you pretend like you're Oprah. I remember that night. I thought you'd lost your magic.'

'Oh, sugar. That'll never happen. Now, chop chop.' He claps his hands before shutting the door, leaving me inside with his words – all that made complete sense.

I grab my phone from my purse. I'll just call and tell him our third date is tonight. Maybe he likes women who don't follow the typical dating rules. I mean, he must if he likes me. What will we do, though? The only thing that comes to mind is The RoseWood. Not everyone is cool watching a stage full of men in sparkling costumes drop it like it's hot. If he's one of those, it'd be best to know now because I could never let a man into my life who didn't respect my brother in all his glory. He doesn't have to know the head queen is Edie. At least not until I witness his reaction to the show.

'Hey, Merc,' Brooks answers immediately, and his voice sends a spark down my spine. He sounds happy to hear from me. 'What's up? I'm working, so I've got to make this fast.'

'What time are you off tonight?'

'Midnight.'

'Will you be too tired to do anything else?'

'That would depend on what we're doing.'

'Date three. If you're up for it.'

He laughs softly into the phone. 'You *really* want to get me in bed, don't you?'

'Yes, so if you complied, this would be much easier. Meet me—'

'Ah, no. Third date – *I* pick you up again. Be outside your building at half after midnight.'

I like that he insists on being a gentleman. 'It's a date,' I say, a nervous laugh leaving my lips.

'Merc—'

'Yeah?'

'You just made my whole week better.'

There's such a fluttering in my chest I can hardly breathe. I don't know what to say. No one's ever said I made their whole week better.

'I think you just made my heart beat, whatever that means.'

'I can't wait to find out. See you tonight, Mercy.'

'See ya.' I slide the phone down my neck to my chest, staring into the mirror.

The curtain opens suddenly, and Hollyn steps in. 'What are you doing? I've been calling your name. Are you – *smiling* at yourself?' She glances between me and my reflection in the mirror. 'Did Edie give you champagne?'

'He said I made his whole week better.'

'Who?'

'Brooks Hudson.'

Hollyn laughs a casual laugh that turns into a full-on swoon as she closes the curtain and shuts us in the dressing room together.

'You're in here giddy over him? What happened?'

'Ed said to call, tell him we're going out tonight, and to stop self-sabotaging. So, I did.'

'Call him? Or stop self-sabotaging?'

'Both?' I lift my shoulders. 'I dunno. I *really* like him, Hols.'

'What's that mean?' she asks excitedly.

'Like I'm excited to see him and learn more about him. I'm not even afraid to continue talking about myself. The way he looks at me like he'd protect me from anything, I like it.'

'I never thought I'd see this side of you.' Hollyn sighs sweetly. I'm speaking her love language, and I knew she'd enjoy that. 'You deserve to feel like this; you realize that, right?'

'I'm starting to?'

Her gaze moves to the dress we all decided was the

one. 'Ed's right; this is it. How gorgeous do you look too?'

'Very,' I say with a laugh.

'You're good with this one, then?'

'It's perfect. I may even wear it again.'

She smiles wide. 'You can do this, Merc. Having feelings for someone can be amazing – if you let it.'

* * *

'Having feelings for someone can be amazing,' I say to myself, mimicking Hollyn as I pace in front of my building. 'Except my heart feels like it's packed its shit and is ready to move in with Brooks Hudson, and that's scary.'

I hear his truck before I see him. Brooks blows the horn, making me jump and laugh simultaneously.

'Hey,' I say as I get in. 'How was wor—'

He kisses me, shutting me up instantly. My brain blinks like a static television. He pulls away with a wide smile. 'Date three, you get a hello kiss. And work didn't compare to having you in my passenger seat. My partner's not this pretty.'

I laugh. 'Hell's bells, you are good at this romance stuff. But you've got some serious dating rules. It's almost like you're an adult who knows what he's looking for and won't accept anything less. That's a language I don't speak.'

'They say immersion learning is the easiest way to learn languages; perhaps you'll pick it up? You seem pretty smart.'

'I have my moments. Here's my idea for tonight. I'll show you my favorite spot in the city, and you show me yours.'

'Show me yours, and I show you mine, huh?' He lifts a single eyebrow, his hand on the back of my seat as he thinks about this. He's parked along the curb, so the only light is from the streetlights above. 'Apartments not included, right?'

'No, we can't choose our apartments or each other's as our favorite places.'

'Deal.'

'The only thing is I have to go first 'cause mine is a business that closes in three hours.'

'Interesting, alright, well, direct me there.'

I make him park a block away, not telling him which business we're going to because there are multiple still open on this road. He opens my door, then offers his hand as we walk down the sidewalk.

This feels like a proper date. One like I've never experienced before, and I can't wait to discover what happens next.

'Is this...'. He steps back, glancing up at the building we're getting ready to walk into. 'The drag place?'

'Yeah. The RoseWood,' I confirm. 'It's a family business.'

'Like the Mexican restaurant owned by family, but you're not Hispanic?'

'Exactly like that.'

'I've never been here before,' he admits.

'You're going to love it.'

His thumb grazes over my hand in his. 'You could have taken me to a train yard, and as long as your hand was in mine, I'd love every second. Let's go.'

26

BROOKS

'Mercy!' The person working the bar beams at the sight of her. 'Oh,' they say, overly interested in who I am, looking me up and down and not attempting to hide it. 'Who is this, doll-face?'

'Geoff, this is Brooks. Brooks, this is Geoff with a G. He's the manager.'

'Nice to meet you, Geoff, with a G.'

The two of us shake hands while he gives Mercy an approving look. Geoff hands Mercy two drinks that seem ready fast, considering we just walked in. The place is loud; the music's bass beats through my entire body, practically forcing my heart to beat in sync. People are at every table, chatting, drinking and enjoying themselves.

'I reserved your favorite spot,' Geoff tells her excitedly. 'He's expecting you, so hurry, or you're going to hold up his entire set, and you know how he gets...'

'Dramatic,' Mercy says with a chuckle.

'Exactly,' Geoff says, waving us away from him.

She turns towards me, waggling her eyebrows, a sly grin on her face as she hands me a drink. 'You've really never been here before?' she asks, nodding for me to follow her.

'I've driven by but never been in, no,' I say, a little nervous as we walk to the other side of the room, across the front of the stage, stopping at a table with a reserved sign on it. Mercy slides into the swanky retro booth, and I do the same, meeting her in the middle of the curve.

'You seem well known here,' I say, glancing up at the dark stage. 'Is that the case for every club in town or—'

'Definitely "or". We've now visited the only two clubs that I know anyone in. This place is special, though, because my favorite person owns it. And in about two minutes, you're going to "meet" them.'

I grin, lifting an arm and laying it across the back of the booth behind her, my fingers brushing against her shoulder. She scoots closer to me, leaning into my shoulder. The woman lights my insides on fire with the flash of a smile. Having her this close, I have to remind myself even to breathe.

New music starts and the stage illuminates briefly. The place has top-of-the-line lighting, a sound system that vibrates the floors, and costumes you'd expect to see at a risqué Broadway show. Men in drag dance themselves into place, then boom, all on-stage movement stops, and the entire room goes so dark you couldn't see your hand in front of your face if you wanted to. I do feel Mercy's hand on my thigh, though. I lay my hand over hers, and she grips it tightly.

A tall, brown-skinned queen in the highest stiletto platform heels I've ever seen, wearing a long robe-type dress that sparkles like diamonds under the flashing lights now pulsating through the room, struts across the floor, stopping center stage. A single spotlight on her as she throws a hand onto her hip, pointing right at Mercy with her free hand. I glance over at her, a smile stretching ear to ear on her face.

'Guuuurls,' the queen says, dragging out the word, a headset mic blasting her voice through the room. 'My little sister is here on a date, and don't you think I'm not calling her booty out on it. This is sugar's *first* third date, y'all. Say "hey, Mercy"!' The last three words all share the same 'ay' sound, making the room bubble with laughter.

The room echoes her, yelling, 'Hey, Mercy,' precisely as she's instructed.

Mercy laughs, lifting her free hand in the air with a wave.

'I wish you luck, sir.' The queen's finger moves to me. 'Don't hurt her, or you'll find out just what kind of damage a size thirteen stiletto heel can do,' she says, obnoxiously winking my way.

All eyes are now on us, but Mercy doesn't seem to mind. The performer struts away from us, stopping midway back of the center stage. The room goes completely black again, the music stopping suddenly, leaving a ripple of silence. With the drop of the first beat, lights flash, and the queen is front and center. She drops her robe, revealing a sparkling, low-cut dress – the room roars.

'And that's my brother,' Mercy says. 'Up until about six months ago, I lived with him and his husband, Carlos, who owns Tequila Mockingbird.'

Carlos, her brother-in-law, owns the Mexican place. All the little details of her life I didn't know are now falling into place, and I find myself liking her more and more.

'Yes, you heard that right. I lived with my brother until I was thirty. When you go as long as I did feeling like no one gave a shit, you hang on tight to those who do. I was afraid to live alone, so he kicked me out like any good brother-father and forced me to face something that scared me.' Her face goes serious. 'Ed's the most important person in my life, and if he hates you, I'm sorry to say that means I have to hate you. Those are the rules.'

I pull my arm from the back of the chair and grab her hand. 'He's not going to hate me,' I whisper into her ear. 'I like you way too much to allow that to happen.'

'This doesn't freak you out?' she asks, a hint of worry in her voice.

She didn't run after hearing I had a daughter or unsuspectingly met my ex-wife – I still need to explain that – so knowing her brother moonlights as a drag queen is alright in my book.

'Not even a little bit. This is easily the coolest thing I've ever done in this city. If anything, it makes me like you more, and I'm a little freaked out by that,' I say, only partly kidding.

After thirty minutes of us watching the most elaborate drag show I've ever seen with a light performance, water raining from the ceiling and choreography that seems impossible for a guy as tall as her brother, the music fades, and the lights come up to where you can see around the room again.

'He wants to meet you,' she says. 'You up for it?'

'Wait.' I grab her arm with a laugh. 'You gotta give me tips,' I say. 'Pronouns, do I call him Edie? Does he have a stage name he wants to go by? Is it "he", "she", "him", "her", "they", or something else? Don't let me mess this up, Mercy.' I laugh nervously. 'I'd never be able to live with myself if you have to hate me.'

She bites her bottom lip through the growing smile on her face. 'When he's at the club in full costume, she's Mz Edee. Otherwise, he's a he, and unless he's here, he looks like a normal guy, only in designer clothes that cost more than my best violin,' she says. 'If you like me, you'll love Edie 'cause he's the good side of me on steroids. Ready?' she asks, scooting from the booth.

I nod, blowing out a nervous breath. If Edie hates me, I will literally die of a broken heart at this point.

'Come on,' she says, extending her hand my way. We make our way backstage. Every other step we take, someone calls her name, excited by her presence, giving me the once-over as I follow her lead.

'Give me one sec,' she says, knocking on a dressing-room door. The name Mz Edee is on a plaque across the top. She opens the door, peeking her head in. 'You decent?'

'Get in here,' a man's voice calls back. She looks

back at me, opening the door and allowing me to walk into a dressing room decorated in all blacks, pinks, purples and blues. Edie walks out from behind a dressing screen, the sparkling robe he lost before his show now wrapped and tied tightly around his waist.

'I can't believe I'm meeting a man you're dating...?' he says to her, partially under his breath, kissing her on each cheek before moving to me, stopping right in front of me and looking me over. 'You like her?' he asks, his face going solemn. Fatherly almost, and I'm the guy taking out his daughter.

'Only a little more every day.'

A grin grows on his face as he and Mercy exchange looks. 'She's kind of a man-eater,' he says. 'You up for that? Girl's a *chall-enge*.' He laughs joyfully – enjoying busting her balls intentionally. 'A mouth like a sailor and stubborn as they come. If you want her to do something—' he looks over at her, his eyes narrowed '—she ain't going to do it.'

'Ed!' she says like she's embarrassed.

I like these two together. I can see the similarities between them. They may not look alike, but they definitely share DNA.

'She's already warned me,' I tell him.

'Oh, she's told you? Is that so?' he asks, strutting

towards a lit-up vanity covered in bottles and potions. 'Now you're warning the boys that you're difficult?'

'I use the word "complicated" – it sounds less crazy.'

He rolls his eyes playfully. 'I'm still trying to figure out where I went wrong with her. My only defense is that I was young,' he says, glancing at me through the vanity mirror as he sits down.

'Whatever you did or didn't do, I think she's perfect,' I tell him.

Mercy visibly swoons, her smile enticing one from me as well.

'*Perfect?* Really?' Edie asks, dropping his jaw open as they exchange looks.

'Told ya,' she says to him like they've discussed me.

'You're not gonna hurt her, are you?' he asks, now looking at me through the mirror.

'Ed,' she hisses at him, jabbing him in the shoulder.

'Hurting Mercy isn't in my plans,' I say.

'I'm using your bathroom real quick,' Mercy says, walking away from us.

Shit. This is where he interrogates me, right? I haven't met a woman's family in a very long time. I don't remember how it works. Ed motions me over to him, waving me closer when I get there. I lean into him.

'You're the cop, right?'

I nod.

'Don't let anything happen to her. She's not as strong as she lets on,' he says in the same whisper.

'I promise.'

'Good!' he says, pulling bobby pins from the front of his wig. 'You've got my blessing, now go, date, giggle, bang.' He rolls his eyes like the word physically pained him to say. 'Whatever it is you do, love.'

'Ew,' Mercy says, exiting the bathroom and smacking him playfully. 'We gotta run; it's Brooks's turn to show me his favorite place in Portland now.'

Ed gasps, a hand on his chest. 'Darling, am *I* your favorite place?'

'You know you are,' she says to him as she leads me out of his dressing room. 'I'll see ya later!'

'I like him,' I say as we walk through the club.

'I think he liked you too.'

'Whew.' I wipe my brow exaggeratedly, watching her smile. 'I was seriously worried.' I pull open the door for her. 'Now I can relax again. My turn?'

'Yes,' she says enthusiastically.

'Gotta warn ya, my place isn't nearly as fun as yours.'

'Will you be there?'

'Yep.'

'Then it'll be a blast.'

The Vera Katz Eastbank Esplanade is a walking/running/biking trail along the river with floating paths and bridge walkways. It's my favorite time to be here when no one is in the middle of the night.

Mercy holds my hand tightly as we walk the trail, stopping at the stairs that lead to one of the floating paths. I sit on the top stair, patting the spot next to me. She sits down, staring out into the city lights.

'I've never been here,' she says. 'It's gorgeous. Why's this your favorite place?'

'Sometimes when I can't sleep – and need a break from work – I come down here and wander. The lack of people at night, the cool air, the life of the city sparkling across the river, and the water all calm me.'

'I can see that.' She takes a deep breath, blowing it out slowly.

We sit silently for a moment, staring across the river into downtown. I knew I'd have to confess what I've been up to with her father, but it feels like the moment is now.

'Mercy, I need to talk to you about something.'

She sucks in a breath, leaning forward with her

hands tucked under her legs like she's expecting bad news. I hope that's not what this turns out to be.

'I, uh... I work with inmates who can help my cases – folks who want to make deals by ratting out their friends. Recently my boss gave me a file he never wanted to look at again. This one is a man hoping to get early parole. I met with him once, and as you and I got to know one another, the pieces of my case and how you are involved started falling together.'

'I'm involved?' she asks, glancing wide-eyed at me.

I decide not to beat around the bush and clear this up. 'My newest informant is Nicholas Alexander.'

She glances over at me, her brow furrowed. 'Nicholas Alexander?' She sighs heavily. '*My* Nick Alexander?' she asks nervously.

'Yes. I didn't know at the time what I know now, but I can tell you this – even Seiver doesn't want to be in the same building as that man.'

She scrunches her face. 'Then you know about my past?'

'I do. But I chose to pull myself from the case, so I'll never bring it up again unless you *want* to talk to me about it.'

'You pulled yourself from the case? Have you ever done that before?' she asks, glancing at me curiously.

'I haven't. But I knew this situation was different,

and with the emotions swirling through me lately, I felt wrong helping a man who took so much from you.'

The way she lets out a relieved sigh says I did the right thing here – both in pulling myself off the case and with telling her.

'You met him?'

'I did.'

'How, uh, how was he?'

'You want the truth?'

She nods, but her face screams she's not sure.

'He made me uncomfortable, and I meet with inmates all the time.'

'Nick's scary?'

'Very.'

'Twenty-two years behind bars hasn't changed much, then.'

'I didn't know him before, so I'm not sure, but Seiver sure doesn't think he's a prisoner reformed.'

'Can he get early parole?'

I drop my head. 'Unfortunately, before I knew you were directly involved in this case, I did secure him a date to attempt early parole.'

'You did?' she asks, clearly worried.

'Merc.' I lean into her, an arm around her. 'I'm

going to do everything I can to ensure that doesn't happen. Seiver is working on exactly that.'

'You're still looking at me the same way you did.'

'Of course I am. Why wouldn't I?'

'My dad is a murderer, Brooks. Shouldn't you be running from me?'

'I'm not running.'

'Why?'

'Mostly because I'm falling for you instead.'

She stares at me, her mouth open slightly and a hint of a nervous smile. 'You're pretty sweet, you know that?'

'Only for you.'

'Honestly, since you already know I might as well talk about it. I've felt so lost since he started contacting me. Now I find out you are involved in all this, which truthfully makes me feel a little safer. A cop is watching out for me and knows exactly what I'm running from; that feels good. Until now, until you, I've felt really alone in all this. Dylan thinks I'm letting Nick ruin my life from behind bars by allowing the memories to haunt me and refusing to heal, but how does one heal after that? I've been trying for two decades.'

'Mercy, I read the file. That kind of trauma lingers for a lifetime. It's going to haunt me. I can't be a part of why that monster gets out. I'd rather protect you from that asshole than help gain his freedom again.' I lean forward, my elbows on my knees, as I fidget with a loose string in my jeans.

'You want to protect me?' The surprise in her voice, it's absolutely adorable. Like she'd never considered someone feeling that way about her.

'Yeah. Protect you, date you, woo you. I want to do all of it.'

She nods slowly, glancing out at the city while she thinks.

'You're really not scared of this?' she asks. 'What if a drug-dealing murderer is in my blood?'

'I don't think that's genetically passed down.' I pull her hand to my lips, her gaze meeting mine. 'My main concern – is that you come out of this OK.'

She's quiet for a long time before leaning forward with me and sliding her hand over my thigh to meet mine. 'Before I become attached to you and admit I feel the same, I need to *see* Nick.'

'You want to *see* him?'

'I have to. I've got some demons I need to give back to him.'

27

MERCY

My alarm goes off, pissing me off immediately. I reach for my phone but realize an arm around me is holding me back. I glance over at Brooks, sleeping soundly next to me. My God, he's cute. He came home with me last night. Since Mother Nature is still knocking on my door, we lay down to watch another episode of *The Winchesters* in my room, and now we're waking up together. I glance under the covers at myself, fully clothed. Whew. Nervously I glance over at him. He's still wearing everything but his shoes.

I veer out of his arms, grab my phone from my purse on the floor, and shut off the alarm.

'What time is it?' he asks groggily, dragging a hand down his face.

'Eight.'

He opens his eyes as I lie back down next to him, now facing him. 'Hey, gorgeous,' he says with a half-awake grin, wrapping his arms around me.

'Did we literally sleep together last night?'

Brooks glances at himself, then at me. 'Looks that way.'

'I've never stayed all night with a guy and woken up still fully clothed.'

'Welcome to marriage.'

I laugh. 'It couldn't have been all bad,' I say, tracing the tattoos down his arm with my fingertips. 'You stayed for eleven years.'

'True,' he says, sliding a hand over my waist and pulling me closer to him. 'But this is better.'

'Most guys wouldn't have stayed the night without getting laid.'

''Tis my first time as a single dude.' His voice is soft and sleepy, and it's doing things to my insides that I like.

'We just popped one another's fully clothed sleep-over cherries.'

'I think we did,' he says with a laugh. His fingers brush against my hand as he moves them up my arm to my neck. 'That's gotta mean something, right?'

'Like what?' I ask slowly, hoping he kisses me, but kind of not because of morning breath.

His thumb grazes my jawline, sending sparks through me. 'I like you way more than I expected to, and every time I look at you, that grows a little more.'

'Is that all that grows?'

He laughs softly, pulling me closer. 'I think you know it's not.'

'Ah... yes, I see now,' I say, feeling something against me, and I'm pretty sure it's not like.

'Merc, I'm falling so hard I'm starting to worry you're close to dumping me. I've never worried about that before because I never saw it coming.'

I shake my head. 'I've no idea why women are dumping you. You're the perfect man.'

'I see you exactly the same way.'

'I am the perfect man, aren't I?' I joke.

Right then, he kisses me sweetly and almost innocently. Afterward, he kisses my forehead and rolls over, sitting up on my bed and grabbing his boots, reminding me that date three never made it to third base, and now it's over. But I'm not unhappy?

'An 8 a.m. alarm. You got somewhere to be this morning?' he asks.

I glance at my phone again. Eight ten. 'Yeah, I have

lessons starting at nine, then Dylan and I have a performance as Violated tonight.'

'Oh yeah?' he asks, glancing at me over his shoulder, seemingly interested.

'Yeah,' I confirm, leaving my bed and walking into my closet, his eyes on me the whole time. Which is a tad embarrassing considering I'm wearing rainbow leggings, a T-shirt that says *How About No*, and zero bra. My C-size girls *need* a bra at all times. 'I can leave you tickets at will-call if you want to come?'

He stands, his boots now tied on his feet. He grabs the black Nike baseball cap off the top of my lamp where he put it to bed last night. I watch as he slips it on his head backward before walking my way.

'Oh, no, mister. Ya can't do that.'

'What?' he asks, slipping his hands around my waist from behind me.

'Your hat.'

'What about it?'

'When you wear it like that, I hear Mariah Carey's "Fantasy" playing in my head.'

'Am I the Ol' Dirty Bastard?'

'Only if we can re-title you as the Old Dirty Bastard I Want to Do.'

He cocks his head like he's considering it. 'I don't hate the idea.' He glances around the closet we're now standing in, his eyes stopping on my shoe wall. 'Wow...' He steps away from me. 'We may have more in common than you think. You like heels?'

'Do *you*?' I ask, lifting an eyebrow.

'Hats,' he says. 'Ball caps are my thing; I've easily got a dozen hanging in perfect rows in my closet.'

'You have a hat wall?'

'It's not as eye-catching as your shoe wall.'

'Now I'm excited to see it,' I say, flipping through my clothes.

'Me too,' he says seductively. 'Are we choosing to-day's pair?'

'*We?*' I ask, but his attention is now on my shoes. 'Do you want to pick my shoes today, Brooks?'

'I do. I want to pick your shoes today. Is that weird?' he asks, rubbing his ink-covered hands in front of his chest with anticipation.

'First a foot rub in the hot tub, now you're drooling over picking my shoes. I think you might have a foot fetish.'

'The only feet I fetishize are the ones attached to this smoking hot violinist I met recently.'

'So, the ones from the hot tub?'

He turns to me, squinting one eye open, a smile that screams he's messing with me. 'Was that you?'

'Ha ha... yes, you may pick my shoes.' I pull a dress

from the closet, holding it in front of me. 'They must either match or completely outstage this. Those are the two shoe rules.'

'Can do...' Brooks scans the wall, taking his time, occasionally referencing the dress I'm still holding. 'These.' He picks up a pair and holds them like they're made of diamonds. 'Yeah?'

The dress he's choosing shoes for is a periwinkle blue wrap dress with an irregular ruffle hemline that hits just below my knees in the back but shows them off in the front. The shoes I'm looking at are pastel floral-print peep-toe stilettos. Not only does the blue in them match the dress perfectly, but I haven't worn these in forever.

'Excellent choice, good sir. If you come to my show tonight, you'll see them in action.'

'I work noon to midnight, but I could probably escape for a long lunch if nothing major happens. What time is it?'

'Eight. Don't feel like you *have* to come if you're busy. I just thought I'd extend the invitation.'

'I *want* to come. In so many ways,' he says with a laugh that makes his cheeks pink. 'I threw that last part in just to appease your dirty mind, which I love.'

'Dirty Mercy appreciates that.'

'I'll do my best to be there tonight.'

The first time the Matthews family showed up to one of my performances, I cried. My brother and Carlos were there too, and Penny made a massive deal out of it. I was following in her musically talented footsteps. Kind of. But that wasn't what it was for me. They showed up – for *me*. And they've been showing up ever since. It's all I ever wanted from my parents. If Brooks walks into that theater tonight while on shift, my heart may finally come off life support.

He stares into my eyes in a way that I'd usually find wholly uncomfortable, but with him, it's not. 'I should go. You have a busy day, and I need to do my first walk of shame.'

I laugh. 'What part shamed you the most?' I ask, following him from my room to my front door. 'It was Aunt Flo's presence for me,' I say as he exits my apartment, leaving me standing in my open doorway.

'I have zero shame. I've never slept so well in my life.' He moves closer to me, static buzzing between us. 'Wanna rain-check third base to a home run on date four?'

'Yes, I do.'

'Perfect,' he says, finishing his sentence with a kiss. 'I'll get that demon-purging appointment set up and let you know.'

My stomach drops thinking about facing Nick.

Even so, I still want to go through with it. I feel like the only way I'll understand what Brooks Hudson is doing to my heart is to finally deal with my past and hopefully leave it behind bars.

'I'll see you tonight,' he says, kissing my forehead.

Dylan's door swings open as I watch Brooks walk down the hall. My heart is floating on cloud number nine, but the giddiness he's left in my chest sizzles out like a campfire in the rain in Dylan's presence.

'An overnight guest *and* public displays of affection? Things must be going well.'

'Where's *your* overnight guest?'

He laughs, closing the door behind him and locking his apartment. 'She respects work hours.'

'Ha ha. I'll be there on time; I'm already halfway ready.' That's not even a lie; my clothes are picked, and that's half the battle.

* * *

Not long after I get to the shop, the best-dressed little girl in the northwest smiles at me excitedly with her ukulele in hand, strumming the chords we learned recently.

'You've been practicing.'

Her uncle laughs. 'I don't think she's put the thing down in a week.'

'Well, I can tell,' I say, kneeling to her level. 'You're easily my best ukulele student.'

'Really?' she asks, beaming with pride.

'Yep. Ready to get started on the next part?'

'Yes!'

Uncle Nate leaves us to practice, and just like last week, she catches on quickly. As we practice the song of my day-mares, I mentally jot down all the feelings coming up for me so I can add them to a letter I plan to write to Nick. Maybe I won't be able to say the things I want out loud, and if that happens, I will torment him with my own written words. Two can play that game.

'Your shoes are pretty,' Ali says as we wind down.

'Well, thank you,' I say, glancing down at them. 'A friend picked them out today. I love your floral tights and boots. You're the most fashionable six-year-old I've ever met.'

'Miss Mercy?' she asks softly while she plays.

'Yeah?'

'After this, do you think we could learn the sunshine song?'

'The sunshine song?'

She nods excitedly. 'My daddy sings it to me when I have bad dreams.'

I'm not sure which song she's referring to. 'Sing it for me?'

Her sweet little voice sings through only one line, and that's all it takes for me to know exactly what she's talking about and play it with her.

She beams. 'Yeah!'

Her dad sings it to her when she has bad dreams. How freaking adorable is that? Hugely so, and nothing like my life as a little girl. My eyes were usually open when I had terrible dreams, and no one ever came to rescue me from them.

'We sure can, sweetie. Do you know what would be fun? To keep it a secret – you can surprise him at your first recital.'

'What's a recital?'

'Every six months, we have a show with all our students. We'll invite your family and have snacks, and you'll play the songs you've been working on. Wouldn't it be fun to surprise your daddy with the sunshine song?'

'Yes!' she squeals. 'But what kind of snacks?'

'A girl after my own heart, worrying about the snacks. They're good ones, I promise.'

Can this girl get any cuter?

28

BROOKS

I blow out another long sigh after the last one goes unnoticed. Yes, I'm being a needy bitch this afternoon.

Andrews glances at me from the passenger seat with a roll of his eyes. 'If you're going to assault my ears, just do it already.'

'We're taking a late lunch,' I tell him. 'I got a thing.'

'Pretty sure the thing you got is work...'

'A different thing.'

'Stop here,' he says, pointing at the Sesame Donuts shop we're just about to drive past. I pull in, park, and watch him walk in. He samples as many donuts as possible before walking out with a box and a brown paper bag.

I'm not planning on telling him details about what's happening between Mercy and me. That would be disturbing, considering he acts as if people pay him to hang out with me. Which is technically accurate, but I know he likes hearing my bullshit deep down. I can tell.

I need his opinion on whether or not it's possible to feel what I feel after such a short time of Mercy and me knowing one another again. Sure, we spent some time in one another's beds years ago, but even so, this feels *so* different. Even what I once felt about Norah can't compare. Andrews has been married for over twenty years. Surely he's got some knowledge and wisdom about the emotions I'm questioning.

When he gets in, he tosses me the brown paper bag.

'What's this?'

'Those are donut holes to fill your word hole, so maybe there will be more chewing than talking.'

I laugh, opening the bag and popping one in my mouth. 'Not gonna work,' I say, now talking with a full mouth. 'You're my work wife, remember? We've farted in front of one another. My manners flew out the window years ago.' I waggle my eyebrows, now pulling out of our spot and heading to the day's destination – a park where my child plays. Isn't that grand? Drug deals happen in the worst places.

Nick's tip that Seiver is making me follow up on is that one of Dominic's dealers is doing big drug drops with rivals at this park. In the drug world, playing both sides of the fence isn't the smartest thing anyone could do. But it happens, and today is supposed to be a drop day; if it happens, Nick's advice could help trigger his early parole. Just thinking about him getting out of jail makes my stomach hurt.

'I told my actual wife your work wife joke, and she volunteered to fill in,' Andrews says, glaring my way.

I laugh out loud. 'Your wife thinks I'm cute, does she?' I ask, stopping at a red light. 'Think she likes me more than you?'

'Yeah, let's discuss it in detail, shall we?' he grumbles, shoving a donut into his mouth. 'Let me ask you,' he says with a mouth full. 'Does your lady friend think you're funny?'

I shrug. 'She laughs when I tell jokes.'

'Then what's the problem? If you can make her laugh, you're halfway there.'

'Halfway where?'

'To convincing her to fall in love with you, moron. I'm assuming that's what all the heavy sighing was about? You're already in love with her and want my opinion? Here it is: I've never met a woman who fell for a guy who couldn't make her laugh.' He shoves the rest of his donut in his mouth.

I jump when a horn behind me honks as the light turns green. Even considering being in love with Mercy has my head on an entirely different planet. I hit the gas, readjusting the cap I'm wearing.

'I can't believe they let you drive a fucking police car,' Andrews grumbles.

Should I tell him her story so he can help with Nick? I know he hates hearing about cases involving kids, but with the right amount of anger, maybe we can make sure this asshole stays in jail where he belongs.

'Seiver saved her when she was eight.'

'What?' he asks. This gets his attention in a way that even halts the donut en route to his mouth.

'Her dad, Nick Alexander – our newest snitch – was a dealer. Typical story, drug deal went bad, someone pulled the trigger, he fled, she was in the house when it happened.'

Andrews stares at me blankly, rage slowly taking over. 'You serious?'

I nod, grabbing another donut hole from the bag

in my lap. 'She watched while it happened, then called 911, and tried to help after the victim's friend *and* her father fled. Unfortunately, the guy didn't make it, and Dad got fifty years in the slammer.'

His stare is deadly as he processes my words. 'Jesus, fuck-ing, Christ,' he snarls.

If one thing can get a rise out of Andrews, it's innocent kids involved in a case. He was on a raid years ago, before I was even a cop, that didn't go as planned, and one of the two children involved didn't make it out. The dealer got wind police were headed his way and set the house on fire with the kids inside. Andrews tried desperately to save them both and nearly killed himself in the process. He's even got a scar on one arm where he was burned that night – a permanent reminder. Seiver warned me when I was paired with him not to bring it up or ask questions. Here I am, reminding him.

The fifteen-minute drive is now silent. Neither of us even eats. I pull into the park and back into a hidden spot against some trees. A playground is to my left, an empty soccer field directly in front of me, and a parking lot on the other side of the soccer field surrounded by trees is where we're expecting our guys to be. It's empty now, but that doesn't mean much.

'Is she OK... now?' Andrews asks, concern on his face.

'With that, no. But she's trying to work through it. When I figured all this out, I was tempted to drive down to that prison and tell Nick how I felt about what he did to her. Instead, I asked Seiver to take back the case. I can't be the lead, but he insists I still do this side of it. When I told Mercy, she admitted she wants to talk to him. Nick. Face to face.'

'You told her that was a bad idea?'

'That's not for me to decide. She's a full-grown woman. Whatever she feels she needs to do, I will support. I made the appointment before we left.'

He side-eyes me momentarily, both of us glancing at the lot we're watching as a car drives in slowly.

'That our guy?'

'Possibly?' We're silent for a few while we watch the car. 'Can I ask you something personal?'

'No.'

'How'd you know your wife was the one?'

He shakes his head. 'I dunno – 'cause she told me she was?'

I roll my eyes. 'I'm serious. There must've been something about her besides her uncanny ability to get you to do what she wants that you fell in love with.'

'I hate that you pretend like we're friends.' He shoves another donut in his mouth, chewing slowly and loudly. 'I got sick once, and you know how I feel about going to the doctor.'

That I do; he was an anxiety-ridden mess for days on end when he needed a colonoscopy recently – he tried to cancel it at work one day until I threatened to call and tell his wife.

'My appendix was close to bursting, and she brought me to the hospital, then never left my side even though she was supposed to leave on vacation that day with her parents.'

'Romantic. Are you saying you just knew?'

'Like a sledgehammer into the sternum.'

'That's... beautiful,' I say, fidgeting with my hat again. Is that what I feel?

'Do *you* just know?' he asks, suddenly more interested in the conversation than he expected.

I glance at him, nodding my head. 'It's not as violent as yours, but I think I do.'

My eyes move back to the car we're watching. The driver's side door opens, and a man gets out. He looks around, tosses a cigarette onto the ground, then walks towards the bathrooms.

I throw the bag of donuts at Andrews.

'Watch my back,' I say. 'If this guy is here to do an

exchange, Nicholas Alexander gets parole. I can't let that happen.' I exit the SUV and make my way to the bathrooms.

Luckily, I have to pee because I've found that working up a piss when I need to follow someone into a public bathroom isn't as easy as one might think. I stroll towards the restrooms, push open the door, walk in and spot my guy at one of the urinals. I step up next to him.

'How's it going?'

He glares over at me. 'We ain't talking while we piss, ya weird fucker.'

Damn. What makes *me* the weird fucker between the two of us? As I'm mid-stream, he finishes up, turning away from me to zip up, and I notice the tattoo on the back of his neck: the numbers one, three, one and two engulfed in flames.

Looks like he's not a member of my fan club – 1312 is an all-cops-are-the-enemy symbol. I let him leave, finishing up myself and exiting the bathroom. I glance at his car, but he's nowhere to be seen, and the tinted windows are too dark to see through.

'Hey,' I hear from my right.

I glance towards the male voice. Thankfully it's not Mr 1312 sneaking up on me. It's Dylan. I know *he's* not dangerous, but he's got a prime opportunity to blow my cover here. He yanks the headphones from his ears by the cord with one hand while jogging my way.

'Uh, hi?' I say, continuing to walk back towards my vehicle. 'I thought you guys were busy with lessons all day?'

'She is. I run to relax before I perform as Violated. Listen, we need to talk,' he says, catching up and walking by my side.

'What's up?'

He shakes his head, something clearly on the tip of his tongue that he holds back but not for long.

'What are you trying to do?'

'Right now?' I ask, confused. 'Work.'

'Do you think letting her face Nick is a good idea?'

Either he overheard me this morning, or she told him her plans. 'I'm not about to control her. If this is what she feels like she needs to do, I support that.'

'Mercy's, uh... how do I say this delicately without sounding like a douche? Damaged? Internally, you know? *Because* of Nick. She thinks she needs to do this to let it all go and be able to love, but I don't even think she knows what love is.'

'She *is* complicated; I'll give you that. But otherwise I think she's perfect – demons and all. I don't want her to tear down walls to let me in. I'd rather learn how to scale them and then go through the storm with her. I think that's what she needs most right now. Someone on her side no matter what she's got going on.'

Dylan drops his head. 'And if this backfires and makes it all worse?'

I sigh heavily, shoving my hands in my pockets. 'Then I'll help her get through it.'

He speaks no words, just stares at me with a blank look on his face.

'I'm not going to let anyone hurt her, Dylan. I promise. Maybe I don't know her as well as the rest of you, but I want to. So, I'll do whatever she needs me to.'

He nods as if he understands. 'We have a show tonight, as Violated. Want a hot tip on how to get her to possibly love you back?'

'You think I'm in love with her?' I ask with a nervous chuckle.

The lift of his shoulders says he's not sure. 'Show up for her even when it's inconvenient. That's what she's looking for.'

Interesting. That I can do. Truthfully, I'd have probably done anything he suggested here since he knows her best. 'Thanks for the tip,' I say. 'I gotta go.' I nod towards the truck, hoping he gets that I'm under-cover and busy right now and not just blowing him off.

'Yeah, no, it's all good. Just, don't let her down, al-right? Her heart can't take it.'

'That's not in my plans.'

He shoves his headphones back into his ears and gives me a nod that says *good talk* before jogging back to the running path that circles the park.

'Who the fuck was that?' Andrews asks when I get back to the car.

'Mercy's business partner.'

As Dylan rounds the corner near the far lot, I no-tice the car that once sat there is gone. If something went down just now with 1312 guy, my and Andrews's attention was on Dylan rather than the people we're here to watch. That could bite me in the ass, but at the same time, it also makes Nick wrong, pushing back his deal.

'I thought he was gonna jump ya.' He laughs. 'I al-most popped popcorn for the show.'

'Ha ha.'

'Walked yourself right into a love triangle, did ya?'

'Nah, he's just worried about his friend. But Dylan is the least of my worries right now. We need to see where that Honda went,' I say. 'Guy called me a weird fucker in the bathroom for trying to strike up a conversation while we pissed.'

Andrews laughs to himself. 'I've been there, and you are.'

29

MERCY

'Why am I so nervous? He slept in my bed last night. We've made out multiple times. Yet to know he may show up and watch me do one of the things I'm most proud of is nerve-wracking.'

'Ass-sweats nerve-wracking?' Hols asks, her face scrunched.

'He's not about to propose,' I snap.

'Bitchy nerve-wracking, then,' Penny says. Ed nods, agreeing with her, earning a glare from me.

'I've got no reason to be this anxious over him possibly not showing. Not to mention that I know he's at work, so he probably *can't* come. But I *really*, really want him to, and that feeling is so freaking scary. I've made this whole thing so big that if he doesn't show, I will feel like an unwanted six-year-old Mercy at the Christmas program all over again. Why is he doing this to me?' I ramble on to the three of them.

'I think *my* ass is suddenly sweating,' Ed says, looking back and wandering away as he does.

'Didn't he promise he'd try?' Hols asks, trying to find the one silver lining – her job as my best friend.

'Yeah,' I confirm.

Right then, the theater door opens, and two men walk in. One is very large and older, with a mustache that hasn't grayed as quickly as the hair on his head. He's hugging the biggest bucket of popcorn this place sells, not waiting a second to dig in. The other – is Brooks Hudson. My heart feels like it skips a beat as he walks my way with a smile.

'My God,' Penny says. 'Is that him?'

'Yeah,' I say in a whisper.

'He showed,' Hollyn says with a tiny squeal. 'This is so romantic.'

'Hey, gorgeous,' he says as he approaches us.

'Hi,' I say, forcing my insides to settle down. 'We were just talking about you.'

'Oh yeah? I'm hoping it was G-rated?' he says nervously.

'Probably.'

He laughs. 'We're on duty, so if I run out midway through, I apologize now.'

'Merc, we need to—' Dylan stops in his tracks when he notices Brooks standing before me. 'Brooks,' he greets him with an approving smile.

'Dylan,' Brooks says, matching his tone.

I glance between them; their gazes are steadily fixed on each other. Did something happen between them? 'Cause this feels awkward.

'You go,' Brooks says, gently squeezing my hand in his. 'If I'm not here when it's over, you did awesome, and I'll call ya later.' He leans into me. 'Next Monday is your meeting.' He presses his lips to my cheek, and my entire body relaxes.

I watch as he and his partner walk away towards aisle seats in the back of the theater. They both nod hello at Penny and Hollyn, who are watching the scene with ridiculous grins.

'You ready?' Dyl asks from behind me.

'Yeah,' I say, taking a deep breath to calm my nerves.

He showed. Even though he might not be able to stay, that alone is enormous. Now to shove away this unknown emotion I'm experiencing and make sure he doesn't regret it.

* * *

The show went amazingly and as Brooks exited midway through, he glanced back and flashed me a smile I can't quit thinking about. Now I'm sitting at the kitchen island in John and Penny Matthews' place, with River, Dax and Hollyn, having pizza and a Friday night like we'd have when we were teenagers.

My head is all over the place, simultaneously hyper-focused on two things. Brooks and Nick. In other words, adoration and animosity. Round and round they go, swirling through my head like a hurricane. There's definite damage happening within, and sadly I won't know what's still standing until it's all over. Monday's the direct impact. God, that's gonna hurt.

'Merc?'

'Huh?' I look up.

'Hungry?' River asks, glancing at the half-gone pizza sitting in front of me.

My jaw drops open. 'Did I just eat half that pizza by myself?'

Everyone nods.

'Is something bothering you, sweetheart?' Penny asks, her worried-mom look plastered on her face.

Should I tell her? If I tell her, I announce it to everyone, which means it's also coming home with me by way of River. Do I want that? Maybe they could help? *Or* they'll think I'm a complete nutjob wanting to face the man who created all this crap that's bogged me down for decades.

Tell them, Mercy. You've already talked to Ed and Carlos, and these people are the closest you have to family beyond them. Do it. Tell them what's happening in your life, and admit you need help. Everybody needs help sometimes. Your time is now.

With a heavy sigh, I bumble through my current problems. Giving them the CliffsNotes version and hoping they don't ask questions I'd rather not answer.

'Now I'm having big feelings for a man named Brooks Hudson. And on Monday, I'm facing Nick and saying everything I need to so I can finally move on.'

The whole room stops. Everyone's gaze shoots around at one another. Finally, John clears his throat. 'You're, uh... you're going to *see* Nick?'

'Holy Moses, you're in love with Brooks,' Hollyn says, earning my attention.

'What? Not once did I mention the word "love".'

'You didn't have to *say* it; Mom and I had to dodge the sparks between the two of you at your show earlier. Must I remind you of a year ago when I had some sudden realizations with your help in this same house. I know your face because it was the same one I probably had when I realized I was falling for Dax.' She leans into him, and like the lovesick fool he is, he plants a kiss on her head between bites of pizza.

'She thinks she's unlovable, and that's Nick's fault,' River says, once again getting it spot on the money. 'She's got to tell her father what he did to her. You get to the good once you acknowledge the bad, and so far, Mercy has avoided the bad – also known as Nick – for decades. When she says what she needs to say, she'll finally be able to let someone love her and probably admit she feels the same way. I'm sure of it.'

Every head turns River's way.

'What?' he asks. 'I smoked a joint before I got here and recently signed up for one of those therapy apps. I think it might be working.'

'Something's working,' Dax says with a chuckle.

'He's right again,' I say to the room. 'If I don't tell Nick what I need to, I can never move on, and him writing me and calling is all one big sign that I need to do it now.'

'Telling that man to eat a bag of dicks won't take away the harm he did,' Penny reminds me.

'I know, but surely it will help?'

'What are you going to say?' Hollyn asks.

I grab my bag from the couch and pull out the letter I've been working on throughout the day. 'I'm writing it all down. I don't plan on even looking at the man while I speak; I just need to get some stuff off my chest, then I'll leave him with words to torment him like he recently did to me. Do you want to help make sure I didn't miss anything?'

My friends agree, and for the next hour, we write a letter that John says any father would be ashamed to hear. I can only hope he's right.

30

BROOKS

'Where are you?' Seiver barks into my ear through the cellphone.

'Starlite Diner, not far from the pen. She's finalizing her letter,' I say, watching Mercy knock back another Long Island iced tea.

She was nervous, and I asked what would help. She said booze and greasy food, so here we are at a silver trailer fifties-style diner that serves exactly three alcoholic drinks and all the greasy food one could consume. She's currently finishing up drink number two.

Was letting her get tipsy before she faces a human monster my most brilliant idea? Probably not, but I'm trying to imagine it being me, and if it were, I'd be downing a bottle of whiskey right now.

'She's writing a scathing letter and spurring her words with a bit of liquid courage,' Andrews says, giving her a proud nod.

'You're letting her *drink*?' Seiver yells, overhearing him.

'She's not driving, and we're right here with her. I won't let her lose control.'

I refuse to let her go home today feeling like this didn't do what she needs it to. She's waited decades to say these words, so if she needs Dutch courage to face Nick, I'll happily pay the tab.

'Well, I'm about to walk into a room with this asshole and let him know he's our bitch now. I'm not announcing he's not getting parole, so make sure that's on her list. That'll be the gut punch. His estranged daughter telling him his parole's been denied.' He laughs an evil chuckle.

Mercy gave me the letter Nick had written to her. Reading between the lines, Seiver decided Nick was planning something and cut all deals after his 'tip' led to nothing the other day. Might Dylan's warning have caused us to miss it? Maybe. But sometimes, a tip not working out saves someone else; in this case, it's the woman I'm head over heels for.

I slide Mercy's notebook my way, taking the pen from her as she watches wide-eyed while I scribble something on a new page. When I give it back, she reads my words and smiles wide.

'Really?'

I nod. I hadn't told her yet because I haven't been working on this side of it. It's taken Seiver all week, but he found a way to keep Nick in a cell, hopefully until he dies.

'Spaghetti and meatballs?' The waitress stops at the end of our table, setting a second plate in front of Andrews.

He ordered *more*? Is he even done chewing the last bite of his club sandwich?

'We'll be there in an hour. I gotta go before Andrews clears this place out of food.' I hang up, setting my phone on the table near my cup of coffee. 'You think this is a buffet?' I ask Andrews, who's sitting on my left.

'You're paying the tab, so yeah.' He scoots his now-empty plate away and pulls the spaghetti his way. 'Miss?' he asks before the waitress can walk away. 'Do you, by chance, have pastries?'

'Not only do I have pastries, but I've got the best marionberry pie in the state. I recommend it warmed and à la mode.'

The smile on Andrews's face is one I've never witnessed before. He's a whore for pie too? The donuts are going to be jealous.

'Shall I bring over a slice?'

'Bring a whole pie,' Mercy says, her gaze meeting mine. 'Sorry, I'll pay for it.'

I laugh, shaking my head. 'I got it,' I say to her. 'You two realize we need to leave here in an hour?'

'Pfft, we could order two pies and make that deadline,' Andrews says, giving Mercy a grin.

'Can I swear at him?' Mercy asks.

'Andrews, yeah, I encourage it.'

'Nick...'

'Oh, absolutely. Let the asshole have it.'

A hint of a grin turns the corners of her lips. 'I'm glad you're here,' she says, reaching across the table and squeezing my hand. 'I don't know if I could do this alone, and I'm not sure it would feel right with anyone else.'

'You still nervous?' I ask as the waitress delivers drink number three, a champagne Shirley Temple.

'More terrified, but maybe this is the magic drink, eh?' She grabs the cherry from the top and puts it in her mouth flirtatiously, watching me the whole time. 'Are *you* nervous?'

Andrews grunts a laugh. 'Pretty sure he's just horny...'

I elbow him.

'What?' he bellows. 'I was talking about that cherry thing she just did. Wow-sa. My wife used to do sexy things like that. You know, back when we didn't spend three hours before bed in separate rooms watching the same shows.'

'Sounds romantic,' I say, grimacing at Mercy.

She laughs, wiping it away when Andrews glares her way.

One pie later, we're escorting Mercy through the prison to the room Seiver's got Nick in. He has no idea he's about to meet the one person whose life was most affected by all this. I doubt he'll even know who she is. Before she enters her worst nightmare, though, I figured I'd lighten the mood and have her meet Seiver first. I thought meeting the guy who saved her all those years ago might help.

With each step, her grip on my hand gets a little tighter.

'You're completely safe, Merc.'

She blows out a breath. 'I'm so scared,' she says timidly, forcing herself to breathe slowly.

'This place is full of guards, cameras and us. We're not going to let Nick hurt you.'

'I'm not worried about that.' She stops walking, turning to me nervously. 'What if this doesn't work? What if you hearing all this makes you see me differently? What if I get in there and can't even speak? What if—'

'Merc.' I grab both her hands. 'You could "what if" all day. It's the perfect way to torment yourself. I know, as I've done it many times. Speak from your heart, then give him your letter, and whatever pain you're hoping to release, you'll know you're done when it happens. If you want me to stay outside the room, I will. Seiver and Andrews will be with you, so you'll still be safe. You can do this.'

She breathes deeply, flashing me a crooked smile. 'I can do this,' she repeats.

Seiver is standing in the hall outside the meeting room when we walk around the corner. As we get closer, Mercy starts to slow. Her eyes are glued to his, and they both have the same look on their faces. Like they're watching a train crash and can't look away. Pretty sure that's just their past encounter flashing through their heads at the exact same moment.

'Is that—' Mercy's voice is small and meek.

'Travis Seiver?' I confirm. 'It is. Travis.' I glance his way. 'This is Mercy Alexander.'

Without warning, she runs the last few steps to

him and throws her arms around his neck, bursting into tears. She told me the story of the day that changed her forever late one night over the phone this weekend. Hearing it from her was harder than reading the case file on it. Her side goes something like this.

* * *

It was a stormy late summer night. Thunder rumbled through the sky, and crashes of lightning lit up the dark night. Nick had sent Mercy to her room, a mattress on the floor without sheets and only a comforter and pillow. A couple of library books were on her bed, and her prized possession, her ukulele, was in her hands. Nick had only one rule: if he closed her bedroom door, she didn't come out until he opened it.

'Gotta protect my baby girl,' he'd tell her. That part pissed Mercy off a lot. He wasn't protecting her. He was hiding illegal activity from her, and even at eight, she knew this.

That night, he attempted to close her door, but it didn't latch and popped open a few inches – just enough for her to watch the scene unfold from her bed.

She heard the three voices but only recognized

her father's. When he got loud, she knew something was going wrong, and she sat in a ball at the corner of her bed, darkness all around her, watching the three men fight. When two loud pops rang out, she pulled her comforter over her head. Chaos followed. Voices she didn't recognize were screaming frantically, so Mercy slowly pulled the comforter from her head and snuck to the door to get a better look at the commotion.

The floors in the house were wooden, and the first thing she saw was a growing puddle of red around a man lying on the floor. She'd never seen that much blood before, so she knew it wasn't good. Her dad had a set of cordless phones in the house and thought he had recently lost one. But it wasn't lost. Mercy had stolen it to help her feel safer, and when she heard the gurgling of the bleeding man, she called 911. He was crying, gasping for his friend to save him, but instead, his buddy bolted. While Mercy waited for the operator to answer her call, she cried, praying for God to take her to heaven to escape this hell.

Seiver was able to dig up the call for me to listen to, and it's the most heartbreaking thing I've ever heard, but at the same time, I was so proud of her. She did nearly everything 911 told her, including following the operator's instructions until the police arrived.

When they pounded on the door, she got scared again, dropped the phone, and ran into her closet, where she sat, strumming her ukulele and singing to calm herself.

Her house was suddenly buzzing with people. The 911 operator dispatched that a call had come from an eight-year-old girl inside the home. Until that moment, Travis had no idea a little girl was inside. He ordered everyone to be quiet so he could find her, and when he noticed an open door to a scantily furnished bedroom, he walked in to hear her ukulele and sweet voice singing a song he didn't recognize.

Mercy remembers Travis talking to her about the books on her bed before he could even see her. He told her he understood how scary this was and that he wasn't there to hurt her.

'Do you like strawberry milkshakes?' was the question that earned a tiny, terrified 'Yes.' Moments later, he'd convinced her to come out so he could help her, and out walked an eight-year-old dark-haired little girl wearing a *Powerpuff Girls* nightgown, stained with blood. Tears ran down her face, her ukulele still in her hand.

'Is he OK?' she asked Travis.

'I don't know yet, sweetie. Is he your daddy?'

'No,' she said. 'My daddy ran away. Am I in trouble?'

'No, honey. You're not in trouble. Let's get that strawberry milkshake,' he said in reply, picking her up and grabbing her comforter, throwing it over her head, attempting to shield her from a scene she'd already taken in. The damage was done, and her father was nowhere to be seen.

* * *

'Thank you,' Mercy says to Seiver when she finally releases him. 'You made me believe the world had good in it that night. And I may have developed a thing for strawberry milkshakes...' A tipsy giggle leaves her lips. 'I can't believe I'm meeting you again!'

'I was just doing my job, sweetheart.' Travis looks her over while he wipes what appear to be tears from his eyes.

'Are you, uh—'

'Shut it, Hudson. That murder was my first big case, so Mercy's always stuck with me. I'm so glad to see you're doing alright.'

'Well, I'm here to yell at Nick twenty-two years later, so... does that count as alright?'

'In life, we do what we have to to survive. You're

doing what you need to live because you're tired of just surviving. Word of warning: he's not a great guy, but you'll have the three of us right beside you. Ready?' Travis asks her.

Mercy glances back at me, her eyes wide like a deer caught in someone's headlights.

'I won't go in if you don't want me to.'

She steps towards me, her hands on my chest as she leans into me. 'I need you with me. Just please don't let this affect how you see me?'

I nod wordlessly. Most of the time, being at the prison is a pain in my ass. This time, it feels life-changing, and not only for Mercy.

Seiver heads in first, then Andrews, then Mercy, and I follow behind them.

'What's this?' Nick groans from the table he's sitting at as we walk in. 'I said no bitch cops!' he barks at Seiver. 'Me and women, we don't jibe. I never met a chick that could be trusted. Every one of them will steal, cheat and stab you in the back.'

Mercy looks back at me, absolutely horrified. I flash her a smile to reassure her it's OK. This is typical talk here.

Seiver laughs at him. 'You made that real easy.'

'What did I make easy?' Nick snaps.

'Looking like a dickbag, and she got to hear it

straight from your lips and not mine,' he says, stopping in front of him.

Standing between Andrews and me is a shaking Mercy, her eyes on Nick while she white-knuckles the letter she wrote him to her chest.

'Nick, meet your daughter, Mercy,' Seiver says, motioning her way.

Nick's entire aura changes. The color drains from his face, leaving him ashen gray, and for a second, I wonder if he's just died sitting up.

'Y-y-you're Mercy?' he asks, his voice much softer. 'My daughter, Mercy?'

The fear in Mercy's eyes changes to fire, and she steps in front of me, not going far but now standing between Travis and me.

'What? No picture of me in your cell? Could I have expected any less from you, Daddy dearest?' She spits the words like poison, and the nerves building in my chest, wondering if this was a bad idea, after all, start to settle. I knew she could do this.

She takes the chair directly in front of Nick, across the table from him. For a moment, she just stares at him interrogation style. She'd make a great cop.

'Cat got your tongue?' she snaps at him. She glances at me with a shaky smile. 'Oh my God, I *can* do this,' she says, proud of herself already. 'Thank you, alcohol.'

The three of us guys all laugh to ourselves. Clearly, the few drinks she had earlier are settling in quickly and mixing with decades-old rage I want to cheer on.

'She's been drinking?' Nick asks, his eyes now on me.

'Booze is what it took for her to face you today.' I step in, unable to keep my mouth shut any longer, and it's been two minutes. I want to end this man. 'Now, you'll listen to every word she has to say, and when she asks you to speak, apologize, plead, grovel. Whatever you have to do to send this woman out of here feeling like she got some closure on the nightmare you made her life.'

'Or what?' Nick snaps.

'Bye-bye, parole,' Mercy says with a sly grin.

A vile chuckle leaves Nick's lips. 'Pretty sure you don't have the power to take my parole, sweetheart.'

'You're right; *I* don't,' she says. 'But *they* do.'

He glances around at the three of us. 'One of these assholes your husband or something?'

Mercy laughs, making Nick visibly uncomfortable. 'You think I can *love*? Or, for that matter, let anyone love me? No. You stole that from me. Along with my trust, childhood, security, self-esteem and innocence. Not to mention my mother.'

'I ain't talking about your mother. We've had this conversation before. You think I wanted to raise a kid alone?'

'Considering one kid you fucked up and another you completely ignored, I'm going to guess you never wanted kids to begin with. I don't doubt you're one of those "I'm real good at pulling out" guys. Did you ask her to have an abortion?'

'You're here, aren't ya?'

She nods her head, her eyes never leaving his. 'I'm *finally* here. I've dreamed of this; did you know that?'

'Of seeing me?'

Her laugh is not joyful. 'No. Of telling you off.'

'Alright,' Nick says, getting tired of this already. 'Let's get this over with.'

'Did you ever wonder what ever happened to me?'

He stares through her, crossing his arms over his chest and refusing to answer her question.

'Would you like to know who I became?'

His shoulders barely lift as he answers her question wordlessly.

'I'm a classical musician. Edie, the son you never had the pleasure of knowing, says I should be playing for the Vienna Philharmonic. He raised me when he

finally saved me from living with strangers and probably aging out of the foster care system. I play five instruments fluently and speak two languages. Yet I
can't let people into my life easily. Especially romantically. I have panic attacks and see not one but *two*
therapists. I'm on antidepressants and anti-anxiety
meds and hardly sleep because the nightmares you
created overwhelm me practically every night.'

Finally, the man shows some emotion when he
breaks their eye contact and stares at the table between them instead. He can't look her in the eyes. I
wouldn't be able to either if I'd done what he did.

'The night my world imploded is burned into my
brain in a way I can somehow still feel the rain on my
skin as I was carried to a police car. By that guy.' She
points to Seiver. 'You ran, and he saved me. Cowardly,
Daddy.'

Andrews laughs but pulls it together when Seiver
shoots him a glare.

'When thunder rumbles, I still see blue and red
lights when I close my eyes. I wake up with cold
sweats after nightmares. I've cried myself to sleep
more often than I want to admit, and I mask my emotions with alcohol and medication. At the same time, I
pretend I'm some fun, tough, emotionless woman
filling internal voids with random penises like it's

helping. When I was fourteen...' Her voice shakes so hard she has to stop speaking. 'I tried to end it all. I thought nobody would ever love me.'

This starts to get Nick as he drops his arms from their defensive stance and eventually looks her in the eye again.

My heart slowly sinks. I had no idea. I want to jerk this woman from her chair and hug the hell out of her right now.

'Let me guess.' Nick's gravelly voice penetrates my thoughts. 'You blame me?' He says the words slowly like they're unbelievable.

She takes a deep breath before she speaks again. 'You're not to blame?'

He shrugs openly. 'I only knew you till you were eight. Couldn't have been all me.'

Her brow furrows, and she drops her head.

'The last time I saw you was in a courtroom. I was terrified of the whole thing but mostly of you.' She swallows hard. 'Yet I just wanted the *only* person in the room I knew – my father – to hug me and say he was sorry he'd turned my life into what it was. I was desperate for you to say you loved me.'

She just wanted her father to love her. Fuck. This is heartbreaking.

'But you didn't. You got teary-eyed for a moment –

right after I took the stand – which sent me into my first panic attack, and after that, you stared at me like it was the first time you'd ever seen me. That bothered me until today.'

'And what changed today?' Nick asks flatly.

'I finally found the courage to face you. But you're even more pathetic than I remember. Why would you *ever* think contacting me for anything would be appropriate? I hoped *never* to see you again; then I get a fucking letter out of the blue twenty-plus years after you abandoned me. Do you know what that does to a girl who'd hoped for a letter from her father her whole life apologizing for messing me up? Instead, you announce you need a place to stay when you get paroled, and you think *I'm* the person who will say yes to that?'

'Going to prison is hardly abandonment.'

Her eyebrows shoot up her forehead. 'Running from a crime scene you knew your daughter was at and leaving her with a dying man is! I was *eight*, Nick! I tried to save that guy because I couldn't bear to watch him die. But he did. He died right in front of me. While I, an eight-year-old terrified little girl, told that stranger he wasn't alone and that he would be alright. That was a lie. I was repeating what the 911 operator wanted me to say.

Nothing was alright. His family never saw him again. His kids have spent their life without a father. And I spent my life practically without anyone at all. *You* did all that.' She hesitates, staring down at the letter in her hands.

'Now that I'm grown, I can't imagine his poor mother when she got the call that her son had made a bad choice and some deadbeat doper killed him. You didn't just steal from me that night, Nick. You tore that family's son away, and you created a scene in my head that lives rent-free while haunting me every single day, convincing me I must not be enough for anyone since my father didn't love me. Do you know what that feels like?'

Nick says nothing, just averts his eyes from her to the table between them again.

'You think you're some kind of badass, but you're nothing but a fucking coward. I thought facing you would break me more than I already was; the truth is, it's making me realize you've *always* been a selfish asshole. Not one ounce of you was good. I just craved a normal family and tried to find anything that made me feel like I meant something to you. I made up versions of you that didn't exist to make it through my childhood. But knowing you're a complete asshole with no remorse can replace all my daydreams about having a loving father. Because you're not that. You never were.'

'I don't know what love is, Mercy.' He speaks, and for the first time since I've met the guy, his voice shakes like he's getting emotional.

'I know. You proved it to me every day you were in my life, and guess what? Now I don't know either. And it's killing me because love is jabbing at my heart like a fire poker stoking coals that are barely burning, and I'm terrified to let him in and even more terrified to let him walk away...' Her gaze moves to me, and Nick follows it.

'She talking about you?'

Travis shakes his head, so I don't respond, just bite my lips together and force myself to stay where I am and not kick this man's ass in front of his daughter.

'What do you want from me?' Nick asks, all his emotions and excuses tucked away.

She shoves the letter she wrote across the table to him. 'I don't want anything from you. Stop writing me. Don't call me anymore and forget I ever existed because, for you, I don't.'

'Fine,' he says. 'We done?'

'We're done when I tell you we're done,' Seiver barks at him.

'I'm almost finished,' Mercy says. 'You know, I hope two things for you.'

'Those are?' Nick asks.

'That this letter haunts you for the rest of your days and that you rot in this hellhole knowing no one outside this place loves you. Exactly like no one on the inside loves me.'

He takes the letter from her but doesn't open it – just stares at his name written across the front for what feels like forever.

'Well, this has been fun,' Nick says with irritation. He glares at Seiver. 'Next time you want to have a surprise family reunion, warn me so I can refuse the visit.' He stands from the table, a guard standing with him. 'Have a nice life,' he says to Mercy before being escorted out of the room and back to his cell, the letter still in his hand.

He didn't even apologize. Fucker. Mercy looks like all the wind was knocked out of her as he walks away. Nick glances back once, and their eyes meet, but Mercy turns to me instead of letting her gaze linger. Tears spill down her cheeks.

'You did good.' I hug her to me. '*So* good, Merc.' God, I hope this worked. For her sake.

31

BROOKS

Mercy requested a few days to herself after the meeting with Nick. After what I witnessed, could I blame her? Absolutely not. She needs to figure some things out, and I've got zero problems with her finding herself after that. I was so proud of her and told her that repeatedly on the way home that day. We still talk daily, but I haven't seen her in about a week. Honestly, I miss the hell out of her.

I have Ali this week, but secretly, I'm hoping to see Mercy at some point. I'll call her when I go to bed later, but right now, I'm playing the most crucial glow-in-the-dark put-put golf game of my life thus far, and Alijah is winning by a long shot.

'Gurl.' I laugh, shaking my head as I step up to my

golf ball. 'Did you go pro overnight and not tell me?' I ask as I putt intentionally badly.

Neon lights cover all the displays – the golf balls glow in the dark, and we're both wearing glowstick necklaces. Hers around her neck, and mine around my baseball cap because that's as far as it would fit. My golf ball cracks against the display, bouncing back at me in a way that I have to either dodge it or take it right square in the nads. Shit.

'Daddy!' Ali giggles at my impending castration, watching me attempt to dodge it ungracefully. 'The ball is supposed to go in that hole,' she says, pointing to the hole she's referring to.

'*Oh...*' I say like I had no idea. 'Maybe this time...' I hit softly, the ball barely leaving the spot I'm at and rolling back towards me.

Ali slaps a hand to her forehead, laughing at me like I'm not doing this on purpose. 'You're so bad at this.'

'What?' I ask like I'm offended. My phone dings in my pocket, and there's only one person I want it to be.

'You're up, girl,' I say, tucking my putter under one arm and seeing her name flash across my screen. 'Hi, beautiful,' I say, utterly giddy like a boy with a crush.

'Is this a bad time? If so, I can let you go.'

'No, I've got a minute. Just getting my butt kicked at mini-golf.'

'Are you losing on purpose?'

'Maybe,' I say with a chuckle. 'How'd you know?'

'You seem the type.'

'What type is that?'

She sighs into the phone. 'The good dad type.'

'I try.'

I'm hoping her week of thinking things over didn't cause her to decide she can't date a single father after what she just went through. I wouldn't blame her, honestly, but I would be heartbroken.

'This is entirely inappropriate, considering you have your daughter right now, and I shouldn't be bothering you, but does she, by chance, have a bedtime?'

'She does,' I say. 'Usually, it's nine, but we've already passed that. What's up?'

'Do you think you might be home tonight by eleven?'

The smile that covers my face feels embarrassing. Thankfully I only know one person here, and she's witnessed worse from me. I take a few steps from Alijah, allowing her to hit her ball a hundred times.

'Eleven sharp?'

She laughs. 'Missed me?'

'Yes.'

'I can't quit thinking about you.'

The fireworks she's activated within my chest are in full finale mode. I can't even find words through the commotion.

'I need to see you,' I say quietly so Ali doesn't over-hear me.

'That's what I was hoping you would say.'

32

MERCY

I fish my laciest, sexiest lingerie, never worn for anyone else, from my top drawer, put it on, and then grab my knee-length dress coat and highest heels. I flash myself in the mirror. Not terrible for a woman who recently ate an entire bag of cookies. I tightly tie the coat around my waist, open my door and look for River. Damn, he's on the couch again. How do I do this without him noticing? Food. River's a sucker for free food.

'Hey, I gotta run to the store; want anything?' I lie. My plan doesn't involve coming back here until well after sunrise tomorrow morning, so I hope he's not starving.

'Um, get me some Doritos and a Coke.' His eyes

stay glued to his laptop, where he's probably working on the documentary about his mother he still hasn't finished.

'Sure,' I say, making my way out of the apartment.

As I close the door behind me, I breathe out a sigh of relief. Whew, step one of my plan done, on to getting across the street without revealing the lingerie meant for one set of eyes only.

The moment I turn towards the stairs, I hear a door open. Considering there are only four apartments on this floor and the other two are past the stairs, I know exactly who it is.

'Where ya headed?' Dylan asks.

'Out,' I say, speed-walking to the stairs and jogging down them as fast as these heels allow.

Ugh, this is nerve-wracking. I've never done this. And by this, I mean going out in public wearing only lingerie under a jacket. I didn't expect it to be so drafty, and the entire trip down the stairs, I'm worried my ass is hanging out in a humiliating way, so I doubt I'll ever do it again.

As I exit my building, I hold my coat tightly, glancing up at the starry sky. A streak of light catches my attention. I stop, trying to decipher what I'm seeing. If a meteorite obliterates Earth at this moment, I will be pissed.

Oh! It's a shooting star! I've never seen one before, but I know what to do because of Dax.

'Please, *please*.let me be able to say the words I want to say tonight,' I say out loud as I walk across the road into Brooks's building. I glance at the man standing at the front desk, trying not to make eye contact, so no questions are asked. Crap. It's Ernesto, the guy who knows me as Sacha Black.

'Good evening, Miss Black. Enjoy your time at home.'

'I will,' I say, half jogging to the elevator so he doesn't suddenly realize I'm not who he thinks I am.

Why do I feel like people can see through my jacket? Maybe because what's underneath doesn't exactly leave much room for imagination. An intentional move. I step into the elevator with a man who doesn't get out, just stares. I glance down at my coat and see the same eyeful of cleavage he's seeing.

'Excuse you,' I say, readjusting my jacket. 'I think you missed your floor?'

The man, too interested in my cleavage, clears his throat as he looks away from me when it's no longer in full view. He jabs at the lobby button, but we're already headed up.

I can't step out on Brooks's floor soon enough, and

the second the doors open, I bolt away from the creeper in the elevator.

Do not skip down this hallway like it's some kind of Yellow Brick Road. Walk like a lady not headed to seduce a man.

Finally, I reach his door. I take a deep breath, knocking lightly so as not to wake up his daughter. When I hear him turn the doorknob, I open my jacket, only – *it's not him.*

'Ye-es,' the elderly man says, nodding his head, his eyes moving down me in a way that makes my skin crawl.

'Holy. Fuck,' I say out loud, closing the jacket tightly. 'What floor am I on?'

'The right one,' he says. 'Matilda! Get out here and see what Daddy needs.'

'Ew.' I half run away from his door, back to the elevator, pulling my phone from my pocket and calling Brooks.

'Are you here?'

'No, but if I flash one more person in your building, security will have me removed.'

He laughs into the phone. 'You've flashed people?'

'Two, so far. I don't think the man who lives directly below you will ever recover,' I say, noticing I'm a floor off when I get back into the elevator.

'You flashed Harold?' Brooks asks, his voice now serious.

'Not only did I flash Harold, but he got a good long look that will hold him over until death. By the way, he calls himself Daddy to someone named Matilda. Should we worry about that?'

'Matilda is his lucky wife. Damn, creepy Harold got an eyeful of my woman before I did?'

I gasp. 'Did you just call me your woman?'

'Um,' he stalls. 'Did you mind?'

'No.'

'Then yes, I sure did.'

I watch myself blush in the elevator mirrors. I think I *want* to be Brooks Hudson's woman.

'In one minute, I'll be at your door. When I know it's you and not some unsuspecting old guy who creepily adds syllables to the word "yes", you'll get a view of what two other men in your building already have.'

He laughs again. 'I can't wait.'

'I'm hanging up.'

'Headed to the door,' he says.

I knock lightly; he opens the door a crack, peering through it with one eye. 'What do you want?' he says jokingly.

When I open my jacket to show him what I want,

the laughing stops; he jerks the door open, grabs my hand and pulls me inside.

'Damn it, Harold,' he says, glancing me over before leading me into his room. 'You are on fire, lady. Stay here; I'll be right back. I'm just going to make sure she's still asleep, then I'm all yours.'

His room is sparkling clean. The bed's made except where he was just in it. His laundry is in the hamper. He even has an organized walk-in closet *with* a wall full of baseball caps – just like he mentioned. At least twelve, all hanging from their designated hooks, and I swear I just fell a little harder knowing he's one of those clean and organized guys. Even his en suite bathroom smells nice, like a spa.

I strip off my jacket and lie across his bed, finding a position that says, *take me, but quietly, so we don't wake up your kid.*

Jesus, Mercy. None of this is sexy.

Brooks comes back in, closes the door behind him, flips the lock and stands against it, staring at me with a massive grin.

'Wow,' he says. 'I knew I needed to see you, but I didn't expect you to be practically naked when I did.'

He makes his way to where I'm at on his bed, crawling across it, now straddling me, one hand on either side of my head. 'Did you put on the sexiest thing you own to distract me from words?' he asks, now glancing down at me in a way that feels way less creepy than when Harold did it. "Cause you could've sewn yourself into a snowsuit, and I'd have still wanted you.'

He still wants me? Whew! So, my bullshit with Nick didn't scare him off? Relief floods through me.

'Really?'

'Yeah,' he says, never looking away from me.

Be. Still. My. Once. Absent. Heart.

I bite my lip hard to prevent a ridiculous smile from taking over my face. I reach up, my hands on the sides of his neck, pulling him to me and kissing him softly. He returns the kiss, dropping down on one elbow and sliding a hand around my waist, pulling me over on top of him.

'Fucking hell, woman, I don't know what kind of spell you cast, but I just want to be with you every second of the day,' he says, between moments of his lips being on mine. 'Clothed, not clothed, all of it.'

'Show me,' I say, pulling his shirt in a way that says exactly how I want him in case the lingerie didn't scream it from the rooftops.

'We gotta do this quietly,' he says, pulling off his T-shirt and revealing all the tattoos I love. 'Can you do that?'

'Maybe,' I say, kissing him again. 'Just keep your mouth on mine, and it'll be no problem.'

'I might not be able to do that the entire time,' he jokes. 'But my mouth will most certainly be somewhere on you at all times...'

* * *

I glance at the clock on my phone, blinking my eyes to figure out if I'm hearing what I'm actually hearing – three forty-seven in the morning. I hold my breath, listening for her again.

'Daddy?' There's a tiny knock at his door.

'Brooks,' I whisper, shaking him awake.

'Huh? What?' He wakes suddenly, propping himself up on one elbow. 'What's wrong?' He reaches for me like he'd do absolutely anything to protect me. It's the sweetest thing I've ever seen.

'Daddy?' Her sweet little voice calls his name again as she attempts to turn his door handle.

'Oh, shit,' he whispers, his eyes snapping open. 'OK, it's fine.' He jumps out of his bed, throwing on his sweats, then turns to me with a nervous grin. 'I gotta be a dad for a few minutes. Look away if need be. I'll be right back.' He leans down, kissing my lips with a small swoony sigh like he can't believe I'm real. I feel exactly the same way.

He opens his door, sliding out and closing it behind him but it doesn't latch and slowly opens a few inches – just enough that I watch him kneel to his daughter's level, the light from the hallway softly illuminating the two of them.

He brushes hair from her face. 'What's wrong, sweetie?'

'I had a bad dream,' she says.

He picks her up, allowing her to wrap her tiny arms around his neck. 'Daddy will never let something bad happen to you; you know that, right?'

'Uh-huh,' she says in a sleepy voice. 'Can you sing me the song I like?'

He walks away from the door as she lays her head on his shoulder. 'You think that will make you feel better?'

'Yes.'

'Let's do it, then.'

Her bedroom is on the other side of the living room, the door across from his. I creep to the edge of his bed, his comforter now wrapped around me like a robe. The last time I watched something out the crack of a door, it was horrifying. This time, my heart feels like it's about to burst. He gets her back into her bed, kissing her forehead, then tucking her in. I did not expect him being a dad to be as adorable as this is.

Brooks walks across his daughter's room, rubbing a hand over his face in an attempt to wake himself up. He comes back into view with an acoustic guitar. He sits on the floor by her bed, crossing his legs beneath him. All his tattoos are on display as he's shirtless, now strumming a tune I recognize. One my newest ukulele student told me her dad sang to her when she had bad dreams. 'You Are My Sunshine'.

No. Freaking. Way.

I sit at the edge of the bed, watching him sing to his daughter – my new ukulele student, Ali.

Brooks isn't rushing to get back to me and has clearly done this a hundred times for her. It's the sweetest thing I've ever seen in my life. A moment I've never experienced myself, but I'm pretty sure this is the way a father is supposed to treat his daughter. If I was any kind of unsure of how I felt about him before, this decides it. There is no way I met this man by accident this time.

Not only can he play guitar like a rock star, but he's a good singer too. His voice gets quieter and quieter as she fades to sleep. Finally, only his strumming of the guitar remains.

After I wipe the unexpected tears from my face, I

grab my phone, jump into his bed and text the words I don't know if I can say out loud but suddenly know for a fact it's what this fluttery feeling has always been. The sound of his guitar wanes, so I set my phone on the nightstand and pretend I'm asleep.

His phone buzzes with my incoming text as he walks back in, closing the door behind him. When he checks his messages, the screen's light illuminates his face, and I sneak a look as his adorable crooked smile grows before he sets the phone down and crawls into bed.

'Merc,' he says softly, sliding a hand over my waist and pulling me to him. 'You didn't by chance just say you loved me via text, did you?'

I press my forehead into his chest. 'Doesn't sound like something I would do...' I lie.

He laughs as he lifts my chin, forcing me to look at him. 'Do you?'

'Yes,' I say softly. 'I do.'

'You are so sweet,' he says, his lips on mine settling my nerves. 'I've loved you since you walked into Oz's bar.'

He has? No way. 'Are you telling me you had a love-at-first-sight moment?'

'If you'd have asked me that six months ago, even I wouldn't have believed it.'

'Want to know the truth?'

'Yes.'

'You sent butterflies fluttering through my body that night, and I was so confused because no one's ever done that to me before.'

'Do you still feel them?'

'They're about to suffocate me,' I joke. 'Promise me something?'

'Anything.'

'You're the dad that little girl deserves. Always put her first. She adores you.'

'You think?'

'Is your daughter's name Ali Blackwell?'

'Blackwell-Hudson, yeah.'

My heart slows. 'Yeah, I don't think; I know because she started ukulele lessons with me a few weeks ago and talks about her daddy all the time. Her uncle Nate brings her by weekly, and I didn't put it all together until right now when she asked you to sing the sunshine song. She mentioned her daddy sings that one to her when she has nightmares.'

Brooks sits up, flipping on the side lamp. 'You've been giving my Ali ukulele lessons?'

'Yeah. She's a total natural.'

He runs a hand over his head – shock on his face. 'Merc, I have to tell you something crazy.'

I sit up with him, suddenly nervous.

'Remember the nutty bathroom tarot-reading woman?'

'Yes...'

'That was, uh... Norah.'

My eyes go wide. 'Norah? Your—'

'*Ex*-wife, yes,' he confirms. 'She's kind of wacky, one of those intuitive, mind-reading, meditating, crystal-wearing women, and months ago, before you and I reconnected, she had a vision of my soulmate. Dark hair, emerald-green eyes, higher than high heels. When you walked to that table at Tequila Mockingbird the day we were there, she knew you were who she'd seen in her dream.'

'Me?' I touch my chest. 'Your ex-wife thinks I'm your soulmate?'

'Yes.'

I nod slowly, thinking about that. Does it make my insides light up? I'm not gonna lie, yeah.

'Is she ever... wrong?' I ask curiously. She sure didn't feel wrong that night.

He shakes his head slowly. 'Less often than I'd prefer.'

'Huh,' I say, holding his comforter over my chest. 'Maybe our timing *was* off before. What should we do about this?'

He smiles wide. 'All this doesn't freak you out? The weird coincidences? The invasive tarot reading? You witnessing me as Ali's dad?'

For a second, I just stare into his light brown bright eyes. 'Yes, all this has freaked me out. But now – being with you makes me feel like I'm finally home, and that's not something I've had often.'

'You feel at home with me?'

I nod.

He scoots closer, moving an arm behind me and leaning his head into mine, speaking right into my ear. 'I am so in love with everything about you.'

'Yeah?'

'Yes, Merc.' He kisses my lips gently. 'Do you have anything you might want to say to me?'

'Lemme grab my phone,' I joke. Before I say it, I take a breath, making sure no part of me is rejecting this idea. Loins, on board. My heart is ready to dive all the way in off the highest diving board. My head, well, it's shoving all kinds of thoughts at me but only one leaves my lips. 'I'm in love with you, Brooks Hudson. Child, job, overly involved ex-wife and everything. I've never loved any other man, and I don't think I ever want to.'

His face lights up. 'Did we both suddenly become believers of fate, and I'm your one?'

I nod. 'You're my one, Brooks. For the first time in my life, I've never been surer of anything.'

And that's how I stumbled upon the love of my life. I didn't think happy ever after was in my future. Maybe because it turns out it's in my present. My past isn't gone, but now I have someone to help me fight it. From the first note I heard him play on that guitar, my heart knew, and finally, the rest of me caught up.

EPILOGUE
BROOKS

Five Months Later...

'Can you guys shut it?' I ask the row of people behind me, all acting like we're sitting in a bar, not a theater for a children's recital. Every one of them clamps their mouth shut. I don't want to miss a second of this. I've even got my father near the stage to film the whole thing so Ali and Mercy can watch it later.

This is the same theater Andrews and I saw Mercy perform at with Dylan for the first time. Now my daughter is performing with her.

'Sorry, Dad,' Ty says. Oz laughs with him, but our

stone-serious mother sitting between them isn't as amused.

'She's not playing something offensive, is she?' my mom asks curiously.

'Don't worry, Mom. The song is six-year-old appropriate.'

'They're up,' Norah says, motioning to the stage where Alijah and Mercy walk to the center.

Why am *I* nervous? I'm only watching my two favorite girls on the planet do what they love most. Play music.

Mercy converses with Ali before they sit, and Alijah strums her first public notes on the ukulele. She loses her nerve a few bars in, so Mercy whispers into her ear, then plays with her until she gets back on track. Then, she shines like the diamond she is, singing the song she's spent six months learning as she plays the tune 'Rainbow Connection'. It makes me so proud that I have to will away the tears threatening to spill over.

'How adorable is this?' Norah whispers, her hands folded in front of her chest. 'We made the cutest daughter.'

'That we did,' I say with a smile when Alijah glances my way. She beams.

'Girl's got talent,' Nate says. 'I knew she did.'

'We should get her in Mom's band,' River says. Penny nods her head, her eyes on the stage and glistening with proud tears. She recently said Ali might be as close as she gets to a grandchild. I seriously doubt that with Dax and Hollyn's wedding coming up.

I thought my family was weird before. Now it's straight nuts. Exes, co-workers, old friends, new friends, drag queens, pop stars and family fill my world, and I don't regret a moment.

We all stand when the song is over, giving Alijah a standing ovation. Our section of the audience is loud. All these people are here for her, and she grins happily, then curtsies just like Mercy has taught her.

Dylan and Mercy stand on stage at the show's end, thanking their students and parents. Sometimes, I still wonder how I tricked this woman into falling in love with me and hope I can keep it going for the next forty or fifty years.

Alijah comes running my way after, a grin ear to ear when she sees the flowers in my hands. Dax's idea. He made bouquets for everyone, so she's about to be swimming in flowers.

'Are those for me?' she asks excitedly.

'They are! You did *so* incredibly well, sweetie. Daddy's never been prouder.' I kneel, hugging her tight before handing her the flowers.

'Thank you,' she says proudly.

I step aside so her many fans can congratulate her while I look for Mercy. I wasn't sure when I'd do this, but after watching her comfort Ali before and during the show, encouraging her to do what she practiced so hard for, I know this is right.

'I'll be right back,' I say to Norah, who nods as she watches Alijah beam with pride as each person there gives her fist bumps and flowers.

'Looking for Mercy?' Cassie asks. She's become a part of Dylan and Mercy's business lately. She and Dylan's relationship is going so well, I wouldn't be surprised if they marry before even Dax and Hollyn do.

'If she's not busy.'

'She's still in the wings,' she says, stacking instruments on the wheeled cart. 'You can go back.'

'Brooks,' Dylan says as I walk past him. 'Your kid was the star of the show. Well done,' he says, carrying some instruments to Cassie. 'You might have a future contestant on *The Next Superstar*.'

Dylan and I have become pretty good friends, and Saturday nights at the bar have got a lot busier with all these new people gathering with us. It's fun. But the one who makes me the happiest is the same woman who just slipped into my line of sight. She glances my way with a smile, holding up a single finger. When she's done, she walks my way.

'Hey, gorgeous.'

'Hi, handsome. Didn't she do amazing?' she asks, almost as excited as Alijah was. Her gaze moves to the box I've just pulled from my pocket. 'What's this?'

'Ali and I wanted to ask you something, but she's busy with her fan club, so it looks like it's all me.'

'What did you do?' The nervousness shows on her face.

I'm not proposing. We're both still pretty firm on the no marriage thing. Who knows, maybe that'll change in the future. I open the box for her, pulling out a key attached to a ukulele keychain. Ali picked it. 'I know you're not a flower kind of girl, so I thought I'd get you this.'

'And this is?' She inspects the key from the box, staring at it anxiously.

'Well, you already own the key to my heart, so this is a key to my apartment,' I say. 'I thought maybe you'd want to move your stuff over?'

'Are you—'

'Asking my girlfriend to move in with me? Yeah. Ali and I looked around the place the other day and realized our apartment was missing one thing. You. What do you think?'

She kisses me, her hand on my chest. 'You didn't actually think I'd say no to this? Did you?'

'I was hoping you wouldn't.'

I've been dating this woman for months now, and still, to this day, every time she touches me, I'm like silly putty in her hands. My insides fizz like champagne, and I can't get enough of her.

'Yes,' she says with a wide smile. 'I'd love to be the woman you wake up to daily.'

'Perfect. Maybe tonight we celebrate with a foot rub in the jacuzzi?'

'Only if it leads to dirtier things this time,' she jokes, wrapping her arms around my neck. 'I love you. I can't wait to move in with you.'

It took her a while to say it out loud easily, but now that she does, I fall for her more each time.

I slide my hands around her waist, holding her to me tightly. 'I love you more every day, Merc.'

She's the one woman who never dumped me. She's accepted all my 'baggage', and I've never been happier. Mercy Alexander is, without a doubt, my soulmate, and my ex-wife will never let us forget she was right. Perhaps our timing was off that first time we met, but now, we're right on track.

ACKNOWLEDGMENTS

To my small circle of writer friends – you know who you are. Though we don't all write in the exact same genres, we all share the same love of writing. Any time I need someone to pick me up, one of you pulls through. I'm not always as great at doing the same at times but I hope to get better. You all inspire me every single day. This job would be me laughing at my own jokes all day without you.

Readers – y'all, if it weren't for you this would literally be me and my imaginary friends and likely some kind of medical diagnosis I don't currently have. It's so fun to share a piece of my heart with you and have some of you connect with the story as much as I did. You are who I do this for, whether it just be my mom (hi, Mom!) reading, or thousands of you, each one of you I am ever so thankful for. I'm excited to keep bringing you the non-sense that goes on in my head when the outside world seems like too much.

Boldwood Books – the wonderful publisher who's

made all this happen for me. Two of six done, easy breezy Aimee's please-dy. Seriously, I'm not a poet. I like mouthy, immature folks, sugary sweet stories, and commas. Just so you know, I wouldn't want to be sharing this experience with anyone else. Let's do River's story next!

A NOTE FROM THE AUTHOR

I lived many years in Portland, Oregon and am a born and raised Oregonian. I write about the Portland I knew, leaving out the newly found issues they're having. Portland can be a magical city with so many cool places to explore. Despite the chaos going on within the city now, it'll always hold a special place in my heart, and I treasure all the memories of my friends and family tromping through the city doing fun things with little worry. Not every venue within my stories still (or ever) exists, but often they are based on real places that I've renamed. I will always try to keep that weird Portland magic that I once knew in my stories.

Thank you so much for reading *Love Notes*. I hope

Mercy's story didn't let you down. I am absolutely in love with these two and how they complement one another's weaknesses. Are y'all ready for River's story next? You're gonna love it.

As always, if you loved the book (or even if you didn't – honest reviews wanted) I'd like to ask you to please leave your review anywhere you'd like, but especially on Amazon. They take reviews pretty seriously around there and the more pre-orders/reviews/buys the more they bring the book to new readers and the higher (lower? LOL) on the ranking lists I go. It doesn't need to be much, just a line or two. Thank you in advance.

Want to say hello? I'd love that. I'm all over social media and very responsive so whether you just want to shoot me a 'hi' or 'I want to option this for film' (LOL manifestation...) I can't wait to hear from you! Follow, friend, email or subscribe to my newsletter to keep in touch and never miss an update. I've got so many fun stories planned for you! Stop by my website https://aimeebwrites.com for info on how to keep in touch.

PLAYLIST
(SCENE BY SCENE)

'Dreams' (feat. Lanie Gardner), David Guetta & MORTEN

Pachelbel's Canon in D (US version), The Chapel Hill Duo

'City of Stars', Ryan Gosling & Emma Stone

'Good Love' (feat. Billy F. Gibbons), The Black Keys

'STRUT', EMELINE

'Ooh La La', Goldfrapp

'Hasta Los Dientes', Camila Cabello & Maria Becerra

'Callaíta', Bad Bunny & Tainy

'Rainbow Connection', Chloe Moser

'Why Me', Jess Glynne

'Nervous', Shawn Mendes

'realistic', corook

'Interstellar on Piano', Andy Morris

'Like She Does', Dayglow

'Feels Right', Biig Piig

'Anxiety' (feat. Selena Gomez), Julia Michaels

'Bad Reputation', Avril Lavigne

'Head in the Clouds', Morgan Olliges

'Make It Rain' (*The Voice* Performance), Koryn
Hawthorne

'Missing Out', The Ivy

'Falling', Emilee

'Mia & Sebastian's Theme', Justin Hurwitz

'Nervous', John Legend

'Chaos', FRANKIE

'Supalonely' (feat. Gus Dapperton), BENEE

'Fall', Big Time Rush

'Love You Like a Love Song' (Jumpsmokers Radio
Remix), Selena Gomez & The Scene

'Past Lives', BØRNS

'Not Falling Apart', Maroon 5

'It's All Good', Josie Dunne

'Where the Sidewalk Ends', gnash & Scott Helman

'Ave Maria', Alexander Markov & Dmitriy Cogan

'I Must Be In Love', Aaron Taos

'Self Sabotage', Abe Parker

'Falling', Florence + the Machine

'Sissy That Walk', RuPaul

'On Guard' (feat. 6lack), Lauren Jauregui
'Fantasy' (feat. Ol' Dirty Bastard), Mariah Carey
'Satellite', Eddie Vedder
'wonder if she loves me', JVKE
'That's What Love Is', Justin Bieber
'Thunderstruck', 2CELLOS
'Make It Rain', Ed Sheeran
'I Need You', MAGIC!
'Shooting Star', Carly Rae Jepsen
'You Are My Sunshine', Nick Lachey
'Rainbow Connection' (String Quartet), Stringspace

MORE FROM AIMEE BROWN

We hope you enjoyed reading *Love Notes*. If you did, please leave a review.

If you'd like to gift a copy, this book is also available as an ebook, hardback, large print, digital audio download and audiobook CD.

Sign up to Aimee Brown's mailing list for news, competitions and updates on future books.

https://bit.ly/AimeeBrownNews

He Loves Me, He Loves Me Not, another hilarious romantic comedy from Aimee Brown, is available now…

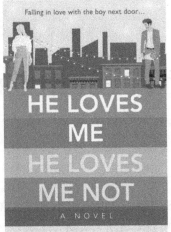

Falling in love with the boy next door...

HE LOVES ME
HE LOVES
ME NOT

A NOVEL

AIMEE BROWN

ABOUT THE AUTHOR

Aimee Brown is the bestselling romantic comedy author of several books including *The Lucky Dress*. She's an Oregon native, now living in a tiny town in cold Montana and sets her books in Portland. Previously published by Aria, her new series for Boldwood is full of love and laughter and real-life issues. *Love Notes* is Aimee's second book with Boldwood.

Visit Aimee Brown's website: https://aimeebwrites.com

Follow Aimee Brown on social media:

 twitter.com/aimeebwrites

facebook.com/authoraimeebrown

instagram.com/authoraimeeb

bookbub.com/authors/aimee-brown

Boldwood

Boldwood Books is an award-winning fiction publishing company seeking out the best stories from around the world.

Find out more at www.boldwoodbooks.com

Join our reader community for brilliant books, competitions and offers!

Follow us
@BoldwoodBooks
@BookandTonic

Sign up to our weekly deals newsletter

https://bit.ly/BoldwoodBNewsletter